MOONSTONE

NIKKI BROADWELL

Airmid Publishing

www.nikkibroadwellauthor.com

✿ Created with Vellum

PREFACE

My heartfelt thanks to Emily Trinkaus, writer and astrologer extraordinaire, for all her support and encouragement during the several years it took to write these books. It was her writing group and prompts that brought the beginnings of this story to the page. And I must give thanks to the ever-present muse as well as the Celtic goddesses who seemed to write these books for me.

My thanks to all my friends and family who have suffered through the many revisions and have offered encouragement as well as the kind but necessary criticism I needed to hear.

Thank you to Lisa Costantino, my first editor who put me on the correct path by cutting huge swaths of unnecessary description from the narrative and helping me understand what the arc of a story really means.

A huge thank you to Karalynn Ott and Verve editorial for the tremendous amount of work put in for the final edit as well as all the personal attention and encouragement.

A great thank you to Stephanie Wilder who serendipitously came into my life at the right time. Due to her and Kismet

Design I have an amazing and wonderful website to advertise my books.

Most of all, my thanks to my wonderful and patient husband who has read and re-read each manuscript several times over. He has helped with line edits, typos and suggestions from day one as well as suffered through every plot change. And when the only subject I could talk about was Wolfmoon he listened and offered advice.

Lastly, I apologize to any and all native Scottish and or Gaelic speakers. I have tried my best to be as accurate as possible with what I've included here but I'm sure I've made many mistakes.

PRAISE FOR THE MOONSTONE:

I love the fantasy genre in literature, and its growing popularity over the last few years has led to a vast selection of books to choose from. However, I do find that there can be a tendency towards stagnancy and repetitiveness, and often-times, you can be only a few pages into a fantasy novel and experience a sense of déjà vu. Then along comes *The Moonstone* by Nikki Broadwell, a breath of fresh air that had me excited from the opening pages because it was obvious, it was right up my alley, although different from anything I had read before...

This is a truly enchanting story written in a magical way with descriptions that flow like a paintbrush bringing a blank canvas to life. The author describes the many different people that Finna meets and the places she visits so vividly, that pictures automatically formed in my head, and I yearned to go there. All is different in the Otherworld, and the mystical quali-ties of everything around them made by skin tingle with excitement and made my senses come alive, as they did for Finna throughout her journey...

There is an air of mystery and the unknown throughout the whole story that kept me turning the pages non-stop. My curiosity was piqued from page one. In fact, I don't think I have ever read a book where I have been so curious to find out what is truly going on. The suspense almost drove me crazy to tell you the honest truth! I am so excited that this is the first book of a trilogy, and I am going to find it very difficult to wait for the second book. This story held me spellbound from cover to cover, and I highly recommend it. Reviewer: Cindy Taylor, www.allbooksreviewint.com

For all those who see with their heart—may your journey be full of magic

CHAPTER I

"**B**ut... my mother's dead!" Finna Lewin held her hand up against the sunlight spilling through the door. A halo of wild red hair and willowy frame were all she could see of the stranger standing on her stoop.

"Your Da worried I would come for ye. He never forgave me for leavin'."

Finna had no memory of her mother but something about Catriona Brice's accent and the timbre of her voice made her heart beat a little faster. Images, like butterfly wings, touched her and were gone before she could catch them. "Please come in," she said, moving out of the doorway. She started to close the door but on second thought left it open to the warm fall day. "Would ye like a cup of tea? I was just about to make a pot."

Catriona smiled. "I would love it. "T'was a long trip to find ye."

"I've only been living here a short time. I tried to keep it a secret from..."

"Not to worry. I have other means to find a person. Your secret is safe with me."

Finna didn't know what to think about that statement as she gestured to the small kitchen table and four chairs. "Please make yourself comfortable." She turned her back to retrieve the tea tin off the shelf, and spooned a few scoops into the teapot. Her hand shook as she pumped water into the kettle and lit the paper and kindling in the wood stove. When she turned around Catriona was seated at the table holding a velvet bag in her clasped hands. Finna was struck by the aura of quiet that surrounded the woman and the way she held her body. She thought about the balance of the pose in terms of her portrait painting, her imagination caught by the slant of light and shadow that played across the woman's face.

"This moonstone is your heritage," the older woman said, bringing Finna back to the present. She placed a drawstring pouch on the table between them. "'Tis been passed down through each generation of women in our family. It symbolizes the ancient sign of the feminine, the moon."

Caught up in her inner thoughts as well as the lilting accent, Finna hadn't taken in all the words. Her public-school education had lessened her own accent considerably and her father's brogue seemed modern in comparison to Catriona's archaic speech patterns. And now her attention was on the woman's clear green eyes, the shape of her face and the way she moved her hands when she spoke. A spark of recognition went through Finna's chest. She sucked in air, realizing she had been holding her breath.

"What did you say? My heritage? Da never mentioned anything about this. He told me you were killed in an accident."

"I left when ye were a wee bairn. I've tried to see ye over the years, Finna, but your Da, he would nae allow it."

2

Memories surfaced as Finna listened: her father, his face angry and red, her father in tears, and her own tears and grief that had been buried so deep she'd forgotten them. A deep longing went through her followed by a spark of outrage. Where had this woman been all these years? "Why did you leave us?" she asked sharply, sinking into the chair across from Catriona.

"Tis a long story. Right now we have more important things to discuss."

The kettle whistled and Finna jumped up. As she poured water over the tea leaves she tried to untangle the muddle of her thoughts. She put the teapot, cups and a small pitcher of cream on a tray and brought them to the table.

"Finna, my nighean, my being here at this moment is for the child ye carry," Catriona said, leaning forward. "All new mothers in our line have made this trip."

"Is that a Gaelic word, 'ny-ee-unn'? And how do you know about the baby? I've only known for a few weeks."

The older woman reached for a cup, poured tea into it and handed it to Finna. "'Tis Gaelic for daughter. As far as your baby, it came to me during a meditation. I am a seer, a blessing and a curse I have to say."

A seer. "Do you mean clairvoyant?"

She nodded. "All our ancestors have had these gifts."

"I don't."

"Maybe ye have nae noticed but ye have them, just as my mother and her mother before her. Look into the wee bag, Finna."

Finna picked up the bag and reached inside. She wrapped her fingers around a smooth object and pulled it out. As she held the pearl-gray oval between her thumb and first finger the cloudy surface began to clear and glow.

"This moonstone was discovered aong the shores of the

3

North Sea many generations ago by Tor, the fisherman who came to marry your seventh great grandmother, Brigid. Brigid was a visionary, named for the Goddess of Fire, and soon discerned the special powers the stone possessed." Catriona paused for a moment to take a sip of tea. "She was pregnant with their first child when she received the message from the ether: *follow the trail in the stone to the Glass Mountain to have the baby blessed by the moon goddess,* the voice in her head told her. 'Twas close to this same time of year when Tor and Brigid set out on that initial journey. Back then there were fewer villages to take them in, but the game was plentiful and Tor was expert with the bow."

Finna stared at her. "So what you're saying is that this stone led them on some crazy journey? This is a ridiculous story. And besides that, goddesses aren't real..." Finna tried to laugh but it came out of her throat like a croak.

Catriona gazed at her without speaking until Finna had to look away. Her head felt thick and she was slightly dizzy.

There was a long moment of silence and then Catriona reached over the to touch Finna's hand where it lay on the table. "I wish I had never left ye. I canna believe Angus neglected to acquaint ye with your ancestry. He knew it all and understood its importance."

Finna pulled her arm back and put her hand in her lap. "So--why *did* you leave us?"

Catriona opened her mouth and closed it. Two lines appeared between her eyebrows. "This life here was nae right for me. And your Da refused to live in the Otherworld."

"The other world? Da never mentioned that to me."

"He wouldn't. 'Twas nae a place he chose to think about. The Otherworld is a parallel reality where the old ways still prevail."

The old ways.

A cloud passed across the sun throwing the room into shadow. Now Catriona's eyes looked dark, almost black. A shiver passed through Finna's body as she stared into space. Parallel universes were a theory some scientists had put forth but they certainly hadn't been proven. As the sun reappeared, streaming across the floorboards in a wealth of golden light, Finna drew in a deep breath. When she looked at Catriona again, her eyes were green, her expression concerned.

"Ye look a bit pale, Finna. Are ye willin' to hear the story?"

Finna nodded. She had to admit she was intrigued. "But what does the stone have to do with anything? Are ye saying it has magical powers?"

"Aye, it does, but what I'm tellin' ye is the history of the stone. Shall I go on?"

Finna looked down at the stone lying in her palm. It looked innocent enough, just a simple moonstone. But as she watched, light played across the surface in amber lines that moved and changed. Her palm tingled. She carefully placed it on the table. "Please do."

"After months of travel, Brigid and Tor ended up at the Glass Mountain." Catriona pointed to the stone. "As ye can see, the surface 'tis nae large enough to show an entire map but it can reveal small sections in its reflective surface; 'tis how they managed to find their way."

Finna hesitated for a second before she picked it up again. As she peered into the milky surface a tiny line began to emerge.

"Ye see? 'Tis the trail we must follow."

The line meandered across the stone's surface like a fissure. Finna dropped it on the table with a shudder. "That is just creepy." Was Catriona asking her to go on some sort of pilgrimage? The little lines were gone now. She must have imagined them.

5

"Finna, I know this is sudden ...but we need to leave soon, so that we can be back before your baby is born. We must reach the Glass Mountain by the winter solstice."

Finna frowned. "Ye can't expect me to leave now. I'm two months pregnant. And how do I know you're who you say ye are? I would be trusting a complete stranger." Finna watched dust motes moving in the sunlight. A memory tried to surface but every time she got close to it, it disappeared. She looked over at Catriona who sat with her back ramrod straight, her eyes focused on Finna. "Maybe after the baby's born and I've known you for a while. But for now I want to stay here." Finna thought about her struggle to find this secluded spot, how comfortable and safe she had felt since moving away from town. "It took me a long time to have the courage to move into this cottage by myself." Finna's eyes filled with tears. Leaving her husband had been one of the hardest things she had ever done.

Catriona continued as though Finna hadn't spoken. "I always hoped Angus would explain the significance of the druidic zodiac to ye, what it meant in the old days, what it means now, the sense of grounding it brings to our year."

Finna's mouth opened in surprise. Had the woman heard anything she'd just said? "This isn't about my Da. It's you who left, if ye are who you say ye are. I don't think you should be implying anything bad about my father."

"I dinna wish to criticize him, Finna. Angus is a good man. I just hoped for your sake that he would explain about the three strands of belief...remembering your ancestors, understanding nature and exploring the connection of everyday reality and spiritual reality..."

"He did tell me some stuff," Finna interrupted. "Not about the otherworld or parallel universes but about the Celtic celebrations when the hill people bring their wares into town."

Finna remembered her father making some offhand references to the Celtic calendar, how it was based on the moon, but she was a teenager at the time, lost in her own world, and hadn't felt particularly interested.

"Finna, in the Druidic calendar of trees your sign is the vine —the fourth day of September. 'Tis an emotional sign and requires much care. I can see already how this fits ye. 'Tis symbolic also of sacred knowledge and spiritual initiation."

Finna had to give the woman credit for knowing her birthdate but she could have asked someone in town. As far as sacred knowledge and so on, it made no sense to her. And her father had never mentioned anything about vines when her birthday came around. She shook her head but the woman kept speaking.

"The moonstone is very special, but in order for its power to be available to ye and your unborn child, it needs to be blessed by the moon goddess, Arianrhod. It will take us several months to get there."

Anger flared at the quiet assumptions the woman was making. "I want to hear about you and my father, not all this nonsense about this stupid stone!" Finna shoved the moonstone across the table where it bounced and then came to rest by Catriona's hand. Finna caught her breath, afraid it would land on the floor and shatter. But then she noticed the slender fingers that now held the stone, the wide silver band glinting in the sunlight. A memory surfaced: her own fat baby fingers tugging at that very ring, reaching up to pull at the russet curls hanging over her crib. It seemed odd that there were no pictures of her mother anywhere--and odder still that she hadn't thought to question her father about the woman who had given birth to her.

"I'm so sorry, Finna," Catriona said, reaching across the table to lay her hand over Finna's. "I wish we could be leisurely about this trip. I should have come sooner. I will explain everything as we travel. As far as provin' I am your mother, look deeply into your heart and ye will know."

Finna tried to swallow the lump in her throat. *Do I believe this strange woman? Where has she been all these years?* But there was something...a familiarity that evoked distant memories, and the moonstone--she didn't know what to think about that. "I need some air." Catriona watched but didn't say a word as Finna jumped up and hurried out the open door.

Finna's heart beat painfully in her chest as her feet sought the well-worn path leading downhill toward a small horseshoe shaped cove. When she reached the beach, she took off her shoes, pressing her toes into the soft sand before following the trail uphill on her right. At the top she sat cross-legged, surveying the pale sand below where wavelets washed gently in and out. Her eyes traveled away from shore toward the snug stone cottage she called home. Built long ago, its whitewashed walls lay in shadow against the green of the low hill behind it, the thatched roof dark, now that the sun had moved toward the horizon.

As the sun sank lower, the indigo water became streaked with mauve and gold. Finna closed her eyes and when she reopened them the sky had turned deep purple; time felt suspended in the stillness of the growing twilight. At the bottom of the hill Catriona sat on a cedar log facing the sea. As she rose and walked up the path toward the house her body seemed to glow as though she was surrounded with light, but the sun had gone down an hour ago. Finna watched her until she entered the cottage, heard the hollow thump of the door as Catriona pulled it shut. Was there something dangerous about her? Could that be the reason her father had lied about her death? Despite finding out about his duplicity she longed for her father's calm certainty. He wasn't here to help with this decision and there was no way to reach him without a trip into the hills; she had to rely on herself.

Guilt surged through her. In her fervor to be independent, Finna hadn't told either her husband or her father where she was living. There was a baby to consider; she felt very irresponsible—like a recalcitrant child mad at the world. Now the rash decision to live alone away from town seemed wrong, when just yesterday it had seemed so right.

Full of uncertainty, Finna walked slowly down the hill. This ludicrous story about the moonstone, the journey to the Glass Mountain, these things were not part of the world she inhabited. None of it made any sense, and yet...she thought about Brigid and Tor... it sounded like a fairy tale but something about it rang true. And the idea of having a mother during this vulnerable time in her life tempted her in a way she couldn't ignore. But was it worth heading off into an unknown wilderness?

On the stoop in front of the door she paused for a moment to look up. Almost hidden by the overhanging thatch was a sign that read *Cead Mile Failte*, a hundred thousand welcomes. This cottage had been here for hundreds of years and the sign had been repainted many times. The little house faced northwest, its east and west facing windows allowing both morning and evening sun to brighten the interior. From the front stoop she could spot the small islands of the Inner Hebrides. The people who built this house so many years ago had placed it wisely.

As she lifted the iron latch, fleeting images of chattering children, mothers and fathers, grandparents, aunts and uncles entering through this door ran through her mind and she could almost hear their laughter. She felt blessed to be here.

When Finna entered the cottage, Catriona turned from where she sat at the table. The square neckline of the elegant linen tunic she wore echoed her face shape, showing off the freckled skin of her upper chest. Her full mobile mouth broke into a smile as she gestured expansively toward the door. "What an entrancing place this is."

Finna nodded, her hands tracing the contours of her own heart-shaped face. She reached around for her dark braid, pulling it over one shoulder, thinking how different her features were from this woman claiming to be her mother. Wouldn't she have the same lip shape, the same face shape or something? Even her hair was a different color. Tucking in the errant strands loosened from her braid, she suddenly felt shabby in her faded plaid shirt and worn jeans.

"Come have another cup of tea, my daughter." Catriona filled Finna's empty cup. "How have ye managed here on your own? Does the father of your child help ye out?"

Finna shook her head. "Alex doesn't know where I am. I don't need much to live. Occasionally I sell a painting." She pointed to a small watercolor hanging over the bed.

Catriona turned to look at the misty landscape filled with purples and blues. "'Tis lovely. Ye didnae inherit that talent from me!" she laughed.

Finna felt heat rise to her cheeks at the unexpected compliment. "I have a big vegetable garden and the butcher's wife and I have an agreement—I do her mending in trade for meat and fish. She has three children so it's a steady job." Finna smiled, thinking about the ripped pants and torn skirts of the two young boys and ten-year-old girl. They were always climbing trees, playing in the mud and generally driving their mother crazy.

"And rent?"

"My friend Lily's family owns this cottage. They were happy to have someone living in it. It costs me nothing." Finna took a sip from her cup, noticing the musky aroma--not her usual brew. "Will ye contact Angus while you're here? If I decide to go, I wouldn't want to leave without saying good-bye."

Catriona shook her head. "Your Da would nae be happy to see me nor would he like ye goin' off to the wilds of the Otherworld."

"Why not? Is it dangerous?"

"Tis very different from what ye are used to. Some folk might think it dangerous, but to me 'tis a place of beauty and peace. 'Tis where I was born and where I've lived most of my life."

"Tell me how you and my father met--why didn't ye stay with him?"

Catriona hesitated for a moment and then a resigned look came over her features. "I used to come to Bailemuir to bring in my herbs and remedies. 'Twas on one of those trips that I met Angus."

"But he seems so much older than you."

"He's twelve years my senior. Maybe I saw Angus as a father figure, I dinna ken. But when he proposed I accepted." Catriona looked into the distance with a sad look.

"But did ye love him? Did ye meet at the market?"

Catriona brought her gaze back to Finna. "Aye. We met at the market. The first time we only spoke a wee bit but the second time he asked me out to supper. He told me he had made up his mind the first moment he saw me."

"You mean to marry you?"

Catriona nodded.

"But you didn't answer me. Did you love him too?"

Catriona laughed nervously. "Finna, all these personal questions! I guess I must have loved him since I..."

"Since you what?"

"Since we had you."

Finna watched her mother's eyes fill and wondered why. Was it all the questions or was Catriona not telling the entire truth?

"But then ye left us. How old was I?"

"Just a wee thing. Maybe two years?"

"Ye don't remember?" Finna watched the woman's face carefully for the telltale signs of lying, but Catriona only looked sad.

"'Twas a long time ago. So much has happened since then. I would rather talk about this trip. Ask any questions ye want about that, just no more about your Da and I. 'Tis too painful."

"But you haven't told me yet why you decided to leave my Da."

Catriona shook her head. "Tis a complicated story."

Finna knew what it was like to love someone and then leave them. But abandoning a small baby? That was something she could never do. She stood up and paced around the small room as unanswered questions swirled in her brain.

"Finna, please sit. We will get to know one another in time. I canna give ye all my history in one short afternoon. 'Tis been eighteen years. Do ye have questions about the Otherworld?"

Finna sighed and then came to the table and sat down. "What is it like?"

"Tis not unlike goin' into the wild Highlands where the brachen fern and heather grow. 'Tis full of light and life."

Finna smiled. She had been across the moors and into the mountains with her father and his sheep many times. It was beautiful, a place that filled her with joy.

THERE WAS NO MORE mention of the moonstone or the journey again that evening. They cooked together, making a simple stew from root vegetables and greens from the garden. As night deepened outside the thick walls of the cottage, Catriona recounted stories about Angus that Finna had never heard. The two of them had spent time in the mountains with the sheep, they had traveled together to Edinburgh to shop and see plays. They had eaten at fancy restaurants. The father she knew was serious, not at all like the carefree happy man that Catriona described. He had been strict with her as a child and she didn't remember ever hearing him laugh. And as he aged he grew even more taciturn. She wondered if Catriona's leaving had made him into the man she knew. Again, the question of why raised itself in her mind. Had Angus hurt her in some way, or had it been the other way around? If that was the case, it might explain why Catriona had left her baby behind. Her mind scattered across time, trying hard to remember any conversations in which her father had talked about Finna's missing mother. But it was only the mention of Catriona's death that came to mind. Again a sliver of doubt had her wondering if this woman could be telling the truth. So far Catriona hadn't said anything convincing. She could have made it all up or even spoken to a person in town in order to get the information. Finna wanted very much to contact her father, to force a confrontation between the two of them and find out the truth of the past.

Before they turned in for the night, Catriona reached out and clasped Finna's hand between her palms. "I wish I had seen ye grow up."

That night Finna dreamed about a woman holding her in her arms, a woman with red hair and smiling green eyes. In the dream she felt satisfied, as though a hollow place inside of her had been partially filled.

. . .

BEFORE FINNA OPENED her eyes the next morning she reached across the bed to feel Catriona next to her but there was no one there. A quick look around the cottage revealed a fresh pot of tea on the table but no sign of Catriona. A nervous feeling went through her—had Catriona left? But then she noticed the pack on the floor next to the table. A second later the door flew open and Catriona swept in, accompanied by a brisk wind and some bright yellow leaves.

"The cove is so beautiful in the early morning!" Her hair lay in tangled coils and she pulled her fingers through it as she came to the table. "I can see how hard 'twill be for ye to leave this special place, Finna." She picked up her empty cup and poured tea into it. "How do ye like the tea I made?"

Finna's stomach tightened at Catriona's unfounded assumption. She hardly heard the question as she turned her attention toward her. "I haven't made a decision yet. This is my home now and I'm not sure that I'm willing to leave it." Her father's face appeared in her mind. Could she possibly find him in the next few days? When she turned her attention back toward Catriona, the woman's eyes had narrowed.

"Finna," she said sharply, "I need to impress upon ye the importance of this trip for your unborn child. I know 'tis a difficult decision and I wish ye had known about all of this as ye grew up so that I wouldn't be springin' it on ye like this. I blame Angus. He should have told ye about your heritage. I certainly talked about it enough when we were together."

She picked up her cup and took a sip, her eyes on Finna. "The Druids call this time of the autumnal equinox Mea'n Fo'mhair," she continued, "and honor the Green Man, the god of the forest, bringing libations and offerings to the trees. 'Tis auspicious to begin our journey now, when the animals start their migration. Samhain, the beginning of the dark time, will be upon us soon."

Catriona looked at the table her voice dropping to almost a whisper. "Your Da and I celebrated these times when we were together. He seemed genuinely interested but maybe he was trying to humor me." She looked up, a wan smile on her face. "Angus wanted me to be happy. But I will never understand why he did nae educate his daughter in the rituals. I can understand not tellin' ye about me. I hurt him deeply but...well enough of that."

So, it was Catriona who left him. That meant it was Catriona's decision to leave her baby daughter behind. "I need to talk to my father," Finna said, her voice low.

Catriona stared at Finna, her eyes unblinking. "There is nae time for that."

"What if I say I won't go until I see him?"

Catriona sighed, pressing her lips together. When she ran her fingers through her hair, pushing it back behind her ears, Finna noticed the bright silver earrings in her lobes, the spiral design of the triple goddess.

"Go and find him if ye must. But dinna be surprised if he tries to stop us. I will answer any questions ye have today but ye must make your decision. The weather will become too cold if we tarry here for long. Your baby is due in March—is that correct?"

"That's what the doctor in town told me." Finna thought about her recent trip to the doctor, the uncomfortable prodding and poking. She wanted a mid-wife to deliver her baby not some old man with no bedside manner. "But why do we need to go now? What is the reason for the blessing ceremony?"

"Our lineage is a unique one, Finna. All new mothers make this trek to ensure the protections offered by the moon goddess. Our gifts need to be safeguarded and without the blessing we would be vulnerable in ways that could be dangerous."

"But what is so special? I don't feel anything—and despite what you say, I know I don't have any 'special gifts' as you call them."

"I am quite sure ye have them. Perhaps they come through your art. And your baby is..." Catriona put her hand up against her mouth.

"My baby is what?"

"The blessing is for the child ye carry, just as ye were blessed when I carried ye in my womb. The ceremony will take place on the night of the winter solstice when the moon is full."

As Catriona gazed at her, Finna felt drawn into her mother's luminous eyes; she tried but couldn't look away. The words droned on around her but Finna didn't hear them. It was as though a universe had opened up inside the woman's eyes--trails filled with dappled light, hills of heather and gorse moved and shifted as the moments went by. And then she felt as though everything she knew had been erased. Her brain felt hollowed out, empty. She pulled her eyes away and took in a ragged breath. "I suppose I need to go and find Da. Will ye come along or do I need to bring him back here?"

Catriona's gaze went toward the window. "I'll come with ye, Finna. But I dinna see a good outcome from this. 'Tis been many moons since we've seen one another and I know he bears a heavy grudge for what happened between us."

"He's in the hills. If he's where I think he is, it should only take a few hours of walking."

"Are ye so sure this is a good idea? It could hurt Angus very deeply. He is a sensitive man and my leavin' was a cruel blow. Think carefully before ye open old wounds."

Catriona's eyes fastened again on hers and this time Finna

couldn't look away. A vision appeared in her mind—her father, Catriona and herself. The hurt she saw in her father's eyes almost made her cry out.

"Ye saw it then," Catriona whispered.

"How did ye do that?" Finna asked, wiping the sudden tears out of her eyes.

"I let ye see into the future, Finna."

Finna stood and began clearing the tea things. She didn't want to hurt her father--she loved him. She put the tray down next to the sink and wiped her eyes again. Sobs bubbled up and then she felt Catriona's arms come round her.

"My sweet daughter. I ken your love for Angus. He is a good man. Come with me in this journey and I'll tell ye all of it—the entire story of why I left and why your Da will nae forgive me."

When Finna turned to face her, Catriona stepped back. Out of the corner of her eye, Finna saw the woman moved her hand in a small circle and then point her fingers outward. A second later Finna's mind cleared. She would not hurt her father, making him face the painful past. And even with all the conflicting thoughts and not being at all sure what the purpose of the journey really was, she had made her choice.

Catriona smiled, pulling Finna into a warm embrace. "I knew ye would make the right decision, child.

Finna relaxed into her arms feeling their hearts beat in rhythm. She smelled the tang of the sea air clinging to Catriona's clothes and hair and warmth spread through her like a healilng salve. But when Catriona released her, a strange sensation went through her belly--*it couldn't be the baby, it was too soon.*

"What is it, child?"

"I hope you'll keep us safe."

"Of course, I will. How could ye think otherwise?"

CHAPTER 2

As the three days of preparation flew by, Finna found herself staring out to sea or caught by the first touch of the morning sun lighting up the hardwoods on the hillside. She removed the delicate curtains she had sewn from lace tablecloths, folding them carefully and storing them in the cedar chest. On moonlit nights she had lain in bed watching the patterned shapes move across the floor. Turning her gaze out the kitchen window, she tried to memorize the curve of beach, the waves rolling in and out. How could she leave this magical spot? There had been no more sensations in her belly but she wondered if it had been some kind of warning. Maybe this was part of her 'special gifts'. She shook her head to clear the strange thoughts. The idea of warnings by the two-month-old baby growing inside her did not sit well.

But apprehension dogged her as she stored bedding and packed. Part of her was excited about the trip and getting to know her mother but she also wanted to hunker down as her belly grew—to spend the winter here until the birth. Her nesting instinct was in full throttle. What if they didn't make it back in time for the birth? A disturbing image of giving birth in the snow flew through her mind, the red of her blood marring the pristine whiteness as she struggled and writhed in the freezing cold. As the images faded, fear cut through her body making her breathless for a moment. Her hands went to her belly, consoling herself with the knowledge of the new life there—she must keep her baby safe.

CATRIONA TOLD her the journey would be made entirely on foot so all their belongings needed to fit into the backpacks they would carry. There were no tracks wide enough for a car where they were going. Besides that, it was a time for Catriona and Finna to get to know one another, Catriona added, putting a warm hand on Finna's shoulder.

No cars? Whenever Finna began to mention her worries, Catriona would place a hand on Finna's chin and tilt her face up until their eyes met. *Trust*, she would say, and in that moment Finna's heartbeat would slow, her worries gone.

Shopping in the little town of Bailemuir for supplies and food, Finna was surprised to see shopkeepers recognize Catriona; she chatted with them as though they were old friends and Finna wondered how long it had been since Catriona was here. Why hadn't she searched out her daughter before this?

As Catriona hurried ahead, Finna stopped to speak to Bethia Cullin, the butcher's wife. "How do ye know my mother?" she asked Bethia in a whisper.

Bethia looked surprised. "Catriona?" she bellowed. "I've known her since before she was married to your Da. She is a skilled herbalist and many of the townspeople swear by her cures." Bethia's round face was rosy, glistening with perspiration in the warmth of the enclosed shop.

"But how long since you've seen her?"

"Oh, 'tis been many a year. When she was younger she would always come for the harvest festivals. After ye were born she came back to see ye once or twice, but your Da, he refused her."

"But...when was this?"

"Finna! Come along!"

"Catriona is a remarkable woman..." Bethia called from the doorway as Finna dashed after her mother. Why hadn't any of these people mentioned Catriona to her before? It was all a mystery.

When they walked by the house Catriona and Angus MacDonald had shared so many years ago, Finna watched her mother's face for signs of regret, but she barely glanced at it.

"I lived here with Da and then my husband," Finna said, stopping. The paint was peeling and a couple of cracks marred the windows. "It's been empty since Da went to the mountains."

Catriona nodded. "T'was a nice enough place to live. I am glad your father stayed...after..."

"After you left?"

Catriona nodded.

THE TWO WOMEN left the house early on the day of their departure, coming into town to access the trail. Just before they came to the end of the roadway and turned to head up the path, a lanky dark-haired man came into view on the other side of the street. A basket of fresh produce over his arm said he had just come from the farmer's market.

"Finna!" he yelled, "I've been searching all over for ye!" He waited for two cars to pass and then raced across the street. Rushing toward Finna he tried to embrace her but she pulled away.

His face fell. "Finna, please. I've been so worried."

"Alex, this is my mother, Catriona."

"Your mother? I thought she was dead," Alex blurted out, staring toward Catriona.

"Alex, that was extremely rude," Finna said primly. "As you can see, she's quite alive. We don't have time to chat, we have to be going."

"Where are ye goin'?" he demanded angrily. "With the baby and all ye need me to take care of ye, Finna. Why did ye leave?"

"Ye know very well why I left, Alex. As for what I'm doing, I'm a grown woman and I can make decisions for myself."

Alex frowned. "And whose baby is it you're carryin'? I have every right to..."

"No, Alex, ye don't."

"'Tis all right, Alex," Catriona interjected. "I shall be takin' good care of Finna and your bairn." As she spoke her hand made a half circle, her fingers pointed toward Alex. "Finna and I are taking a wee trip together. We need to become acquainted after all this time." She smiled reassuringly and then glanced at Finna, winking.

"Are ye sure you're feelin' up to a trip, Finna?" Alex asked quietly, his eyes straying toward her belly. "I was hopin', ye know, that we could be together while ye...during this time before the baby comes. I miss ye so much...I'm so sorry for everything," he continued, and then looked down, a flush turning his neck and face red. "I...I spoke to Angus, and he said..."

"When did ye see my father?"

"He came into town a couple of weeks ago. He was as worried about ye as I've been--he didn't know where ye were. He was surprised that we were apart with ye bein' pregnant and everything. He thought ye needed lookin' after."

Finna's lips compressed as she imagined her father and Alex discussing her situation. She felt the soft touch of Catriona's hand on her arm.

"Alex, I need to go now."

"Ye will contact me when ye get back? I'm livin' with my mother until...until we can...ye know, patch things up."

"I'll contact you." At this moment she had no intention of contacting him. His condescending attitude infuriated her.

"'Twas good to see ye, Finna, and to meet ye, Mrs., um..."

"Just call me Catriona. Give my best to Angus when ye see him again."

"I will. I love ye, Finna. Let me know as soon as ye get back."

Finna didn't answer as she turned to walk beside her mother. Catriona had done something back there that causeed Alex to behave differently. His anger had been palpable and then he became as docile as a kitten. As they climbed the hill she glanced over her shoulder to see Alex staring after them, his dark hair falling across his eyes. A sharp pang of regret went through her. Why had she been so mean to him? Her hands went to her belly where life was beginning, new life that she and Alex had created.

"Finna, maybe 'tis none of my business, but what happened between the two o' ye? Are ye married?"

"We're married, not that it makes a bit of difference. He...I guess ye could say I lost my trust in him."

"He seemed a decent enough fellow and 'tis obvious he loves ye."

"Loves me? I hardly think so."

"Sit down here." Catriona pointed to a grassy spot next to the trail and took off her pack. "Tis good for the soul to get these things out, my daughter. Otherwise, they fester and hurt ye in other ways."

Finna took off her pack and gathered her thoughts. She wanted to talk about it, wanted to vent the anger that was right on the surface. But seeing Alex had confused her all over again. Had she done the right thing in leaving him? She turned toward the older woman. "He was drinking too much. I guess it was partly my fault because I was a virgin. I didn't know anything... Da never told me about...about...well any of it." Finna put her hands on her flushed cheeks as the words poured out.

"I am so sorry." Catriona placed her arm around Finna's shoulders and gave her a squeeze.

"We *loved* each other; we had been going out for months and months. He courted me and we had already planned to get married but we hadn't set a date. He didn't want to wait—he told me everyone nowadays was having sex before they were married. But my Da had always drilled it into me to wait until I was married and I was afraid. Alex and I argued a few times about it, and then one night he..."

"Did he hurt ye?"

"No. But I wasn't ready. I told him yes when I meant no. And because he had a few beers he didn't notice how I was feeling. I didn't want my first time to happen like that."

Catriona's arms came around her and Finna let herself be held. Until now there had been no one to talk to about this. After a minute she pulled away and got a tissue out of her backpack and blew her nose.

"Afterwards I told him to go away, that I didn't want to ever see him again. About a month and a half later his mother came to see me. She said Alex was devastated. By then I knew I was pregnant and I had to tell her. I was so worried and didn't know what to do. She told me Bailemuir was very provincial and if we didn't get married, I would be shunned. I decided she was probably right, at least about the shunning part, not that I really cared. But for the baby's sake, ye know. I already felt so bad to have conceived a child when I was feeling so cut off from him." Finna's eyes welled and she pressed her sleeve against them.

"After the wedding Alex moved in with me and he was so sweet and understanding. He was thrilled about the baby. He had a job at the mill just outside of town and seemed more settled, content with his life and with me. But just as I was beginning to trust him and feel happy that we were having a baby together he did it again—got drunk at the pub after work. He wanted to have relations but I locked myself in the bathroom. When he left for work the next day, I packed my things and went to stay with my friend Lily."

"I know ye probably do nae want to hear this, but I think ye need to contact him after this baby is born. He is the father after all, and I can tell how much he cares for ye. And he has a lot of guilt about what happened. Alcohol can bring on all kinds of behaviors. He has a problem that he hasn't yet recognized."

"How do ye know that? He could have cleaned up his act and he didn't, why should I give him another chance?"

"I am nae saying ye have to live with him, only that he has a right to know his child. And who knows? He may take a hint and quit the drink. By the time ye see him again ye might feel differently."

Finna didn't say anything. If Catriona had been around, she probably would have known more about sex and wouldn't have ended up in the situation to begin with.

"I have nae business giving ye advice," she heard her mother say. "With me around ye would have been more prepared. I suppose I'm trying to make up for my absence."

Finna didn't reply. This was the second time Catriona had read her thoughts. They reached the top of the hill where the trail narrowed and Catriona went ahead.

"Can you tell me exactly where we're going?" Finna squinted into the distance but all she could see were trees and the path disappearing around a bend.

"Our destination is an island off the shore of the Caer Sidi where the Goddess Arianrhod's castle lies—in the Glass Mountain. This track we're on will eventually lead to the tunnels between the two worlds. Do ye remember what I told ye the other day about the origin of the moonstone?"

"I think so. I'm just having a hard time understanding any of this. What is the care city? Didn't you say the moonstone was found on the shore of the North Sea?"

"Aye. The stone was discovered in this world, your world, but the map it shows is not of this world. Your ancestor, Brigid, knew this intuitively and found her way. We are going to the Otherworld, Finna. The Caer Sidi lies in the farthest point north where the river joins the sea. 'Tis the most magical and protected realm in the Otherworld and includes Arianrhod's island. 'Tis also home to the Tuatha De Danann and the special forests that house the aurochs and the red deer."

Finna tried to imagine what this place might look like. *The tuath e de* what? And what was an auroch, anyway? A shaky feeling went through her body making her feel slightly sick. As they came around a bend a clear view of the mountains loomed in the distance.

"But how long will it take us to get there?" Finna asked, focusing on the massive peaks in the far distance.

"The Glass Mountain is far beyond these mountains. It could take us more than three months of travel."

Three months? Had Catriona mentioned this earlier? I'll be five months pregnant by then. There's no way we'll get back in time for the birth. What am I doing? She stopped in the middle of the path.

"What is it, Finna?"

"I can't put my baby in danger. I need to go back." Even being with Alex seemed better than wandering into the wilderness with this stranger. They hadn't come far--she could find her way back.

Catriona placed her hands on Finna's shoulders. "There is nothing to fear, my daughter. We must continue for this baby's sake."

Finna pushed her hands away. "But why?" she shouted. "Why is this so important? And what if we don't get back in time? I don't want to have my baby somewhere in these woods. I have a midwife in town who's promised to help me when my time comes."

"First of all, if something happened and we didnae get back in time, I am also trained in midwifery. I have delivered many a bairn. But we will be back in time, I promise ye that. As far as the importance of this journey, 'tis part of our family's destiny to have each child blessed before their birth. It keeps the magic of the lineage strong and protects us from evil. Ye have to trust me."

Evil? What evil? Catriona's eyes bored into hers and Finna saw her hand move oddly, the same movement she had noticed her make with Alex. A second later Finna's legs seemed to give out and she sat down heavily on a log at the side of trail. Her head hurt and she put her hand on her forehead. What had she been thinking? She had to continue on this trip for the sake of the child. Out of the silence she heard her mother's voice.

"I made this very same trip when I was eighteen."

"You were pregnant with me at eighteen? I'm already twenty." Finna thought about how young she'd been two years ago. She had only just met Alex, was still taking in wash from her neighbors to earn a bit of money. When she wasn't being courted by Alex, her social life consisted of hanging out with her friend Lily. Most men scared her when she even had the chance to have a conversation with them. When she met Alex, it was only because he literally ran into her when she was carrying a basket of laundry. Things went flying and he spent more than fifteen minutes helping her sort the strewn bits of clothing. If he hadn't made it his business to pursue her, she never would have gotten to know him. And the first time he took her to the pub she was completely tongue-tied. She had grown up a lot in the past year and a half.

"Aye, Finna. I was nae so sheltered as ye have been and more prepared for the love between a man and a woman. It can be very special. Giving birth, becoming parents, these are things that should be shared. I do take the blame for nae being in your life to give ye the education that ye should have had by now. But Angus made sure of it."

"Did Da go with you to the Glass Mountain?"

"Nae. This is why 'tis so important for me to be with ye during this trek. 'Tis right for the mother to take the daughter..." Catriona gazed into the distance and wiped her eyes.

"What about your mother?"

Catriona looked at Finna, her face bleak with pain. "My mother is dead."

"Oh. I'm so sorry."

"And there is another reason for how important..." Catriona paused, her forehead creasing as she looked down.

Finna had a funny feeling in the pit of her stomach, as

though she knew something but couldn't bring it to consciousness. "What?"

"'Tis a long story I'll tell as we travel."

"Is it about my baby?"

Catriona didn't answer, just took her hand. Finna allowed herself to be led and they walked on in silence, the only sounds the dull chitter of pebbles being dislodged on the path and their labored breathing.

"What did you mean, my father 'made sure of it'?"

A moment went by before Catriona answered. "Your father forbade me to come back. I tried a few times to see ye but Angus forced me off. Do ye nae remember? Once when you were three and again on your thirteenth birthday. I brought ye a present to commemorate ye becomin' a woman. After that I gave up. Ye know how stubborn Angus can be. He must have known this day would come. 'Tis a good thing ye were on your own or I may nae have gotten by him." Catriona's laugh sounded bitter.

"So that's why ye talked me out of seeing him before we left—ye knew he would stop us."

Catriona's eyes turned dark with sadness. "Nae. But t'would have been hard on all of us."

Finna's thought about that birthday and the woman who wore a dark hooded cloak and appeared mysteriously carrying a package tied up in bright ribbon. It was a terrible time in her life. She had been too embarrassed to talk to her father about what was happening to her body. If it hadn't been for Lily, she wouldn't have known what was going on. The memory of her father yelling at Catriona was what remained from that day. It was one of the few times she heard him yell, and it scared her enough that she never asked who the stranger was. "I remember that you brought me a present. Da never gave it to me."

Catriona frowned. "I am sorry for that. 'Twas a special protection necklace that a friend of mine made in the shape of the serpent."

Her father had done the best he could but it was hard to raise a girl child without a woman. She looked down at the glowing stone lying in her palm. When had she pulled the moonstone out of her pack? As her fingers closed around the smooth oval a sense of protection filled her from head to toe.

"This time I had to scrye to find ye and then I was afraid to approach because I knew ye would be angry and confused about my absence. I only came forward now because you're with child and I needed to lead ye on this journey. A journey that is *absolutely necessary*," she emphasized, looking pointedly at Finna. "Your father was always afraid of what I am."

Scrying. That word was one that she had read in books about witches. "What you are? What does that mean?"

"I have some unusual abilities as I've told ye. They run in the family."

"Well, yes, you told me you're a seer but...does that mean you're a witch?"

Catriona laughed. "I'm an herbalist. I make potions, do a little healing, and some other things."

Potions? Finna had a strong sense there was more to the story. An uneasy feeling came over her and she wished she had insisted on seeing her father. She hadn't even said good-bye. What if she never saw him again? Despite his lies about her mother he was one of the few people she trusted. The only thing she couldn't abide was how he treated her like a child, insisting that she stay with Alex as though she was incapable of taking care of herself.

It was the year Finna turned seven that Angus had divulged that her mother had abandoned both of them. She remembered because she asked him about her mother after being teased at school for being motherless. Before that it hadn't really occurred to her that anything was amiss. The taunting had been hard for her, making her feel as though she lacked some essential quality that all the other children had. She would never do that to a child.

It was a few years later that her father told her Catriona was dead—she had fallen off a high cliff and broken her neck. After what she knew now, Finna supposed he was afraid if he didn't make up some story, she would start asking questions again. But how could he lie so easily? That image stayed with her--the high rocky cliff, the broken twisted body at the bottom. These nightmarish scenes plagued her dreams for years.

"Don't dwell," Catriona murmured.

Fifteen minutes went by in silence as they kept up a steady pace. Finna felt calmer now, the disturbing thoughts left far behind. "So, tell me more about this Otherworld. Aside from the heather and gorse, what's it like?"

"The people live as they did before technology."

An image of filth, bloodied swords and various gruesome devices of torture came to her mind. "Ye mean like the Middle Ages? That sounds horrible."

Catriona gave a little laugh. "Nae, Finna. There has never been war or poverty in the Otherworld. All beings live in harmony. Everything they need for a full and abundant life is found in the environment and given freely. Everything is alive. 'Tis difficult to fully explain. Ye will have to experience it for yourself."

When Catriona's eyes met hers, Finna tried to adjust her horrified expression to one of calm. From her history studies it was hard to believe a place existing before technology could be harmonious. "Has my Da ever been there?"

"Angus did accompany me as far as the village of Clachencreid, but he didn't feel comfortable and headed back within a couple of days."

"Was that after or before I was born?"

"After. He wanted to take ye out with him but I kept ye here with me while I gathered some herbs before I went back to Bailemuir. After all, the Otherworld is my home. I wanted to live here but this was nae possible with your Da. Angus was nae open to the faerie world."

Faerie world? What did that mean? A chill went through her body and she wondered again about the folly of this trip.

"Faerie world doesn't just refer to fairies, it means a world separate from the world one is used to," Catriona said, pulling a sweater from her pack. "Put this on, child. Ye look cold."

Finna pulled the hand-knit gray sweater over her head, the soft wool immediately taking the chill away. They had been climbing steadily for some time and the path had narrowed to just an overgrown track with a steep drop-off to the left. Below them in the far distance to the north lay a valley surrounded with steep rocky cliffs. Cloud shadows tripped across the fields and farms, illuminating the tiny shapes of sheep grazing. A river meandered lazily along the bottom, shining like silver in the distance. "How old were you when your mother died?"

"I canna talk about her, Finna."

"But she would be my grandmother."

"It would be best if ye never thought of her again. I didnae get along with her. I was fifteen when she died."

"At least tell me her name."

"Her name was Adair."

"And what about my grandfather? Is he alive?"

Catriona shook her head. "Fergus was his name and he died the same year as my maithair."

Catriona's face had paled and there was an expression in her eyes that kept Finna from asking more questions. As they came around a bend, the ominous looking peaks in the distance took Finna's attention. They were jagged, like broken teeth, their sides steep and dark. "Is that the Otherworld?"

"Nae. We must first go through the tunnels--the boundary between the worlds."

CHAPTER 3

T he significance of the journey began to dawn on
Finna. Every morning she took the moonstone out of
her pack just to reassure herself, staring at the tiny
trail in the luminous surface. It didn't frighten her anymore
and she had begun to feel comforted by the hum it gave off as
she held it tightly in her palm. The two women had fallen into
a pleasant routine in which many hours were spent in silence.
Most nights they sheltered in abandoned huts that shepherds
had used over the years. They were clean and dry and usually
contained straw on which they could spread their blankets.
The trails they followed led them past clear running streams
where they bathed and gathered watercress and other fresh
greens to augment their diet of nuts and cheese. There had
been no rain and the days continued, pleasant and warm.

It was around this time that the dreams began. At first,
they were vague with a portent of something bad, but as the
nights went on, they became clearer. A shadowy figure wanted
her baby. Finna thought the person might be Catriona. Many
nights she woke screaming, bringing Catriona rushing to her

side. In the mornings after a nightmare Catriona talked to her, assuring her that all would be well. It wouldn't take long before Finna laughed at her own insecurity, agreeing that it was all due to hormonal imbalance.

But despite Catriona's assurance that they would stop once Finna became acclimated to the dietary changes and the higher elevations, the dreams continued.

"Your red blood cells need to increase to supply oxygen in the thinner air. And being pregnant is a stress on your system as well."

Fine for you to say, Finna thought grumpily, trying to rub the cramps from her calves.

As the days went by, Finna's thoughts strayed to Bailemuir, feeling remorse about leaving her father and Alex. All her anger with Alex had been replaced with a fervent longing for his company. And she was positive her father would be distressed to learn his only daughter had chosen to head off with his ex-wife. Or were they still married? So far Catriona's accounts had been very sketchy. Every time Finna broached the subject Catriona managed to skirt around the issue or head off to gather something for dinner.

For the past few mornings Finna had awakened full of thoughts of heading home. The dreams were scary and dark and she had a strong feeling of foreboding that she couldn't shake. Her body was feeling the stresses of the pregnancy and her mind could not calm down. But before she could voice her concerns, Catriona was by her side, encouraging her to talk about the dreams while she rubbed her back or combed and re-braided her hair. Finna watched for the witch-like movements of her hands and wondered about the strange tasting tea Catriona had her drinking daily. But Catriona's hands stayed by her side and she drank the same brew. Ultimately it was the long overdue mothering that kept Finna going. Just the feel of the woman's hands in her hair made her feel loved and wanted.

It was a week or so later that the night terrors finally disappeared. Catriona told Finna that her body was growing stronger, she was getting close to her second trimester and her hormonal levels were coming into better balance. Without the dreams to mar each morning, Finna began to enjoy the bright leaves clinging to the hardwoods, the dew-covered meadows of flowers and the grassy grazing pastures used by shepherds.

The often ran into men tending their herds and Catriona was able to obtain cheese or bannock to tide them over. The luck of meeting these herders had Finna wondering how they would have managed without the extra food, but Catriona was serene, confidant that the universe would supply them with whatever they needed.

"I'm going to gather herbs and mushrooms," Catriona told her one evening as they settled into an abandoned hut. "I won't be long. Maybe you can make a fire while I'm gone."

"But I don't know how," Finna called plaintively as her mother disappeared into the forest. Finna sighed, looking around for sticks and bigger pieces of wood to burn. It was always Catriona who made the fire, Catriona who brewed the tea and prepared their dinners of gathered greens, cheese and bannock. She had become dependant, she realized, like a small child. But maybe that was to be expected since this was the first mothering she'd ever had.

Her thoughts were far away when Alex stepped out from behind a tree. She let out a high-pitched shriek, dropping the twigs she was carrying. "What are ye doing here?"

"I've been following ye," Alex said quietly. "I want ye to come home with me. I don't trust her--what you're doing is dangerous for our baby. Look how thin ye are, Finna." He grabbed herwrist, wrapping his fingers around it. "Ye should be gaining weight, not losing it." He looked her up and down. "Is the bairn still with ye?"

Finna's hand went to her lower belly. "Of course she is."

Alex laughed. "A wee lass then," he said before turning to look over his shoulder. "Do ye really believe she's your mother?"

"Ye don't think she is?"

Alex's brows moved together in worry. "Ye don't look anything like her," he hissed. "Her hair's red, she's got green eyes--yours are gray-green and look how dark your hair is." His hand went to her braid, lifting it, his eyes on hers.

A moment later she was in his arms, not sure if he'd pulled her there or if she'd walked into them. Her tears came as he pressed his cheek to hers.

"Dinna cry, my sweet. Ye should nae have come out here with that woman. Ye need to be thinkin' of the child now."

In the distance Finna heard her mother singing—a lullaby she recognized. She moved away from Alex, wiping the tears from her face. "Just because I don't look like her doesn't mean she isn't my mother. I remember her. And besides, Bethia knows her. Why would she lie to me?"

"She's a witch, Finna. Your father even said so."

"Angus said she's a witch?"

Alex nodded. "He said she knows things and does things that aren't normal. He was afraid of her and it's why he kept ye with him. He wanted to protect you." Alex pushed the hair out of his eyes, moving closer. "How do you think she convinced ye to leave at a time like this?" He pointed toward her belly where a small bump protruded against her sweater. "My Gods, Finna, how can it be good for ye to walk for months on end? You're exhausted and not eating properly. What the hell is the purpose of this trip, anyway?"

"I know what I'm doing, Alex." But in truth she wasn't at all sure--her father, a man she trusted over everyone, had called Catriona a witch.

"Your Da said and I quote, *'If it's Catriona, she's taking Finna to a very dangerous place'*. He asked me to bring ye home."

Alex reached out for her but she pushed him away and backed up.

Alex grabbed her arm. "Are ye going to let your own Da worry about ye? And what if ye miscarry?"

Finna wrenched her arm away from him. "I'm not going to miscarry. My mother is taking good care of me."

Alex frowned and took a step toward her. "Finna, I know I hurt ye. Please try to remember how things were before..."

"Go home, Alex. Tell my Da I love him and not to worry. I think you should get out of here before Catriona sees you," Finna added, looking around.

"If she's so all-knowing she must have realized I was following by now."

At that moment Catriona appeared from under the trees. "Hello, Alex," she said. "I was wondering when ye would show yourself. Will you share our evening meal?"

Finna glanced at her in surprise.

"I know how ye feel but the man must be hungry. He will leave after that, won't ye Alex?"

Alex glanced from Finna to Catriona in confusion. "I'll leave whenever ye wish."

Finna twisted to stare at him. What was it about Catriona that had him bowing and scraping?

Catriona smiled happily. "I found some greens for the soup tonight." She led the way back to camp where the pot had already been filled with water. She added the miner's lettuce, wild chives and watercress and then gazed at Alex. "Let's get the fire started, shall we?"

Alex made the fire as Catriona constructed a lattice of green twigs. She rested the ends of the woven sticks on the rocks surrounding the firepit and then placed the pot of water on top. As the water warmed, she added several scoops of herbs from her pack. "'Tis amazing how many nutrients there are in simple herbs and greens." She pulled a muslin wrapped cheese from her pack and offered it to Alex. "Take as much as ye want, Alex. We'll soon be in Clachencreid where I can replenish our supplies."

As they ate Catriona regaled them with tales of her early escapades. Her mother described herself as a hippy, wandering through her life without a care until she became pregnant with Finna. Before her arrival in Bailemuir that fateful year when she turned eighteen, she had spent her days gathering herbs and distributing them to villages across the Otherworld. According to Catriona there was no real illness in this mystical world, but the people needed the special herbs to maintain their connection with the spirits and to ward off any negativity that crept into their psyches.

Finna had the distinct impression that the stories were for Alex. There was no mention of Adair or what had happened there, no mention of why she left two-year-old Finna and retreated to her home. Catriona told of the fairy-tale romance between herself and Angus, barely alluding to the fact that she was pregnant when they decided to marry. And after hearing about how independent her mother's life had been, the sudden marriage sounded oddly out of character.

When Finna glanced over at Alex his face held a rapt expression, his attention hanging on every word her mother uttered. As Catriona talked about leaving home at fifteen and managing alone in the woods by gathering mushrooms and nuts, Finna realized how sheltered her own life had been. A trip or two to Edinburgh for a concert or the ballet was the most she had done.

After they put the food away, Alex obediently gathered his things together. He had a big pack and a sleeping bag that he hoisted onto his back. "Thank ye, Catriona," he said, holding out his hand. "I trust ye to take good care of my wife and child."

Finna stood up. "I can take care of myself."

Catriona let go of Alex's hand and touched Finna's shoulder. "Everyone needs looking after in some fashion, Finna. I'm quite sure ye could manage on your own, but I'm not sure ye would find the Glass Mountian without me."

"Glass Mountain? Is there really such a place?" Alex asked.

Catriona smiled. "Yes. Ye may nae understand this, but there is a purpose to what we're doing here. Finna comes from a long line of powerful women who have all made the very same trip."

Finna pulled the moonstone out of her pack and held it out to Alex. "This stone has been handed down from generation to generation. See the map there?"

Alex leaned over her, staring at the stone. "What the hell?"

"It shows us the way."

"Enough," Catriona said quickly. She grabbed the stone out of Finna's hand and slid it into her pocket. "'Tis time for ye to be on your way, Alex, and we need to sleep."

"I guess 'tis good-bye, then," Alex said. "Take care of her Catriona and thanks for the food." Alex headed for the trail.

Finna watched him, waiting for him to look back and wave, but he didn't turn and soon faded into the dark as though he had never been there.

"Come Finna, 'tis late and we need to rest."

That night the dreams came back. Finna woke several

times shaking and in a cold sweat. A person or persons lurked in the shadows waiting for the opportunity to steal her baby. In the dream she carried the small bundle close, her breath ragged from running.

"Finna, are ye all right?"

"I had the dream again."

Catriona kneeled beside her in the dark. "I'm nae surprised. Alex being here stirred up your emotions. The dreams will pass." Catriona stroked her hair until she fell asleep.

THEY HEADED out early the next morning. Alex's revelations about her Da sparked several long conversations about Catriona and Angus's relationship. Catriona confessed that early on Angus was nervous about Catriona's uncanny abilities but he also loved her. Later when she tried to get him to live in Otherworld, he became standoffish and began complaining about her lack of propriety.

"I know he still loved me, Finna, but my lifestyle was a wee bit too much for him. Honestly, I think he was jealous in a way. He always had to play by the rules and I know he longed to let go once in a while. But after what I'd done, I couldn't blame him."

"What did ye do? Ye mean leaving me behind?"

Catriona's face turned red and she put both hands on her mouth. "I...yes, that's what I meant."

Finna waited but the conversation seemed to be at an end as Catriona strode quickly up the trail ahead of her. She still didn't know why Catriona had returned to Otherworld without Angus and more importantly why she left her baby daughter behind.

. . .

LATE THE NEXT AFTERNOON, after they had bathed in a cool stream and were settling down for the night, Catriona wandered off into the trees. She was gone so long that Finna became alarmed and decided to go look for her. The sun had set but it was one of those warm fall evenings when dusk seems to last forever.

As Finna searched through the copse of beech trees, she caught a movement out of the corner of her eye and turned to see Catriona in a clearing about twenty feet away. She was dancing. Her hands undulated gracefully through the air as her bare feet stepped and lifted off the ground. Her skirt revealed slim legs as it rose and fell with her slow sinuous movements, her hips rotating back and forth with an inner rhythm as she twirled and rose on her toes. Now her head was pulled back, exposing her long neck, her hair a shimmering wave down her back. It was as though Catriona could hear some inner tone and rhythm, some music that Finna was not privy to.

Finna stood transfixed until the dancing came to an end. She left then, afraid to let Catriona know she had been spying on her. She felt like she had intruded upon something very private. The utter freedom of her mother's movements made her want the same for herself. She felt like a gray and dull moth compared to the butterfly that was Catriona.

FINNA FOLLOWED her mother up a narrow path along the edge of a deep ravine. It had been a week since Alex's unexpected visit but to Finna it seemed as though months had gone by. It had been a strenuous day and Finna felt nauseated and weak.

When she stopped abruptly Catriona turned back. "Are ye all right?"

"I think I'm going to be sick." Finna's insides churned as she bent over next to the trail with her hands on her thighs.

"Here, chew these," Catriona said, handing her a piece of root and some seeds. "It's ginger and anise, good for nausea."

She was skeptical as she put the herbs into her mouth but a few moments later was surprised to discover the nausea gone.

"There's some color coming back into your cheeks. Keep them in your pocket if this happens again. I was lucky with ye. I didn't have that problem."

Finna looked at her mother through watery eyes. *Was there anything that bothered this woman?*

"The higher elevation is probably contributing to the morning sickness. It will most likely pass once we get through the mountains."

Finna hoped she was right.

As they struggled up a steep rise and around a bend, the distant mountains came into view. The temperature had dropped and Finna pulled her scarf close around her neck.

"We should find a place to spend the night, we won't reach the village until tomorrow."

"Where could we shelter up here?" Finna examined the rough boulders and scrub that lined the trail, longing for the rolling hills and paths filled with dappled light they had left behind. It had been too many days since she had bathed, she thought, running her fingers through her clump of unbraided hair.

"Around the next big bend is the cave—the opening to the tunnels that lead to Otherworld. We need to hurry since the rainstorm ahead will reach us in less than an hour." Catriona pointed to dark rolling clouds in the distance and a moment later, as if on cue, wind gusted, throwing bits of dry grass and dirt into the air. "Time to start climbing," Catriona called cheerfully, leading the way up an impossibly steep deer trail.

When Finna's calves protested Catriona grabbed her hand, helping her navigate the protruding rocks before releasing her to go ahead. How could she be this winded? It was humiliating to see her mother striding up the hill ahead of her.

As the trail leveled out, the mouth of a cave came into view —a dark spot above a jutting ledge of stone. The cold air whipping around them was suddenly warm and fragrant. "Is the warm breeze coming from in there?" Finna asked in surprise.

"'Twas one reason the ancients chose it."

"But why is it warm?"

"No one really knows. Perhaps the moisture inside has something to do with it. The ancients could tell ye, but all their knowledge has been lost with the exception of the paintings and carvings that have endured inside the caves."

Catriona swung herself onto the ledge, holding her hand out to Finna. "Let me help ye. 'Twas a steep climb." Thick blackberry bushes and mountain laurel grew on either side of the opening, a testament to the warmth. Once Finna had scrambled onto the flat rock she noticed a faint glow coming from inside. Finna peered into the darkness. "Where is the light coming from?"

"There's phosphorescence inside the cave caused by a certain type of bacteria—nae enough light to read by but helpful for finding our way. We won't need a torch once we're inside. " Catriona folded her long legs under her and removed her pack. "We can eat here," she announced.

Finna struggled with her pack as she fought to catch her breath. "How is it that you never seem to get tired?"

"Oh child, I have been walking these mountains since I was

a wee girl. I'm just used to it. Your condition is causing a lot of your fatigue. How are your legs feeling?"

Finna wiggled her ankles back and forth. "They ache."

Catriona dug in her pack, pulled out a tiny burlap pouch and handed it to Finna. "This formula contains agrimony for mood, and since you're pregnant, just a pinch of wood betony for the nerves. It also contains solomon's seal for aching muscles and joints." Catriona relaxed against the cave wall and began to eat some cheese, handing a chunk to Finna. "I've pushed ye too much today," she muttered. "We'll go further into the cave at nightfall. There's a good place to sleep just a short walk inside."

After eating, Finna took a small pinch from the bag and put it in her mouth. It was only a few minutes before the ache in her legs was gone. Her mood lifted as she realized they were finally about to enter Otherworld, a day she thought would never come.

THE STORM ARRIVED JUST as Catriona predicted, sending torrents of rain from the quickly moving dark clouds. At the first drop, they gathered their things and headed inside. The phosphorescence growing on the stone brought the pertro-glyphs on the walls into focus. Stick people with spears and arrows, wolves, deer, oxen, horses and some other animals that looked like large upright apes gazed back at her as she walked along. In between the animals a design had been repeated over and over—an oval with rays, like spokes in a wheel. Each depiction was slightly different, sometimes larger, sometimes done in charcoal, and other times very pale ochre. "What's this?" Finna asked, leaning in to examine it.

"'Tis the moonstone, Finna."

"The moonstone? But these drawings are ancient—way before Brigid or the others you spoke about."

Catriona nodded. "The druids have told me that the stone was used by early tribal priestesses. It was their talisman and passed down from one to the next. How it came to be on the shore is a mystery, although there is a theory that our line are the direct descendents of the tribes known as the people of the stone."

An image of scantily clad, red-haired warrior women went through Finna's mind. She turned from the wall as she picked up the scent of rose combined with the spicy scent of narcissus. "What is that wonderful fragrance?"

"'Tis the night blooming lilies. They only grow at the boundary between the two worlds. The first hall is nae far."

Finna squinted into the semi-darkness to see where this "first hall" might be, but all she could discern was an eerie glow emanating from somewhere up ahead. She followed Catriona around a small bend in the tunnel, surprised when an enormous arched doorway appeared. Spirals and intricate whorls and knots had been carved into the wood and she stopped to run her fingers over them before stepping over the threshold into the vaulted room.

"Come, Finna," Catriona beckoned from the other side of the vaulted room.

The light was strong here, as though hundreds of candles had been lit. Sweet perfume wafted from the luminous white flowers clinging to the cave walls, their large lotus-like petals facing the glow that emanated from the curved ceiling. In the center of each flower long yellow stamens waved back and forth like sea creatures.

"How is this possible?"

Catriona smiled. "These flowers are in symbiotic relationship with the bacteria. What harms them is too much carbon dioxide. If more people were to discover this place, the light would begin to disappear and then the flowers couldn't grow." As Finna stepped further into the room, Catriona took hold of her arm. "Ye might experience slight dizziness or disorientation as we cross over the portal."

An understatement, Finna thought as everthing began to shimmer. A wave of nausea went through her as she tried to get her bearings.

"'Twill pass. Your body needs to acclimate to the different vibrations."

By the time she reached the center of the room the dizziness had subsided. Now the flowers looked clearly delineated, as though each petal had been carefully cut out of paper. Their heady perfume pulled her towards them.

"They don't seem real." She reached to touch one of the petals, her fingers repelled by the little currents of air that surrounded them.

"Ye canna pick them or touch them, Finna. It will disturb their precarious hold on life. But you may breathe in their perfume. It has many healing properties."

Finna backed away as she examined the intricate veins, the translucent petals. "They're so beautiful." The flowers leaned toward her, waving as though from a breeze.

"Come now, child, we must find our beds, the time grows late."

CHAPTER 4

That night Finna dreamed about the moonstone. It hung in the air, glowing with a greenish hue. All around was a sort of fog that obliterated everything else. She tried to grab the stone but it was always just out of reach. The more she tried the further away it seemed to get. In the dream she knew that without the stone she would not find her way.

She woke with a start, forgetting where she was for a second. Catriona was gone. In the profound silence she listened carefully for her mother. It was hard to tell if it was day or night with only the glow emanating from the ceiling. She tried not to be alarmed, but the thump of her heart was loud in her ears. There was no chance she could find her way out of these labyrinthine tunnels by herself. Without thinking, her hand searched through the pack, her fingers closing around the stone. At once she was calm—but where was Catriona?

It was only a few moments before her mother appeared out of the darkness. "Where have ye been?" Finna cried.

"I'd heard a rumor about a cave-in so I went to check it out. It is there as I was told—along the tunnel that leads to the village of Clachencreid."

"What happened?"

Catriona didn't say anything for a moment. When she spoke, her voice sounded troubled. "Something came through here and broke the protections."

"Something? What does that mean?"

"I dinna ken what it was. I just know it got through the magical barriers put in place by the ancients. There are life forms in Otherworld that canna survive anywhere else, just like the flowers in this cave. Things are always changing, growing toward a lighter and more balanced way of being. The magic still exists here. If the coarser thought forms creep in, this place will change as they have in the outside world, your world."

"Coarser thought forms?"

"Greed, deceit, hatred-- I'm speakin' about the hypocrisy that causes war and disharmony among beings. Genocide and cruelty has been encouraged to grow and thrive in the name of religion and political ideologies."

By now they were in the dark of the tunnel and Finna felt a rising panic about what lay ahead. Maybe her father had been right to protect her from all of this. Alex had repeated her father's words and now they rang in her ears—*she's taking Finna to a very dangerous place.*

"Will we be spending time in Clachencreid?" she asked hopefully, hearing the dull sound of her voice echo off the stone.

"A day or possibly two. My friends Mikdal and Herska live in Clachencreid and are planning to help us with our preparations."

A real town. Two days with friends in a house with a fireplace and a bed and maybe a bath. Warm food. "Clachencreid. I like that name."

"'Tis Gaelic. It means, 'where the heart dwells'."

"What kind of preparations?"

"Oh," Catriona said lightly, "we'll need some more herbs and warmer clothes. Where we're going is much colder and there are things at work there that require a clear mind."

With that ominous description of their future Catriona headed down yet another tunnel in what Finna assumed was the direction of Clachencreid.

WHEN THEY FINALLY EMERGED FROM the darkness into an arching stand of birch and alder, the sun was barely visible between two mountain peaks and disappearing quickly. The trees formed an imposing entrance, their branches twisted into a lattice high above. It was the time of day when the dark usurped the light, the witching hour, and all the plants, trees and rocks looked luminous in the golden dusky light, as though surrounded with a halo. Finna wondered if she was imagining things. "Wow!" was all she could think to say.

"Aye, Finna, everything in this world is vibrantly alive. 'Tis why ye can see the radiating energy. Here the spirits still reside in the creeks, rivers and trees. They guard the water and keep it clean and pure. Ye can hear them if ye are quiet, and if you are lucky, you might see them as well. These things have dimmed in your world, partly because of pollution and partly because man has lost his connection and belief in the magic that exists within all life." Catriona raised her hand, pointing toward the trees. "Look at the birch and alder. They're leafless now, but birches are a symbol of new beginnings and the alders are for protection. Various parts of both trees are used for medicines and the birch bark is used for tanning hides."

When Finna placed her hand on the papery bark of the closest birch a slight vibration through her fingers. "Is the light completely gone from my world?"

"There are still some areas that retain the light, places where people acknowledge and appreciate the sacred. Where ye live is one of them."

"Maybe that's why I chose it, and why it was so hard to leave. But I've never seen things glow the way they do here."

"Tis nae so obvious there, but if ye still your mind and look around, ye can see. It just requires more effort than it does here."

"Why didn't my father want to live here? It's so beautiful."

"The idea of this kind of aliveness frightened him, although he would never admit it. To him rocks are inanimate and trees are just trees. This place is not for everyone. 'Tis a good thing or it would be overrun."

Beyond the trees Catriona stopped to examine a section of charred stumps and blackened limbs.

"What happened here?" Finna asked.

"Possibly what I was saying earlier, the destructive forces that have been getting through the magical barrier. These trees will regenerate," she said, turning back toward the trail. "We need to hurry. The sun will soon be down."

Before following her mother down the hill Finna turned back. She wanted to take one last look at the tunnel, to reassure herself of the way out, but instead of the opening there was only a sheer wall of dark rock. A shiver went down her spine as her eyes traveled its length, unable to discern any hint of where the tunnel had been. It must be part of the protections, she thought, trying to shake off the uneasiness in the pit of her stomach.

As they came further down the hill, Clachencreid came into view, a cozy village nestled between two dark mountains. Voices and laughter could be heard in the distance as lights blinked on one by one.

"Don't they have electricity here?"

"In this world the people and beings live according to the old ways. Because there are no electric lights they can still see the dark night sky and watch the phases of the moon and stars as the seasons change. Everything that happens here is in accordance with the natural rhythms of nature. Ye will see all of this as we travel."

A rugged, uneven trail led toward a wider road that crossed a stone bridge into the heart of Clachencreid. A dozen or more sheep grazed on the steep hillside on the other side of the river. "How many people live here?"

"Clachencreid has around two thousand people. When we leave this village we will be in wilderness. 'Tis quite a distance to the next settlement."

Finna's mouth went dry. She tried to quell her nerves but had a flash of heat as her stomach heaved, sending acid into her mouth. Remembering the herbs, she reached into her pocket and found the ginger root and chewed a small piece.

The path switchbacked several times before the two women arrived onto the main road. Men and women were going about their evening chores, carrying buckets for milking and herding small groups of sheep and goats along the road-way. The clothing seemed hand-made and old-fashioned, long full skirts covered with aprons or loose fitting pants and loosely woven overshirts. On the other side of the river, children raced after one another, their laughter ringing out in the crisp air.

Across the bridge Catriona turned to the right heading along the well-traveled main road. Several people walked by them, heading out to the fields to catch the sheep. All of them seemed to know Catriona, smiling and saying hello as they gazed curiously at Finna. The place seemed like a storybook town with its thatched cottages and small gardens filled with bright fall flowers and leafy vegetables. A young woman passed by them going the other way, her hands folded around a wooden dish filled with apples, grapes and squash. In the middle of her forehead, a blue spiral caught the light from the hanging lanterns, glowing dully. She didn't smile or nod as the others had, her steps measured, her eyes downcast. "What is she doing?" Finna whispered when she was out of earshot.

"That is Enid, our spirit sister. The blue spiral is the ancient symbol for the serpent—it represents ethereal energy, and expansion of consciousness. This mark indicates that she's taken a vow of silence in order to listen more closely to what the earth has to tell her. She's been chosen to bring offerings to the spirits of the stream and trees. The people here hold everything in reverence and this keeps the spirits strong." Catriona looked ahead, squinting into the deepening dusk. "We're almost there and I for one am looking forward to some warm food and a real bed tonight. It will be good to see my old friends."

The atmosphere felt hushed despite the laughter and noise of the bleeting sheep and goats and the lowing of cows on the hill in the distance. Finna turned, watching Enid kneel at the edge of the stream. Her fair hair fell like a curtain to hide her face as she placed the plate reverently on the grass. When Finna turned away again to follow her mother, she felt held somehow, as though the place itself enfolded her.

CHAPTER 5

From the kitchen came the sound of water being poured, a match being struck, the heavy clunk of cups on the wooden table. The smell of cooked cereal filled the air. Finna peeked around the corner to see Catriona stirring an iron pot on the woodstove. Her feet and legs were bare under her light shift, her unbraided hair loose around her face.

She turned as Finna walked through the doorway. "I hope I didnae wake ye."

"No, I woke myself up from a dream." Finna shuddered as she recalled the same dream images that had plagued her on the trip. The shadowy figure who followed her relentlessly. She shook herself trying to get rid of the dream remnants as she looked around. This thatched cottage was so much like hers that she felt a pang of homesickness. Herbs hung from the beams and shelves held cups and plates and jars full of beans and oatmeal and other grains.

"Ye look cold. Come in next to the fire. Mikdal and Herska have gone to the bakers to get some bread. Herska didna have time to bake yesterday."

Finna walked over to the pot-bellied stove and stood next to her mother. It was obviously later than she had thought-- the lack of light came from being sheltered in the valley between the mountains. Her mind went back to their arrival the night before—a blur of greetings followed by a delicious stew, bannock with fresh churned butter and home-brewed beer, after which she heated water on the stove and washed herself as best she could as the others talked quietly in the other room. Her hair had taken several pots of water before it seemed clean, the hand-made soap less than adequate for the job. After that she fell into the soft bed and was asleep within minutes.

By the time Mikdal Fagan and his wife Herska arrived home the tea was made and Catriona and Finna were sipping from earthenware mugs. The older couple arrived carrying parcels of apples and cheese, their cheeks ruddy from the chilly air. Mikdal was a blacksmith with hands rough and calloused and a deeply lined face in which blue eyes peered out, bright with unexpressed laughter. Small and bird-like with wiry brown-gray hair braided and tied back, Herska's smile was tentative and shy but not any less warm.

"We need to get some heavier clothing while we're here," Catriona remarked. "The northern mountains are much colder than what we've been used to so far."

"I have a few warm leggings and oversize sweaters that ye may take," Herska said, with a sidelong glance at Finna. "Ones I dinna need for myself. I have also knitted some hats and gloves. Tamar in town sells high fur-lined boots that will keep your feet and legs warm and dry." Eyeing Finna's ankle high boots she raised her eyebrows. "Are those waterproof?"

"No, but it hasn't rained so far."

Herska shook her head. "Ye canna count on dry weather

during this season. Ye could have all manner of cold—ice and snow, wind. 'Tis the time of change."

Finna shivered at the warning look in the woman's eyes. It seemed too early for snow.

"DID YE ALSO REMEMBER the herbs we spoke about so many months ago?" Catriona asked her.

"Aye. They are bundled and ready."

Finna listened to this exchange with confusion; apparently Catriona had planned this trip months ago. How could that be? She looked from Herska to Catriona. They seemed to be communicating on a level beyond words, their eyes locked together. She could almost hear a conversation. Mikdal broke the trance with a cough and went to the table to set out breakfast. Fresh eggs cooked in their shells, bannock and butter and apples and cheese accompanied the oatmeal Catriona had made. They ate in silence after Herska gave thanks for the food and for the wonderful visit from her 'dear friend, Catriona, and her sweet daughter'. Finna had many questions but felt too shy to ask them; she felt like she was in a foreign country and didn't speak the language.

Herska's warm sweaters and leggings were large enough to accommodate Finna's growing girth with tons of room to spare. She looked at Herska's small frame wondering why she would have made sweaters so large. Had she also known about Finna ahead of time? The dense wool smelled of lanolin and was wonderfully soft against her skin.

After breakfast Mikdal left the house with the promise of a present for the trip, returning a short time later with two pairs of boots. They were made of grayish-brown sheepskin, about knee high with straps running across the front to tighten them and lined in soft fleece with protective leather soles.

Finna gasped in delight as he handed her a pair.

"I found your size, I think." Mikdal's blue eyes twinkled.

At that moment he reminded Finna so much of her Da that she wanted to throw her arms around his neck. It wasn't often that her father had that expression, but when he did it was like the sun had just come out from behind a cloud. "Thank you, they're absolutely beautiful!" She slid them on marveling at the softness and how they hugged her feet –a perfect fit.

"I didnae make them. My talents lie in metal, not wool and leather. Glad ye like them."

"On our way through the village we can stop at Tamar's shop and I will introduce ye," Catriona said, pulling on the new boots. "He's the local cobbler."

"He's expectin' ye. I told him ye were in town," Mikdal said winking. "And dinna forget the honey. I wrapped it carefully."

Catriona smiled, reaching out for the muslin wrapped jar. "Your bees make the best honey I have ever tasted."

"Tis from the lavender that grows on the hills," Mikdal answered, waving his hand vaguely in the direction of the door.

They began to pack away their newly acquired belongings in the now bulging knapsacks and prepared for their departure. As Finna watched Catriona and Mikdal studying a worn map she realized there would be no time to question these old friends of Catriona's. She had been hoping to gain a bit more understanding of what this trip was all about. From where she stood, Finna could see the look of concern on Mikdal's face. When she walked into the kitchen they abruptly stopped talking.

"Did I interrupt something?"

Catriona turned toward her. "We were just discussing certain routes to take, or should I say, not to take," she added, looking at Mikdal.

Finna gazed uneasily from Catriona to Mikdal but neither of their faces betrayed any fear. She tried to let go of the clenched fist that had taken up residence in her stomach. *Mikdal should come with us,* she thought. There was something solid about him that she found very reassuring. But when she asked him he looked at Catriona and then shook his head. Just before they left, Finna pleaded with him again, but he just replied that this was not the time--Catriona was a strong and resourceful woman and not to worry. He patted her on the shoulder and smiled in a fatherly way.

After saying their good-byes, Finna and Catriona left the cottage. They had only made it to the main road when Catriona turned and asked Finna to wait a moment. She needed to say hello to a friend of hers before they left. As she hurried off in the opposite direction Finna walked back to the cottage to wait. She started to go inside but then overheard the urgent conversation going on between Mikdal and Herska.

"Do ye nae think Finna has a right to know?" Herska asked.

"Of course I do, but ye ken Catriona. Maybe she's afraid of what it means, the responsibility that lands on her shoulders."

"But the importance of this outweighs all other considerations. Ye should have told Finna about Adair yourself."

"I couldnay do that, Herska. I have to respect Catriona."

"And her brother is at the settlement now. Does she realize how dangerous he's become?"

"I showed her the new route to take to avoid the settlement but I canna force her to heed my advice."

Herska laughed. "She's got a stubborn streak just like yours, as well as a blind spot when it comes to her brother." A moment went by and then Herska's voice continued. "I didnae expect her to ever connect with the child after everything that happened. Do ye think Finna has inherited Catriona's gifts?"

"'Tis hard to say but ye can be sure Finna's bairn has-- especially with the healing abilities of both grandparents."

Healing abilities? Finna had never noticed her father having any special talents in that regard. Her cheeks burned as the conversation continued. It made her uncomfortable but at the same time she couldn't pull herself away, especially since her name and her baby had been mentioned.

"I wonder about this trip she's taken on. She left her child and acted like it was the easiest thing in the world. 'Twill be hard for her now. I'm sure she feels a lot of guilt."

There was a lull and Finna moved a short distance away from the open window, feeling a bit sick to her stomach. She leaned forward with her hands on her knees and breathed in and out, hoping she wouldn't throw-up. Villagers walked by and stared at her curiously.

When the conversation resumed it sounded as though Mikdal and Herska had moved into the other room and it was harder to make out the words. Finna heard the name, 'Fergus'. She crept closer. Suddenly their voices were loud, as though they were right next to the window. She ducked and huddled against the cottage wall. If they noticed her out here...

"But I do hope she heeds your advice, Mikdal. If they run into Brandubh it could get nasty and dangerous, especially for the girl. And the bairn needs to be protected above all else. Should we follow them?"

"Nae, Herska, she's a seer, she'll figure it out and she has many friends. Ye know Catriona is like a daughter to me but we have to let her find her own way...if we intervene we could cause more of a problem. Remember the faisnich..."

Remember the *what?* Finna puzzled over the strange word.

"Of course ye would feel that way, husband. She spent so much time with us after what happened to Fergus and..." their voices faded again and then Finna saw her mother hurrying toward her. She ran to meet her, hoping Catriona wouldn't notice her eavesdropping.

"Sorry to take so long," Catriona said breathlessly. "I should have brought ye with me. I could have introduced ye to my friend, Tannith. Mikdal told me she was here to see her aging mother and I just had to say hello. Are ye all right? Ye look flushed."

"I'm fine," Finna said but she was not fine at all, she was shaky and still had a sick feeling in her stomach.

"Here Finna. Take some of these," Catriona offered, handing her a small pouch. "And try a bit of the honey—it works well for nausea. We have a long way to go today."

Finna reached into the bag pulling out small pieces of a root that smelled like licorice. Chewing distractedly she unwrapped the jar. She stuck her forefinger into the fragrant honey, licking it clean as she followed Catriona down the dirt road.

Shops were opening, the shopkeepers hanging out their wares. Finna admired the hammered tin lanterns hanging on hooks outside the metalsmith as they passed. Next was a pottery, not yet open, and then a shop containing weaving supplies and wool in different stages; a woman sat outside working with something that resembled a metal dog brush, carding wool. People stood together in groups talking and waiting to begin their shopping as the sun came into view, rising from behind the eastern mountains. The light spilled across the valley, casting a warm glow on the already radiant faces of the villagers. Everyone called out greetings as they went by, some acknowledging Catriona by name. The people all seemed full of joy, contented and happy but it didn't get rid of Finna's unsettled feeling.

Tamar lived on the edge of town in a small stone cottage. He was in the doorway when they got there and was obviously delighted to see Catriona. He grabbed her and kissed her on the mouth and then pulled her close for a long embrace. When they pulled away from each other laughing, Catriona turned to introduce Finna. Tamar was much older but looked like Alex, with the same thick thatch of dark hair and piercing blue eyes. He could almost be Alex's father or maybe an uncle.

"I wanted to thank ye for the lovely warm boots," Finna managed to say as she examined his familiar features.

"I was so glad to contribute something for your journey." Tamar smiled and grasped Finna by the hand. His voice was deeply timbred--rich with the heavy brogue of the village. "And 'twas a delight to see ye again, my friend," he said, pulling Catriona close once more. He kissed her again, lingering a bit too long for Finna's taste but she figured it must be the custom here.

As they turned to go he said he hoped to see them on their way back. "Be safe," he called as they walked away up the trail.

"Tamar looks a lot like Alex, doesn't he?" Catriona remarked.

"You noticed that too? I wonder if they're related. Is that possible?"

"Why not? What do ye know about Alex's background?"

"Actually not a lot. His father died when he was fifteen and he never spoke of his grandparents." Finna thought about her courtship with Alex. Mostly they frequented the bar in town or went for picnics. Alex was reluctant to spend much time with his mother who he described as a busybody. Finna thought the term harsh and enjoyed the older woman despite the way she doted on her son. To Finna her behavior seemed justified considering her being a widow and Alex an only child. "You and Tamar seem pretty close."

Catriona turned toward her with a surprised look. "We've been friends for a long time, Finna."

The slight tone of annoyance and dismissal made Finna feel chastised, like a small child. This wasn't the first time she had heard it.

As they left the protected valley behind the air grew colder, accompanied by a chill wind. Finna pulled the wool hat she had gotten from Herska down over her ears. Now was the time to question Catriona about what she had overheard but she was embarrassed to admit her eavesdropping, and reluctant to have Catriona angry with her. But names had been mentioned--names that she wasn't familiar with, alluding to things Catriona had not mentioned.

The trail rose in front of them, taking them away from the safety of Clachencreid. The meaning of the name fit this rustic, homey place. A hollow place opened up inside Finna as she thought about how long it had taken them to get here and how far they still had to go. She placed her hands on the hard bump of her belly and then hurried after her mother's retreating figure.

It was surprising to see the village so far below when they finally emerged out of the trees. The sun had reached its apex and the warming light was very welcome. A circle of stones stood off the trail in an open space next to the path, drawing Finna into their protection. "Let's stop to eat in this sunny spot," she called, heading toward them.

"A good choice. This has been a place for travelers to rest and receive energy for many a year." Catriona slid the backpack off her shoulders and placed it on the ground and then began pulling out the food supplies.

Despite being nervous about her mother's reactions, Finna couldn't contain her questions any longer. It was all she had thought about since leaving the village. "I overheard Mikdal and Herska talking about someone named Brandoof," she blurted out.

Catriona whipped her head around. "What did they say?"

"They said he was dangerous. Who is he?"

A long moment of silence went by and then Catriona said, "He is my brother."

"But...you never mentioned you had a brother."

"I know. I should have told ye about him." Catriona bent over her knapsack, her long hair covering her face. "Brandubh, my brother, he...he's an enigma. He...well...I don't really want to get into all of this right now. Let's have our lunch. All of this will spoil our digestion."

"What about Brandubh? Has he done something?"

"'Tis a long discussion. Can it nae wait until we've eaten?"

"No, I don't think it can...they mentioned the name Fergus too, who's he?"

Catriona's face blanched. "What else did ye hear, child?"

"I'm not a child. I deserve to know about you and your family, my family. I've given up my safe life to head off into god knows where and ye won't even be honest with me!"

"Finna, please. I havnae told ye these things because... because I have put them behind me. Fergus is, was, my father. As far as my brother goes, I will tell ye. He's a priest. He was ordained in Edinburgh. I went to visit him a few times before...before..."

"Before what?"

"Before he turned." Catriona pushed the hair back from her face distractedly. "He always had this side to him, this dark side, but something changed after he became a priest. I dinna know why but he became even more arrogant and determined

62

to do whatever he wanted. He craves power. 'Tis all he seems to care about. I havenae seen him for a long time."

"But he's involved in something bad here in the Otherworld."

"I dinna know that for sure."

"I heard Mikdal talking about it, Mother." Finna put her hand over her mouth. It was the first time she had called Catriona 'mother'.

Catriona noticed it too and came over and put her arms around her. "Finna, my dearest nighean. I am so sorry for all of this but I...I didnae wish to overwhelm ye."

Finna pulled away. "I have a right to know what I'm getting into. Don't you have any concern about your grandchild?"

"Of course I do! That's the entire reason I came for ye in the first place...this bairn..." her voiced trailed off and she started again. "Ye must understand that I would never purposely put ye or your bairn in jeopardy."

"But since you didn't know about Brandubh being close by, that makes it all right? Herska said he was dangerous. Why would she say that?"

"Herska does nae know if he's dangerous or not. I have hopes for my brother. We were very close growing up."

When a sudden exhaustion moved through her body, Finna sat down on a low rock, hugging her arms around herself protectively.

Catriona sat down next to her and placed a hand on her knee. "Ye have every right to be angry but dinna use it as an excuse to lose trust in what we are doin'. I was wrong to leave ye with Angus, I see that now, but at the time 'twas the only thing I could do. I canna undo the past but I can bring ye safely to the Glass Mountain. Nae need to worry about things that may or may not happen, Finna. Herska and Mikdal have been like parents to me and they're very protective. Now, enough of that--the word for mother in Gaelic is mathair. Would ye be willin' to call me that?"

Finna looked into her mother's hopeful face and nodded. "I'm not planning on going home...ma-har... although the thought has crossed my mind. I just want you to be more forthcoming."

Catriona clapped her hands, dispelling the somber mood. "Good pronunciation, my nighean. Now, we shall eat our lunch and have a short rest. We still have a long way to go today." Catriona had a thermos of tea she had brewed before they left the village and handed Finna a cup. "Drink this, it will help."

As they ate Finna placed her hand on the stone behind her. She could feel a kind of pulse or vibration. "What *is* this place?"

"'Tis a resting place where the sun and moon converge at special times of the year. 'Twas built by the ancients as a place of spiritual succor where they came together for the equinoxes and solstices. They gathered here and at other locations for their sacred rites to take advantage of the special alignment of energies. See these marks?" she pointed to a series of horizontal and vertical slashes on the stone. "This is Ogham, the language of the Druids who lived here long ago."

"What does it say?" Finna asked, running her fingers across the indentations in the stone.

"I canna translate but there are some Druids living here who can. There have been many theories regarding the meaning. These marks are most likely a guide to those who came after, maybe a secret message, or maybe a road map of sorts. Many travelers have found peace among these old stones. Take in what they offer, Finna, ye will need it later on."

Finna looked around at the worn stones. Some had moss and lichen growing on them, some were pockmarked and broken from weather and time. She felt a certain kinship with them, as though they were living beings. Birdsong came from the massive beech trees on the other side of the field, winter chickadees and some others that she didn't recognize. As she closed her eyes, a vision of white robed people carrying flowers and walking slowly among the stones came to her. She watched them place the flowers on the ground in front of the largest stone and then gather in a circle. And when she opened her eyes to the meadow of pale yellow grasses blowing lightly in the breeze, snow covered mountain peaks in the distance, all under a warming sun, she felt restored.

"We need to reach the closest peak there before sunset." Catriona pointed into the distance, her brow furrowed.

Finna looked again at the far-away mountains. "There?" Her newfound peace left her as she took in the enormous distance.

"'Tis where Mikdal told me the new trail begins and there's an old mine where we can shelter for the night. I know it looks a long way off but we'll manage it."

Just before they left Catriona gathered some grasses and a few wildflowers from the meadow and placed them in front of the largest stone. "A way of giving thanks," she said, as they packed their things and headed toward the path.

THE TRAIL WOVE through scattered oaks and birch and Finna saw evidence of other standing stones here and there through the trees. She wanted to investigate but Catriona shook her head and kept going. As they came into a meadow of wildflowers, they startled a small herd of wild boar that melted quickly into the underbrush on the other side. Finna followed Catriona across the meadow and entered beech woodland where the smell of mushrooms permeated the cool, moist air.

"I need to collect a bit of this fungus, Finna. I'll only be a moment."

Catriona headed toward a tree trunk and picked off parts of something that resembling a huge beehive. "What is that?"

"'Tis agarikon. It has antiviral and antifungal properties. 'Tis difficult to come by since it only grows in old growth forests." She placed a small amount of the tree mushroom into her pack and came back to the path.

Finna thought she saw a herd of tiny horses coming toward her from the left side of the trail but before she could get a good look at them they wheeled and took off, galloping back the way they had come, leaving little puffs of dirt in their wake. When she stopped and looked back there was nothing there. "Did ye see that?" As Finna hurried toward her mother she was stopped in her tracks, struck by the violet shimmer around Catriona.

"The horses? Aye. Rhiannon has become enraged again and taken it out on her herd."

"Rhiannon?"

"The horse goddess." Catriona laughed. "The last time this happened 'twas the stallion refuing to allow Rhiannon on his back."

Finna tried to wrap her mind around the reality of a goddess, and especially a vindictive one. "So she shrank them? How will they survive?"

"They will be back to normal as soon as they give in to her demands."

Feeling suddenly weak and shaky, Finna went to sit down. Too many weird things were happening. She stared at the vibrating color shifting around her mother and then noticed a faint shimmer around her own hand. She must be hallucinating.

"'Tis nae hallucination, Finna," Catriona said before Finna

could organize her thoughts. "Our light is always there but the denser atmosphere in your world renders it invisible."

Finna waggled her fingers, watching a glimmer of the palest blue in the air behind them.

LONG SHADOWS LAY across the trail. Now the peak they had been heading toward loomed up in front of them. The lichen and small plants with pink bell-like flowers growing amongst the rocks helped dispel the otherwise desolate feeling of the mountainside.

"Mikdal said the mine was downhill from where the new trail begins. I am nae familiar with this area. For some reason this is a trail I've missed on my many trips." Catriona looked worried as she searched through the underbrush.

Finna sat down on a flat rock next to the trail to catch her breath. She had almost forgotten about the moonstone and pulled it out now to check the milky surface. A line appeared almost immediately. "There's a map in the moonstone," she called excitedly.

Before Finna had time to examine the emerging map, Catraiona had taken it out of her hand. Holding the stone in front of her, the older woman led the way down the hill. The ground leveled off, and then the entrance to an old mineshaft came into view at the side of the trail. Catriona pulled a candle and a box of matches out of her pack, lighting it before she entered the dark tunnel. Finna followed, close at her heels, trying to stay in the circle of light as the shaft descended. In but a few minutes the shaft ended at a doorway into a small room. Catriona used the candle to light an oil lamp left behind by some former occupant, revealing beds of straw covered in burlap, a tattered shirt, pieces of a woven basket and broken pottery. Finna let out a heavy sigh of exhaustion and took off her pack, setting it on the floor next to one of the makeshift beds. She had just closed her eyes when Catriona's distraught voice shattered her peace.

"Help me, Finna!"

Against the darkness of the tunnel, glowing red eyes and a mouth full of sharp yellow teeth hurtled toward them at an alarming rate. Finna screamed, the sound echoing off the walls of the enclosed space, and then ran to help Catriona push against the entrance stone. The animal had almost reached them when the stone rolled into place with a heavy thunk, sending Finna flying backward. The eerie howl from the other side made the hair on the back of her neck stand up. The creature's long claws scrabbled against the stone as it whined in frustration.

"What *was* that?"

"One of the beasts that belong to the Wildmen who live in these mountains. I am nae sure why 'twas so vicious toward us. They often hunt the young boar and other animals around here but never humans." Catriona's face had visibly paled, her eyes wide with alarm.

After the adrenaline rush, Finna's strength ebbed quickly away. She sat down heavily, her head in her hands. After her heart stopped pounding, she reached for her pack, bringing out apples, cheese and bannock in hopes of replenishing her energy. Kneeling, she arranged the food between herself and Catriona, watching her mother carefully. When Catriona came to sit down cross-legged beside her daughter, the color had returned to her cheeks. The older woman smiled, reaching to tear off chunks of the freshly baked bannock.

Slowly, Finna's heartbeat returned to normal. It was as though Mikdal and Herska's essence was with them, providing strength through their food. Finna looked over, mentioning this feeling to Catriona.

"Aye, I feel it too, they are very special people and what they have to give comes through in mysterious ways."

After they finished eating Catriona closed her eyes. Finna didn't want to disturb her so she crawled into one of the straw filled nests in the corner of the room pulling her heavy sweater around her. Despite the lingering fear about the beast, it did not take long for sleep to claim her.

WHEN FINNA AWOKE, Catriona was sitting in the exact same spot. The soft light from the lantern brightened her russet hair.

"Good morning," her mother said, opening her eyes.

"Did you meditate all night?"

Catriona didn't answer as she brought out the rest of the cheese and bannock from the night before. She opened the thermos, pouring tea into the cup and handing it to Finna. "Today should be easier, we dinna have far to go."

Finna put the cup to her lips, tasting cinnamon and some other spices. "Where do you find cinnamon here?"

Catriona smiled. "I bought that back in Bailemuir. It has several health benefits."

"Such as?"

"It regulates blood sugar, helps brain function and contains minerals that are good for ye and the baby. And besides that," she added with a chuckle, "it tastes good."

"Do we have a destination today?" Finna asked after taking another sip.

"Some friends of Mikdal and Herska's live along this trail—we should be there by early afternoon."

"What about the beasts?"

"They are less likely to bother us in the daytime. They're nocturnal hunters--their eyes are more adapted to the dark."

Finna's mind went to Alex and her father, both overprotective and stubborn. Alex tried hard to persuade her to go home with him--who could blame him? She was carrying their child into a place where goddesses wreaked havoc and vicious beasts roamed freely. At this moment she wouldn't mind if the two of them were sitting next to her. She could put up with their meddling ways in exchange for their size and strength in battling those horrible animals. Her hands went to her belly expecting to feel a large bulge but it was still almost non-existent. When would she begin to show? And how would it be in a few months when her stomach grew large? Would she still be able to walk the distances they had been covering every day? In her mind's eye she saw Alex and her father sitting beside her. In her fantasy Alex picked up her hand and told her not to worry. She leaned into him feeling the muscles of his shoulder, his strong arm around her. Tears filled her eyes.

"What is it, child?"

Finna wiped at her eyes as she gazed into her mother's pale and worried face. "Nothing. Just thinking about the beasts."

"They're long gone. Ye need to eat a good breakfast and then put on your warm mittens and boots, 'tis a cold day and there could be snow."

The night before had been clear with no hint of bad weather coming in. How did Catriona know this? There was no window and the shaft opening was covered with the large stone they had rolled into place the night before.

"Ye never know what the weather will be like in these mountains and I have to say that it seems even more unpredictable than it has in the past." Catriona arranged their breakfast on a white cloth she had pulled out of her knapsack.

After eating, they packed up their things and moved the

stone out of the opening. It was so well balanced that it rolled sideways with ease. Before heading out, Catriona pulled out a small handful of herbs and held them out to Finna.

"What do these do?"

"They will protect us from the beasts for one thing, they eliminate our smell so they canna track us. They also allow one to go longer without food--very nourishing to the system. 'Tis a combination of high john, agrimony, oatstraw and a few others that are good for circulation."

Almost as soon as Finna began to chew, a warm sensation crept up from her toes and spread through her body. Carrying the lantern in her hand, Catriona turned and smiled. In the soft lantern light, Catriona's eyes looked bright, her skin aglow. Her thick red hair was pulled back and braided with a few wisps left to soften her jawline. Her mother was beautiful and even dressed in thick wool pants and a heavy sweater she managed to look elegant. Finna's hands went to her own hair that had come out of its braid from her restless night of sleep. She pulled off the tie and rebraided it quickly as she followed her mother up the tunnel.

Crisp air greeted them as they emerged into the pale morning light. Turning right, Catriona hurried up the hill following the path from the night before. "We must get to the main trail as soon as possible."

"I thought this was going to be a leisurely day," Finna said, looking around nervously.

"I didnae mean to imply that. We must be watchful."

"But you said the beasts are nocturnal."

"There are many forces to be reckoned with here besides the beasts, Finna."

Stomach churning, Finna hurried after her mother. She recalled Catriona's earlier description of the Otherworld: *...not unlike the wild Highlands...'tis full of light and life.* This was not reminding her at all of her trips with her father where she awoke in the morning to hear the sheep baaing, the hollow comforting sound of their copper bells clanking. Hmm.

It wasn't long before they arrived at the main trail and Catriona began to walk at a more normal speed. Finna tried to catch her breath, wanting to sit for a minute, but Catriona didn't even glance her way as she swung off down the new trail. They walked quietly for another twenty minutes, the silence spreading over them like a soothing blanket. A minute later an ear-splitting yowl rent the air, followed by a shrieking wail that sounded like an animal being torn apart.

Finna grabbed her mother's arm. "What was that?"

Catriona shrugged and shook her head.

"Ye don't know what it could *be?*"

"We need to go on quietly, no more talking."

The path narrowed again, heading slightly downhill. Finna followed Catriona, her heart pounding in her ears. As they came around a bend Finna thought she saw something moving on the path ahead of them and grabbed Catriona's arm again. They both stopped and held their breath, straining to see in the gray mist suddenly forming around them. When an amorphous dark shadow moved across the trail, Catriona sucked in her breath, holding a warning hand on Finna's arm.

A great rumble of thunder split the silence and almost immediately rain poured down. The silver birch, aspen and straggly scots pine trees offered no protection from the drenching downpour sending Catriona hurrying to the thick brush at the side of the trail. She crawled beneath the branches, pulling Finna after her. For a while nothing could be heard over the dull roar of the downpour, but when something ran by on the trail Finna grabbed Catriona's sweater, her hands clammy. All her dream images came rushing back—was this the figure who was always after her? A fluttery feeling went through her belly and she looked down as though she could see inside to the small being inside her. It seemed too early to feel the baby but when it happened again she counted the weeks—the baby was around three months now. Was three months when they quickened? The one visit to the doctor had given her very little imformation regarding pregnancy and she hadn't been thinking clearly when she spoke to the midwife.

When the rain lessoned allowing them to hear another eerie howl, Finna cringed, her hands over her ears.

"'Tis far away now," Catriona said, crawling out and holding up the branches.

Reluctantly Finna followed, her breath coming in short gasps.

Catriona scanned down the trail and then bent to brush the mud off her boots. "Mikdal did tell me about something... a shadow creature that has taken up residence here. It preys on fear."

"How can you keep from feeling fear?" she asked, adrenaline racing through her.

"Ye must recognize the fear and let it go before it takes over."

"I don't know how to do that." Finna pulled her damp sweater protectively over her belly.

"I will teach ye. I've been all over these mountains and had some close calls but never been harmed."

"What happened when Mikdal ran into this....this shadow?" Finna asked, hurrying after Catriona.

"Mikdal is able to make himself invisible, something I have nae mastered."

"Invisible? Are ye joking? Do you take herbs for that?" Despite her fear, Finna laughed.

Catriona turned, her expression serious. "This canna be

achieved with herbs. 'Tis accomplished by a concentration of mind."

"Have you tried to learn it from him?"

Catriona shook her head. "I would have to spend many months of practice and so far havnae had the time or felt a pressing need."

After those words, her stride lengthened, and Finna had to run a few steps to keep up. At the edge of a large meadow Catriona stopped, signaling for quiet. A few deer on the far side looked up when the two women came into view and then resumed grazing. When Catriona stopped at the side of the trail to examine a plant, Finna walked around her, leading the way along the narrow trail and following the edge of wet grass. Soon the sun appeared through a hole in the clouds, illuminating the grasses and turning the raindrops into tiny prisms. As the rich aroma of wet earth and wildflowers rose into the air, Finna's senses came alive. The croak of a frog began and then another answered. Soon a cacophony of sound filled the silence. A snake slithered across the path, disappearing into the weeds on the other side of the trail. She stopped to take it all in, breathing deeply as she closed her eyes for a moment. When she opened them, Catriona had passed her and was already disappearing around a bend. She ran to catch up, heading down a steep trail. To her left, a narrow river wended its way along the bottom of a deep ravine.

Catriona waited, allowing Finna go by her on the narrow animal track. 'Be careful here, the rocks are treacherous."

Finna wtched her feet for a few steps and then gazed into the canyon, getting lost in the beauty of the rocky hillsides and the sun glinting off the water at the bottom. She didn't notice the dead deer until she had stumbled over it. A shriek escaped her lips before she could stop it and she stumbled backward. "Do you think this is what we heard back there?"

Catriona knelt next to the carcass. "The body is still warm. Whatever killed it didnae want it for food. It might be what we heard."

Finna bent closer, noticing the open staring eyes and the jagged bloody rip exposing the glistening insides of the belly. She moved to the side of the trail and threw-up, heaving again and again.

"Finna, take some ginger."

"I can't," she said thickly, lying back on the ground.

"Finna take this. It will stop the spasms." Catriona forced the ginger into her hand.

"How much farther are Mikdal's friends?" Finna asked, her teeth chattering.

"I havnae been on this trail so 'tis hard to say. At least another hour or two."

Finna's heart sank. She wouldn't make it. "Why are we on a trail you aren't familiar with? I thought you'd explored every bit of this place."

Catriona shook her head. "Mikdal recommended this route, Finna. I'll give ye some herbs for stamina. I was going to taper off with these but after what just happened ye need them."

"Are they going to make me sick again?"

"Nae, they will give ye strength as well as clean out your mouth."

Finna took a pinch of leaves and handed the packet back to Catriona. She chewed up the sweet herb and swallowed it with a big drink of water. She smiled wanly at Catriona, who was watching her with some concern. "So far so good."

"These herbs are very reviving and good for the baby as well." Catriona pulled a cloth out of her pack and gently cleaned Finna's face, wiping the cold sweat off her brow. "Lie down here." Catriona pulled out a dry sweater for Finna to change into. "You're too weak to go anywhere right now."

Finna closed her eyes, images racing across her mind: the dead staring eyes of the deer, the beast in the tunnel, its red open mouth filled with sharp teeth, the shadow creature on the trail...and then the conversation about Catriona's brother and the betrayal she felt. Another spasm went through her as she registered the terrible danger she had placed herself and her baby in...she was literally sick with fear. Her body shook with nerves and cold and Catriona came over and covered her with another sweater.

"Try to rest a bit. I will keep watch."

"Are ye strong enough to continue?"

Finna heard Catriona's voice as if from a distance. She opened her eyes.

"We need to go now. We don't want to be here after dark." Catriona helped her up.

"Do Mikdal's friends live in the valley down by the river?"

"From what Mikdal told me they live further up this trail," Catriona answered, motioning for Finna to follow. "Their dwellings are rudimentary, barely what I would call houses. But according to Mikdal this way of living suits them."

"Is it a man and a woman, a couple?"

"I dinna know if ye could say a man and a woman, but they're friendly."

"What are they then?"

"They are called the Amuigh, which roughly translates to "outside."

"Ouside what?"

"Ye can judge for yourself after ye meet them. I am nae

familiar with this group-- I've only met their kind in the south-eastern section of the Otherworld. They are able to live here because of the higher vibrations."

Finna followed Catriona along the trail, struggling to keep up. *Higher vibrations?* What did that mean? Everything felt the same as it had but when she looked at her hand the aura was no longer visible. Maybe her being ill had done something to her senses.

They soon came to an area full of berry bushes and hazelnut trees lined up in rows. Fields had been cleared beyond the rows of trees and by the look of things some kind of earth vegetable was in the process of being harvested. Finna squinted ahead trying to see through the swirling fog. Around the next bend a shape appeared out of the mist. It looked like a large ape walking along the path in the other direction. Finna screamed and grabbed Catriona's arm. "What's that?"

"We have arrived," Catriona said quietly, her voice calm. "Wait here, I'll go ahead and introduce myself. They are a shy tribe."

By now the light was fading fast--Finna felt depleted and chilled to the core of her being. As she sat down with her back against a tree she watched similar creatures about thirty feet away digging in the dirt with short sticks. They were around five feet tall and looked to be part ape and part human, with fur-covered bodies and deepset eyes. Finna whimpered, wishing she were home in her little cottage away from all this weirdness. Her hands went to her belly and she wished fervently that nothing bad would happen to her or her baby on this trip.

"We have beds for the night and a warm meal being prepared for us," Catriona said happily, appearing next to Finna.

Finna took her mother's outstretched hand, wondering

again about how weak she felt. Was it the pregnancy or this place?

"You're beginning your second tri-mester, Finna. 'Tis natural to feel fatigued. I think ye have done very well so far."

Finna looked at her mother in surprise. She was positive she had not spoken her thoughts out loud.

Catriona nodded. "I've always had an uncanny ability to read thoughts, especially with family members. "Tis hard to keep a secret from me," she laughed.

Finna followed her down the path to what looked like a large pile of sticks. As they drew closer a being emerged from an opening on the side and Finna was face to face with a creature that seemed oddly familiar and yet utterly alien at the same time. Catriona began speaking softly in a language Finna couldn't understand. The cadence seemed almost musical, the sounds like notes instead of words. Without turning, Catriona reached back for Finna's hand and pulled her forward, placing it in the Amuigh's hand and covering their clasped hands with her own.

Nothing could have prepared Finna for what stood in front of her. Her own imagination, which was pretty fanciful, could never have conjured such creatures. Finna stared into the deepest eyes she had ever seen. A shining wise intelligence gazed out at her. She smiled and mumbled 'hello'. The being said some words in a melodic voice.

"This is Mena, she is the daughter of Cay who is matriarch of the tribe."

"Hello, Mena." Finna smiled in what she hoped was a friendly manner although she felt very self-conscious as well as fearful.

Mena continued to gaze at Finna and said, *Feennna*, making it sound like a musical note. Mena didn't smile but still managed to convey a profoundly welcoming presence as she turned and led the way into the dwelling. On the other side of a hanging burlap door, a twig fire sent its warmth into the rounded space. Another member of the tribe sat hunched over next to the firepit occupying the center portion of the surprisingly spacious hut. Her gray fur looked rough, her deepset eyes not as clear as Mena's. She also greeted Finna by name but in a deeper more resonant tone. She spoke her own name, 'Cay', pointing to her chest with long gray fingers. Finna nodded and smiled thinking how grandmotherly Cay seemed. A vision of young Amuigh sitting in her lap went through Finna's mind and she let out a delighted laugh that brought a curious look from Cay.

Finna watched the smoke curl up from the fire, surprised to see it forming spirals before it left the dwelling by the small hole in the ceiling—the symbol was the same as the one on Enid's forehead. She sat down next to her mother, filing the question away for later. While Catriona began pulled cheese and meat out of the backpack, Mena brought over a basket filled with fresh berries and hazelnuts. She urged them to eat and they helped themselves to the nuts and berries and some of the reddish mashed goo from the pot that hung over the fire.

Finna didn't know what was expected in this strange setting and tried to pay attention to any signs from Cay and Mena. Was it all right to eat this much of their food? She realized she was starving as she crammed the sweet potato-like mush into her mouth. Finna listened to her mother chattering with them in their language, wondering what they were talking about.

After Finna had filled her belly her eyes drooped, fatigue taking hold of her. The last few days had sapped her enegy. As her head nodded, Cay reached for her hand with gentle fingers, leading her to an area in the back of the dwelling where the ceiling sloped down. Finna lowered herself onto the bed of woven leaves, barely able to keep her eyes open. The warmth and the smell of the fire mingling with the distinctive odor of damp fur immediately lulled her into sleep. The last thing she remembered was the musical sound of their conversation before she drifted off.

CHAPTER 6

S he woke in the morning to the sound of their voices, as
though the conversation had never ceased. Catriona,
Cay and Mena had been joined by two others, who
were larger and distinctly masculine.

"Guid mornin', Finna. Ye had a long rest."

"What time is it?" she asked, pushing herself up on her
elbows.

"The Amuigh dinna measure time. 'Tis between dawn and
mid-day judging by the light."

"Don't we have to continue on our journey today?"

"We will remain here one more night. Ye need to rebuild
your strength."

The view through the small gap between the burlap and
the doorframe revealed snowflakes falling straight down from
a charcoal sky. She sat up, pulling her sweater close around her
body.

"Come sit by the fire, I've made tea." Catriona held out a
cup. "I mixed our black tea with herbs for energy."

Rubbing the sleep out of her eyes, Finna came close to the

fire. She took the proffered cup, sipping as she sat close to the flames. While Catriona pulled out the remains of the cheese and some apples from her pack, Cay brought over a bowl of ripe berries, putting it down next to Finna. Her grandmotherly attitude showed itself again as her fingers touched Finna's head before she went to sit on the other side of the fire. When Finna looked up, Cay was watching her, encouraging her to eat by bringing her own fingers to her mouth, and patting her stomach. Finna munched on a few berries, trying hard not to feel self-conscious about the newcomers. No one had introduced them. The berries were sweet and succulent, and before she knew it the bowl was empty. She looked up, aware for the first time that she was the only one eating. "Mother, did you have your breakfast already?"

"Oh aye, I ate hours ago with our hosts. This is Beag and Ard," she finally said, gesturing to the new Amuigh.

Finna smiled and held her hands out. They each grasped one, staring into her soul with their perceptive eyes. It was a very long minute before they let go. Finna took in a deep breath, watching in surprise as the four Amuigh rose as one and headed out of the hut. Finna looked questioningly at Catriona as the burlap flap fell back in place.

"The snow has stopped so they are going back to work."

"What are they doing?"

"They are gathering stores for the colder weather and drying their fruit. They also grow tubers that they dig up around this time of year. It's what we ate last night, a sort of sweet potato. They're vegetarians, living off what they grow and can gather from the forests. They live as our hunter-gatherer ancestors did, moving from place to place as the seasons change, but they have certain areas where they always return, like this one. We are lucky they were here, 'tis nearly time for them to head into the valley to escape the heavy snows and ice."

"Will we encounter that kind of weather?"

"Aye, Finna. "Tis winter."

"But how will we survive?" Finna heard the whine in her voice as an image of ice storms and bleak frozen expanses went through her mind. All she had to keep her warm were wool sweaters and if they got wet they were not much use.

"Dinna worry, I am prepared."

"Are you? It doesn't seem that way to me considering what we've already been through. I have my baby to think about, you know."

Catriona's eyebrows went up. "Nothing bad has happened to ye, Finna, aside from the morning sickness, which is perfectly natural. We have warm clothing, good boots. Ye have been spoiled far too long. Be grateful for what ye have."

Finna opened her mouth to reply but then closed it. What Catriona said was true. She was spoiled and acting like a child. But being pregnant in this alien place scared her. Every day there was something new she had to get used to. Today it was the Amuigh, tomorrow, who knew? What if she got sick? What if she broke her leg? This backward place didn't have doctors or ways to treat injuries. Her pre-natal vitamins had been left at home, forgotten in the cupboard over the sink. Was the baby getting proper nutrition? Alex's admonitions returned to her: *you're too thin...you're not eting properly*. Was she too thin? There were no mirrors here, but her belly was growing, she knew that. It wasn't as though she felt hungry all the time. She had stuffed herself last night and the supplies her mother still had in her backpack were definitely nourishing.

She glanced at Catriona who was staring at her pointedly. "I am an herbalist and a healer," was all she said before she got up and left the hut.

. . .

THE REST of the day was spent outside with the Amuigh gathering food. Catriona and Finna were given rudimentary wooden digging tools and told in what areas the tubers were growing. The steady conversation of the Amuigh was like listening to dozens of windchimes.

When it grew dark the Amuigh carried their baskets into a storage hut full of racks of drying berries and burlap sacks full of tubers. The pleasant smell of fruit and earth wafted around them. At Cay's insistence, Catriona and Finna filled their knapsacks with as many tubers as they could fit. Mena gave them dried berries that Catriona wrapped in paper. By the time they followed Mena and Cay to the hut the sky was completely black and a cold wind had begun to blow. With no ambient light, the darkness here was sudden, like a velvet curtain coming down. Inside, Cay and Mena built up the fire and brewed sweet tea in a large hand-formed clay pot. Mena covered the dwelling opening with another layer of heavy burlap to keep out the wind and it stayed surprisingly warm inside.

THAT NIGHT FINNA slept fitfully with dreams of shadowy beings, odd gnarled trees with limbs filled with icicles and a mountain of ice so sheer it looked like glass. When she woke in the morning the fire was out and Catriona was nowhere to be seen. Panic rose in her throat--she jumped up, pulling the burlap aside to look out. All she could see was a snow-covered hillside, no smoke from any of the huts, no beings and no Catriona.

❄

"WHERE HAVE YOU BEEN?" Finna tried to control the quaver in her voice but was unsuccessful.

"I was walking with the Amuigh. Today is the day they chose to leave."

"What do you mean? They just got up this morning and decided it was time to go?"

Catriona nodded. "They take their cues from something that is far beyond our limited senses."

"Did they tell you anything else?"

"Aye, they imparted a lot of information. Their knowledge of this area is vast. They told me the easiest and least dangerous trails to take. I drew myself a little map from their descriptions." Catriona held up a small piece of brown paper full of pencil marks.

"Why can't we just use the moonstone?"

"We can but 'tis helpful to have another option. The stone is sometimes unreliable."

"Unreliable? I thought it was magic."

Catriona pressed her lips together. "'Tis, but from what Mikdal told me the route it shows could be dangerous now. The stone knows nothing of the changes wrought here."

Finna puzzled over this. If it was magic it should know the current situation, or so it seemed to her. "Will we be going soon?" Finna looked uneasily at the dark gray sky.

"The weather will hold today. This I know from the Amuigh. As soon as ye have eaten we can gather our things and travel on toward the Glass Mountain."

"The Glass Mountain... I had a terrible dream about a mountain of ice!"

"And so it is; maybe your psychic powers are beginning to unfold." Catriona's eyes looked very green in the frigid air.

Together they went into the hut and gathered their belongings together. Finna ate cheese and bannock and drank a little of the cold tea Catriona had saved.

"It feels desolate here since they left."

"Aye, it does. They are very gentle beings. Come now quickly, we have a long day of travel ahead of us." Catriona bustled around, putting the remaining food into her pack and returning the cups to the low shelf against the wall. Finna followed her out the door and toward the trail in the opposite direction of the Amuigh.

THE TWO WOMEN followed the snow-covered path northeast, away from the village. Finna's former world seemed far away now, almost as though she had entered a different lifetime-- and in some ways she had. They had been away for over a month, it was getting close to the Celtic New Year and the beginning of the dark time. She had only a vague idea of the date, not that it mattered anyway. Except for the need to reach the Glass Mountain by the solstice and the birth of her baby in March she didn't have much use for dates anymore.

Something had happened since the revelation that her mother could read her thoughts. It wasn't that she purposely kept her thoughts secret; it was as though they skittered into her mind and left like furtive creatures searching for the dark. Somehow her consciousness knew that if they hovered for too long her mother would discover them. And some of these were musings she wasn't ready to share.

Small scots pines, a smattering of silver birch and oaks dotted the sides of the trail as they headed north. Taller evergreens in the distance looked almost black beneath the crisp white on their boughs. The silence was complete, only broken by the occasional chirp of a chicadee or the whump of snow falling off the limbs. The trees were not dense and open fields were visible beyond them, filled with yellowed grasses poking through the layer of snow. To their left, the ground sloped off to meet a narrow creek that gurgled beneath a thin layer of ice.

A sound came to Finna's ears, high, like the tinkling of bells. "What is that?"

'Tis the 'Ghillie Dhu'--the spirits who live in the birch trees."

Finna looked up at the bare branches. "I don't see anything."

"They don't show themselves very often. They protect these trees." Catriona waved her hand around.

"What do they look like?"

"A blur like wings of a hummingbird. They move from place to place in a reality much faster than this one. There are many beings living here that we humans canna see."

At a certain distance away from the trees, the sound disappeared, leaving a piercing silence in its wake. Finna didn't want to break the spell of this place but other questions were hammering at her and refusing to go away. "I never learned why the moonstone is part of the blessing ceremony," she finally said. "What will it mean for us afterward?" Her breath formed a white fog as she spoke and she wondered how cold it was today. Her fingertips felt numb and she stopped to pull gloves out of her pack.

Catriona stopped and faced her. "I've been wondering when you'd summon the nerve or curiosity to ask. The moonstone is blessed by the moon goddess whenever a new being from our line comes into the world. If ye carry it with ye, the stone protects and allows ye to see with your heart instead of your head. It makes it possible for the one blessed to walk through this life connected to the higher realms and to the spirits that dwell in the streams, trees, and plants--in all life. It has other intrinsic powers that I spoke about before we left on the trip, uses that seem to emerge, as they are needed.

"So, since I was the last one blessed that means I'm protected, right?"

"From most things, aye."

"What does that mean—most things?"

"It means that I havnae been this way for a long time."

Finna's stomach clenched. Catriona's tone was the one that said, *do not question me further.* "How far are we from the castle?"

"At least another month's journey." Catriona looked over at Finna. "Are ye all right, child? I know your feelin' tired but is that all?"

"Can we stop for just a minute? I feel dizzy." Finna found a rock and sat down, placing her head in her hands.

Catriona came over and began to rub Finna's back and shoulders, using her knuckles to knead the sore muscles. "The baby is growin' and ye have less stamina. I have some herbs for ye but we need to taper off with these." Catriona took off her pack and pulled out a small drawstring bag. "This is a combination of ground mushrooms for clarity, rose hips to call in good spirits and passion flower for your nerves. They work better as a tea but 'tis nae possible at this moment."

Finna took they herbs from her, chewing them gratefully. After a few moments of rest Catriona helped her up. They continued along the path until it abruptly ended. In front of them was a tangled thicket and gnarled trees so close together it seemed impossible to get through. "This reminds me of my dream." Finna looked over at Catriona who was searching the area and then glancing at the map.

"We may have taken a wrong turn."

Finna looked over Catriona's shoulder, perusing the map. "Where did we start from?"

Catriona pointed to a spot marked in heavy black pencil. "That is the Amuigh camp."

"What about the moonstone?" When Finna pulled the stone out of her pack she could feel it vibrating. She held it in her hand watching a trail emerge, zigzagging across the smooth gray surface. Two tiny figures appeared on one end of the crooked line.

Catriona folded the map and put it in her pocket. She frowned, peering down at the stone. "I think we took the wrong fork right there," Catriona said, putting her finger on a tiny point along the line.

"But where is that?" Finna asked. "I can tell from the stone where we are now but I can't..."

A sudden gust of cold wind blew little eddies of snow off the trees. Finna took her eyes from the stone to watch the branches bend and sway as the odd wind moved through them. They rubbed together making an eerie creaking sound. When she looked at her mother, she seemed to be swaying with the branches. Finna rubbed her temples—her mind felt addled, as though the snow was blowing inside her brain. A second later Catriona grabbed her hand, leading her quickly down a hill. The wind was making a high-pitched whistling, which hurt her ears, confusing her. She pulled back, convinced they were heading the wrong way. Catriona ignored her, leading purposely down the path to where the trail split. The wind was stronger here, shrieking up from the canyon below, whipping against their faces and making their eyes tear. It ripped at their clothes like something alive. Finna tried to say something but the wind tore her words away, flinging them into the air.

Despite Finna's whimpering, Catriona continued to drag her down the hill. Something skittered across the path ahead of them and Finna shrieked, trying as hard as she could to loosen her mother's grip. Catriona turned, her face a pale mask. She shook her head, continuing in the same direction. There was no point in trying to talk; the wind pulled their words away before they had even formed in their minds. Finna felt like a hand had fastened around her throat--she was suffocating. Struggling to breathe, she pressed the moonstone there until the feeling passed but she was left shaking and weak.

They soon found themselves in a dark wood. Catriona pulled Finna behind her into a small hollow where they huddled down, pulling their scarves up to cover their faces. Finna, paralyzed with fear, could scarcely breathe. They stayed until the last of the wind whistled away, leaving them covered in little snowdrifts.

As the last of the wind died away Catriona stood up and dusted the snow from her sweater. "Come." She walked rapidly back to the open trail.

Terrified to be left alone, Finna hurried after her. "What *was* that? The wind seemed almost alive!"

"Aye. Did ye feel its power over your mind?"

"I couldn't think and I couldn't speak, I felt like I was choking."

"Aye, 'tis what it does. It sucks human breath away and creates a vacuum in the mind."

"I don't understand. If this place, the Otherworld, is so special and untouched, why are there such evil forces here?"

"The winds are nae what I would call evil. In a way they are like a test, making sure the beings here are able to keep their minds alert and immune. The Otherworld has always contained both the light and the dark but any negative energy like fear and anger can pull the dark forces in, creating an imbalance The Otherworld is very sensitive to energies. If the balance is off it becomes ill, just as the human body."

Finna checked Catriona's expression for signs of fear or

worry. There was definitely a look of concern around her mouth and lines had appeared in her forehead but mostly she just seemed anxious to continue. Finna, on the other hand, felt terrified and unsure and wondered how she could go on. Catriona's explanation of the winds had not alleviated her anxiety. Her stomach hurt and she was sick with worry about her baby. It took all of her will to keep herself from bursting into tears.

She heard Catriona's voice say, "Check the moonstone, Finna, and see where we might find shelter for the night."

As she looked into the milky surface, a small line appeared, leading down a non-existent trail. Finna searched to find it and finally gave up. Her body felt odd, cold and hot at the same time.

"Finna, ye must hurry! 'Tis too cold, we must keep moving."

When Finna didn't move Catriona came back and grabbed her hand. "Please Finna, there is nae time to lose."

Finna looked up at the darkening sky, dismayed to see snowflakes beginning to fall. "I thought you said it wouldn't snow today," she whined, feeling betrayed by everything including the weather and Catriona.

"What did ye find in the moonstone?" Catriona's voice was loud and angry as she grabbed the stone out of Finna's hand.

"Ye didn't prepare me for this!" Finna yelled. "And I'm sick of being treated like a child."

"I won't treat ye like a child if ye don't act like one. Open your eyes and see what's all around ye, girl. Look at the snow falling, the way it's landing so softly on the branches. And the light—it looks violet--can ye see? For an artist ye are very unobservant."

Finna looked where Catriona pointed, noticing the violet shadows on the snow for the first time. The dusky evening light and the crystalline flakes falling soundlessly all around seemed suddenly magical, as though she had stepped into a fairytale. The muted whoo-hoo of an owl broke the silence and then a second later there was an answering call in the distance. It was quite dark now and when she looked up through the snow at the sky, there were open spots where stars winked blue. As she turned to share this with Catriona she saw a light moving through the trees and a second later a woman materialized, carrying a lantern. She wore a dress made of cobwebs, silvery and soft and dark spiders clung to her mass of silver-gray hair. Her topaz eyes sparkled like crystals.

"I am Vasilia, goddess of the wind. I have come to lead you to shelter."

Finna gaped at her, unable to speak.

"I am nae surprised to see ye here, Vasilia," Catriona said, walking into the light of the lantern. "We experienced your winds earlier today."

Finna thought from her mother's tone that Catriona and Vasilia must be old friends but Vasilia's expression remained neutral as she pointed toward the trees. "Follow me."

Catriona turned toward Finna and smiled reassuringly before she followed Vasilia between two trees and down a steep slope.

Vasilia led them to a shallow protected cave next to a creek covered in a thin sheet of bluish ice. The overhanging bank on the far side had been severely undercut at some previous time when the water was high and ferns and ivy hung down, covered with a dusting of white.

"You will be safe here," Vasilia said. "But you must take care," she added, looking directly at Finna out of her strange golden eyes. "You will be more susceptible to the winds if you are overly tired. Sleep well this night."

Finna began to say thank you but Vasilia had already faded into the trees like a wraith.

She turned to ask Catriona about Vasilia but before she could open her mouth Catriona said, "Everyone is looking out for us. Do ye nae feel the support from this special place?"

Finna was glad of Vasilia's help but she wouldn't go so far as that, after what they'd been through today. She smiled at her mother, trying to keep her thoughts neutral. She didn't relish being chastised anymore tonight.

CATRIONA FELL ASLEEP QUICKLY, softly snoring into the dark night, but Finna lay awake, thinking over what Catriona had said and also Vasilia's warning. It was true: the more tired she was the more fearful she became which led to acting like a child and expecting Catriona to take care of her. As her body relaxed, she drifted, hearing the eerie howling of wolves and the skittering of creatures foraging under the snow. She became aware of essences floating around her, mysterious thought forms and currents that permeated her skin. When she finally fell asleep it seemed as though murmured voices were caressing her.

"NOT THE BEST place to sleep I suppose, but not the worst." Catriona stretched into a backbend with her arms above her head. Behind her the newly fallen snow made puffy quilts over the bushes and rocks.

Finna sat up feeling a sharp twinge in her back. The ground was hard, her night restless trying to get comfortable. Catriona was now bending forward her hands touching the ground.

"I think I heard wolves last night."

Catriona straightened and then swept her hands up and out, bending sideways. "The wolves will nae harm ye. They often hunt at night so they call to each other. I have spent many a chilly night in their company and stayed warm because of it."

"Do we even know where we are?" Finna asked, trying to ignore what Catriona had just said. The picture that her words conjured was frightening indeed. She pulled the moonstone out of her pack.

"Vasilia didn't take us far off the main trail. The moonstone will guide us back."

"Have you met Vasilia before?"

"Nae. She must have heard about..." Catriona stopped.

"Heard about what?"

"Our journey. She is the ruler of the path and the journey and especially helpful to those who travel alone."

Catriona took the stone from Finna, gazing into it. "We need to pass across the high valley between this mountain range and the one that stands between us and the Glass Mountain. In the winter it can be inhospitable so we must try to make it all the way across before nightfall."

"The winds?"

"I canna promise anything, Finna. Do ye nae remember Vasilia's words of warning?"

"She told me I needed to get enough rest but how can I when I hear wolves howling and I'm trying to sleep on frozen ground?"

"Ye are a bit grumpy this mornin', child. I didnae have a problem last night. Maybe ye selected a rocky spot. Now come and have a bite to eat."

THEY SET off shortly after this conversation with Finna trying very hard to put her fears and grumpyness aside. Catriona had actually been more tolerant than usual and she didn't want to push things and get into another yelling match.

Catriona took the lead, following the tiny trail in the moonstone. The sun had risen and shafts of light glistened across the snow. Finna watched birds flitting through the branches, making little beeping noises like finches. That and the crunch of their boots were the only sounds.

"Finna."

Catriona's voice was startling in the silence, making her jump. "What is it?"

"Vasilia's visit has me rethinking our plan for the day. We can take a short detour to a village nae far from here. I have friends there who will put us up and we can get a good night's rest and have a warm meal."

Finna didn't argue. Even with the warming rays of the sun she felt cold. Her body ached from rolling around on the ground—a soft bed sounded delightful. She huddled into her sweater and followed Catriona up the trail.

It was mid-morning before they came to a fork in the path. A smaller trail led east toward a hardwood forest. "'Tis the path to Tiadhan, the village I mentioned."

"What is the meaning of 'Tiadhan'?"

"It means 'small stone' or 'little hill'. The town is built partially within an ancient stone circle that sits on a small rise."

The path led them through a copse of birch with bright yellow leaves. Finna listened for the Ghillie Dhu but there was only the sound of the breeze rustling through them. The azure sky was filled with small puffy clouds and the temperature had risen dramatically. Finna stopped to take off her heavy sweater. On the other side of the grove, a meadow of wildflowers came into view. It seemed late for such blooming but the entire area seemed much more temperate than where they had been. A stream meandered along one side of the meadow, disappearing into a small pond surrounded with low hanging willows.

Finna's spirits rose. "It's so warm here! Can we bathe in the pond?"

"I suppose we can. 'Tis fed by a warm spring so it should be quite pleasant."

"Do you have soap in your pack?" Finna asked, pulling off her heavy shirt. "My hair could use a good washing."

"I have a bit of the crushed bulb from the amole, also called the soap plant. It lathers well."

Catriona dug in her pack and handed Finna a small packet. "I need to replenish this, I'm almost out."

"Where do you get it?"

"It grows in the dryer climes of the east where my home is."

Finna stepped gingerly into the water, feeling the squishy layer of rotting vegetation between her toes. She put her head back to wet her hair and then worked the amole into her scalp. A water snake glided by, looked at her blandly and then disappeared into the weeds on the other side. Catriona splashed into the pond and Finna listened to the scrubbing sounds of her hands on her scalp. Insects droned by, making her sleepy. When she opened her eyes again she saw Catriona's naked form collecting something from the far side of the pond. A light mist hung in the air around her and the sun sparkled through it, casting colorful prisms.

"What did you get?" she asked, as Catriona came toward her.

"Willow. "Tis good for fever, and aches and pains. 'Tis an important one to have in one's medicine stores."

Finna watched her mother walk unself-consciously back to where she had left her clothes. Her every movement was fluid and with the sun glistening on the dampness still left on the surface of her skin, she looked like a goddess. Finna imagined for a moment what that must feel like, that free and uninhibited confidence. She climbed out of the pond and picked up her clothes, wishing she could find that easy grace.

After dressing, they walked across the meadow and into another small grove. A couple of enormous trees with heavily ridged bark stood next to the path and Catriona stopped. She placed her hands on a trunk for a moment, then broke off some small dried twigs that she placed in her pack.

"What kind of tree is this?" Finna looked up at the wide arching canopy. Instead of being straight, the trunk leaned oddly to the right.

"'Tis black poplar, good for making matches because the wide grain in the wood absorbs paraffin. This area is rich in a variety of plants and trees that I use in my medicines as well as other practical applications. Can ye feel the energy here?"

Finna cocked her head to one side. "It just feels good to me, peaceful, I guess."

"Look at the brightness of the trees. There is joy here." Catriona smiled.

Finna looked around as they walked, trying to feel the subtle energies. She did notice something, a soft whispering, but she assumed it was the wind.

"These oaks and elms have been here many years. This one especially has given me a lot of medicine over the years." She placed both hands on the wide trunk of an ancient oak and closed her eyes for a moment before she broke off a small branch and peeled back the outer bark. Using a small metal tool she cut away the inner bark and placed it in her pack. "This is good for stomach ailments."

They left the hardwoods behind, following the trail up a small rise and into an ancient yew forest. The trees towered above them and not a whisper of wind could be heard. Part of a poem came to Finna—a stanza she had memorized in school from *Evangeline* by Longfellow—about the Acadians being forced off their land by the British for refusing to be involved in the fight against the French. She had always loved the language and the sentiment, although the story was very sad.

"THIS IS THE FOREST PRIMEVAL. *The murmuring pines and the hemlocks,*

Bearded with moss, and in garments green, indistinct in the twilight.

Stands like Druids of eld, with voices sad and prophetic.

Stand like harpers hoar, with beards that rest on their bosoms.

Loud from its rocky caverns, the deep-voiced neighboring ocean

Speaks, and in accents disconsolate answers the wail of the forest.

This is the forest primeval; but where are the hearts that beneath it

Leaped like the roe, when he hears in the woodland the voice of the huntsman?

Where is the thatch-roofed village, the home of the Acadian farmers—

Men whose lives glided on like rivers that water the woodlands,

Darkened by shadows of earth, but reflecting an image of heaven?

Waste are those pleasant farms and the farmers forever departed!

Scattered like dust and leaves, when the mighty blasts of October

Seize them, and whirl them aloft, and sprinkle them far o'er the Ocean.

Naught but tradition remains of the beautiful village of Grand-Pre.

Ye who believe in affection that hopes, and endures, and is patient.

Ye who believe in the beauty and strength of womans' devotion,
List to the mournful tradition still sung by the pines of the forest;
List to a Tale of Love in Acadie, home of the happy.

THE OTHERWORLD REMINDED her of what Longfellow partially spoke to: reverence for a land and people who were innocent. *Acadie, home of the happy.*

ONCE THEY LEFT the yew forest, a hill with a wide expanse of enormous stones came into view. A number of small houses had been built within the circle and more houses, like stepping stones, led down to where the ground leveled off. From there, the town proper headed off in a horizontal line in both directions. Sheep grazed in rocky undulating fields divided by low drystone walls and in the far distance to the north, low purple hills stood out against dark clouds scudding across the otherwise pale blue sky. The shadows had grown long in the late afternoon sunlight.

The two women came into the village just as the sun disappeared behind the forested hills to the west. Tiadhan was bustling with activity, villagers hurrying along the street with wheelbarrows filled with branches and baskets of goods and produce over their arms. Laughing children ran by with dogs barking at their heels. Lanterns had been lit along the main street and shopkeepers stood in doorways calling out greetings to one another.

As Finna and Catriona walked past the open door of the

metalsmith, a man rushed out. "Catriona!" he cried, seizing her around the waist and lifting her off her feet to swing her around. "'S fhada bho nach fhaca mi thu." Finna stood by awkwardly trying to say the strange words to herself and wondering what they meant.

"'S fhada gu dearbh," her mother answered, smiling.

The man turned to Finna and then back to Catriona. "Co tha seo?"

"This is my daughter, Finna. And she does nae speak Gaelic, if ye please. Finna this is an old friend of mine, Duncan Kincaid."

He looked from Finna to Catriona. "Your daughter?"

"Aye, Duncan, my daughter."

"Is she mine?" he whispered, suddenly serious.

"Nae, of course not," Catriona said, coloring. Her eyes darted to Finna and then back to Duncan.

Finna watched her mother and then looked at Duncan. His wiry red hair was shoulder length, his face square-jawed and dark from the sun. He had a scraggly beard and bright hazel eyes. Despite his unkempt appearance he had the look of someone who found delight in everything, with lots of laugh lines around his eyes and mouth.

"Finna, 'tis a nice name. It means fair, did ye know? My mother's name," he continued, turning toward Catriona with a puzzled expression.

"Dinna read anything into the name, Duncan. My husband was responsible for the naming of this child."

"So who is this girl's father, your husband, if ye dinna mind me askin'? Ye wer nae married the last time we were together."

"Ye have never met him."

"What happened to that other fellow, the one who was married to someone else?"

"Duncan, please," Catriona put her hand on his arm, a pleading look in her eyes.

Duncan turned back to Finna and held out his rough hand. "Tis good to meet ye, *child*," he added mockingly, looking her up and down. He glanced at Catriona as he took Finna's hand and then he burst out laughing. "Ye look just like your mother did when she was your age! And I did nae consider her a child at the time," he added with a sly wink. "Can ye come to my house for a wee blether?" he asked, looking from Finna to Catriona. His merriment was infectious and Finna smiled.

"Aye, Duncan, but can ye put us up for the night?"

"Of course. 'Tis so good to see ye again, it's been far too long and I am glad to meet this unexpected daughter of yours." He turned to inspect Finna once more, letting his eyes travel from her face to her feet, lingering at her belly.

"Ah, and a little one on the way, I see. I wondered why the rosy glow. Catriona, ye will be a grandmother!" he grabbed Catriona's hand and began to dance with her.

"Stop it, Duncan," she cried, attempting to pull away from him. Two spots of color had appeared on Catriona's cheeks and her eyes were unusually bright. Duncan, his hand on the small of her back, directed her in a wild waltz. As he twirled her, Catriona's long hair flew away from her face.

Finna left them, walking away to inspect the small stores lining the busy street. It felt good to be in a town with real shops, normal looking people and the possibility of a good nights sleep. People passed by, couples with small children and others with baskets over their arms, chatting amiably and stopping to say hello to her almost as if they knew her personally. She nodded and smiled even though she didn't understand the foreign words. There was a feeling of prosperity and joy in this village and it showed in their happy expressions.

Catriona ran to catch up. "Wait Finna, I dinna want ye to

become lost," she said breathlessly. "This is a big town. I've known Duncan a long time. I hope ye can tolerate him, he can be a bit overbearing. I was fifteen when we met."

A moment later Duncan caught up to them and took Catriona's hand, tucking her arm through his. "The town is getting ready for Samhainn," he said, as they walked together down the street. "We have a weeklong celebration here, Finna. Your mother knows all about it and has participated in the past. Remember the last time, Catriona?" He looked at Catriona with an impish grin. "We had a right merry time." He pressed her close for a minute, chuckling and then turned to Finna. "All the last crops will be brought into the square to be distributed. We always have a bonfire accompanied by dancing and singing."

"And much ale drinking," Catriona added, her lips curling in a smile.

Finna listened to the two of them, the easy rapport they shared. Her mother seemed like a different person in Duncan's company. And for his part, Duncan seemed about to burst with energy and enthusiasm.

"Aye, the ale drinkin', how could I forget that?" He smiled wryly at Finna and winked. "Anyway, on the night of Samhainn, the goddess of the harvest, Habondia, arrives with her consort, Cernunnos. They sit on a throne in the square and we bring them the best of what we've grown. In return they promise fertility and a good harvest for the following year. This last celebration of the year ushers in the dark time. Maybe the two of ye can stay until after the festival?"

Without waiting for an answer he pointed up a small street to the left. "My house is up there. Aye, Catriona, I still live in the same wee house, but there is plenty of room for the two o' ye." He led the way up the narrow winding street, stopping in front of a tiny thatched roof cottage. The road continued on, meandering into the standing stones at the top of the hill above them. "I just missed having a house inside the circle. But I still feel the ancient spirits from here." He opened the low door, stepping back to let the women go by him.

The interior was dark. The windows let in limited light during the day but now they were only squares of black. Duncan lit a couple of oil lamps and then went over to the fireplace and began to build a fire. The room had a sleeping pallet against the far wall with a small wooden blanket chest next to it. On the wall next to the fireplace hung cooking utensils and a few pots. Cups and plates were housed in an open cupboard, as well as a teapot and some clay jars. A rustic table with two chairs stood in front of the cupboard.

"I have another room for ye to sleep in," Duncan said, getting up from the fireplace and pulling back a blanket on the wall. "There's a bed in there and most importantly, some privacy."

Duncan picked up one of the lanterns and handed it to Finna before she went into the tiny room. Taking off her pack she massaged her shoulders where the straps had dug into them. Aside from the sleeping pallet the room was bare, without even a window. It wouldn't be a place she'd want to hang out in. She unbraided her hair and combed through it with her fingers. The mattress of straw was not thick but it would provide a soft place to sleep, she thought, sinking down to test it out.

As she re-worked her hair into a braid she heard Duncan say, "I'll make some tea." And then she heard mumbled conversation in Gaelic between her mother and Duncan. When she came out they had their heads together and were talking in low voices. Steam came from the iron kettle hung on a metal pole over the fire.

Catriona motioned Finna over. "Duncan has some warm food for us. Are ye hungry?"

Finna nodded eagerly as she came over to the table. She was famished.

FINNA AWOKE in the night to sounds from the other room and made her way to the curtain and pulled it back. Moonlight shone through one of the windows revealing her mother and Duncan twined together on the sleeping pallet. Their naked bodies looked pale in the dusky blue light as they undulated in a languid rhythm. She heard her mother's soft cries of pleasure and the deeper tones of Duncan's husky whispers as their bodies moved together and apart. She was disgusted but unable to turn away, her mind twisting in on itself. *How could her mother just fall into bed with this man? And with Finna only ten feet away!* It was disgusting, appalling. She crawled back under the quilt and plugged her ears with her fingers, trying to forget what she had witnessed.

When Finna woke in the morning her mother was sleeping innocently beside her. She got out of bed and made her way othrough the small cottage, heading toward the privy. Passing by Duncan she glanced down. He was wearing a woolen undershirt now and sleeping peacefully. His lips curled up at the corners in a half smile and his right arm was flung nonchalantly above his head. She sucked in her breath as the image of the two of them came back to her.

Finna found her way to the outhouse and relieved herself, all the while thinking of what she would say to her mother. Her anger and disgust would be hard to hide. She took her time, trying to come up with a suitable sentence or two but nothing seemed quite right. When she came back in, Catriona was at the fireplace in her shift, her long wavy hair, loose around her face.

"Guid mornin', Finna!"

Her mother looked radiant, full of health and happiness with no trace of guilt in her open expression. Before Finna was able to answer, Duncan rose from the pallet, yawning widely. He stretched and then came over by Catriona to help with the fire.

"Guid mornin' everyone," he said jovially with a big grin. "So nice to have a bit o' company. Here, let me do that." He took the log from Catriona and placed it in the fire. When his fingers grazed hers they looked at each other for a long moment and then he leaned over and kissed her gently on the lips.

Finna's mouth fell open. It was one thing for them to have sex while she was asleep but to blatantly flaunt it in front of her this morning was too much. She went into the other room to dress. When she came out again the tea was made and Duncan and Catriona were sitting at the table.

"Come have some tea, Finna," Duncan said, getting up from the table. "Sorry about the lack of chairs." He held his chair out for her.

Finna didn't look at him as she came to the table and sat down. Her mother poured tea into an earthenware cup and handed it to her. "There's milk and honey on the table." Catriona pointed as she took a sip of her tea. "Did ye sleep well?"

Finna didn't answer.

"What is it? What's wrong?" her mother asked worriedly, reaching toward her.

"I ...I saw you...last night..." Finna said in a low voice.

Catriona glanced over to where Duncan crouched in front of the fire. "Oh that," she said with a light laugh. "I told ye that Duncan and I are old friends."

Finna stared at her, unable to speak.

"Drink your tea while I fix breakfast, we need to get an

early start today." Catriona got up and began preparing bannock and cheese on a plate she removed from the cupboard.

Duncan came over to the table. "Finna, I'm sorry if what we did offends ye. There's no need for that. Catriona and I... well...we've known each other a long time. We didn't expect ye to wake up last night. I'm sorry, but we...we care for each other, that's all." Duncan gazed toward Catriona, a pleading look on his face.

"But I was right there, only a few feet away, how *could* you..."

"Finna!" Catriona grabbed her by the shoulder, turning Finna to face her. "What I do is my business and has nothing to do with ye. You're a grown woman, not a little child. Ye should understand these things. I enjoy Duncan and he enjoys me. If we wish to express our feelings physically this is our business. I will not make excuses for myself to my daughter, do ye understand?" Catriona's eyes flashed as the power of her voice reverberated in the small room. When Finna looked up, her mother's brows were pulled together, her lips compressed into a thin line. All at once she felt small and stupid and very naïive. Her mother was right. It wasn't her business. "Sorry, Mother," she said, looking down at the table.

Catriona softened immediately. "I'm sorry too. We still dinna know one another very well, do we?" She reached over and placed her hand on top of Finna's.

Breakfast was a quiet affair and afterward Catriona and Duncan left the house together, leaving Finna to tidy up. She watched them head up the path to the stone circle arm in arm. She still felt humiliated and embarrassed about her behavior and wished she could take the whole thing back. As she cleaned the dishes and placed them in the cupboard she pondered her reactions, wondering why disgust had been her first emotion. But in her own defense she had never seen anyone make love and especially her very own mother. It was a shock to see the woman she looked up to engaged in such an animal-like act.

Finna was seated at the table when Duncan and her mother returned. "Can we stay until the harvest festival, Mahair?" she asked, trying to make up for her bad behavior.

Duncan smiled and looked hopefully at Catriona.

"Nae, Finna. The time grows short and we may get held up in other areas on our way. We could be delayed due to bad weather now that the snows have begun. I think it best if we move on."

"I'm sorry to hear that," Duncan said. "Despite the earlier upset 'tis been a pleasure to have ye here, Finna. Ye could have been mine," he said wistfully, gazing at Catriona. "I have never married, although I did ask your mahair to be my wife a long long time ago. Did she tell ye?"

"Duncan! That's old history! We were nae suited."

"Ye said that but I never understood it, Catriona."

"Well, I'm not going to explain it to ye now."

Finna listened to the two of them argue about the past, wishing she had a man to argue with. It took a close relationship to quarrel like that. She wondered why her mother didn't think she and Duncan were suited. They almost looked like brother and sister with their red hair and square-jawed faces. Their babies would be redheads with fiery temperaments. It occurred to her suddenly that her mother was still young enough to have another baby. Did she use birth control? Because if not she could be pregnant right now. Her own child could be a playmate to her mother's child—what a weird thought that was! She laughed aloud, causing Catriona and Duncan to stop their argument to peer at her curiously.

"Sorry, just thinking about babies," she said.

Before leaving, Finna insisted on doing some shopping in town. She needed some

powder to clean her teeth and a bar of soap and some cloths to wash with. While she shopped, Catriona and Duncan talked with friends in the street, their lilting Gaelic coming back to Finna. Most of the people here did not speak English but Finna managed to make herself understood by pointing. The barter system had her confused though, and she finally had to call on Duncan for help. Finna watched him gesturing and obviously bargaining as he worked out a deal in trade. Duncan was a metalsmith and had many fine lamps and hanging tools, as well as wrought metal poles for hanging over the fire.

"I got these for next to nothing," he said, handing her the package as they left. "Just a small decorative hanger that Galitin has been wantin' for some time."

The shopkeeper, Galitin, was a plump woman in her late forties who obviously thought Duncan was hilarious, laughing nearly the entire time he was with her. "She lives above me inside the stones and asks me to tea to take in the energies from time to time." He looked at Catriona. "I think she has designs on me," he said with a wink and a smile.

"So why don't ye take her up on it, Duncan? Ye could have a wee bairn and a good woman to cook and take care of ye."

"Can ye see me with her, Catriona? For one thing she's fat. For another she's old. For the spirits sake, she's way too old to have a bairn!"

"Oh Duncan, ye are so particular." Catriona laughed as she looped her arm through his.

"'Twas ye, Catriona, who spoiled me for anyone else," he said despondently.

CHAPTER 7

I t was after midday by the time they left Tiadan. The path
was wide enough for two and Finna matched her gait to
that of her mother's. "Where exactly is your home,
Mahair?"

Before answering Catriona stopped to place her hands on
the trunk of an aspen next to the trail, wait a minute or two
and then strip a bit of bark. She put the bark into a cotton bag,
depositing it into her pack before she turned. "I've been living
in the east--'tis many days walk from where we are now. I
needed to spend time alone and that particular area is very
good for herb gathering. There are a few small villages close by,
but my house is far from town. My only visitors are deer,
badgers, foxes and rabbits."

"Can we go there? Maybe on our way back?"

"'Tis too far, a good three-day trip from anywhere we
might be. I imagine we will be in a hurry once the blessing
ceremony is complete. Your baby will be close to term by the
time we get back."

Finna thought about how long this trip was going to take.

It was still over five months before her baby was due. For the past few days she felt so well that she kept forgetting she was pregnant at all.

As they walked on, new revelations about her relationship with her mother surfaced. Something bothered her about her mother's lack of inhibitions—as though Catriona had no feeling of shame. But then again, why should she? Was there something shameful about the human body or the sexual act itself? Somehow part of her believed this. Her relationship to her own body had been suppressed due to being brought up by her father. And the experiences with Alex had hardly helped. But there was more to it--maybe she didn't want this newly discovered mother of hers to be involved so closely with another, to be anything other than a loving presence in *her* life. And rising up in the back of her mind despite her attempts to ignore it, was jealousy. She was envious of the easy intimacy she had witnessed as well as the shared physical pleasure. It was something she had no experience with--she longed for that with a man.

The path began to rise, leading them into a very different landscape. Instead of the groups of towering trees, small scraggly pines and other dwarfed species were scattered here and there. By the look of them, the climate was so inhospitable they could barely survive. The temperature dropped as they climbed and Finna was now bundled in her warmest sweater, a hat pulled down over her ears. In the distance, under a forbidding yellowish-gray sky, a wide valley stretched between the low mountains. It resembled an endless river of low scrubby grass that had yellowed and dried. Dread entered her, coming to rest in her upper chest and she missed the comforting forests and meadows they had left behind.

• • •

THE PATH MEANDERED down the hill, linking up with two paths heading in different directions. Catriona took the one heading straight across the valley.

"Keep close to me and focus your mind on the trail. Try not to let your thoughts go down treacherous paths, ye canna afford to be in a negative frame of mind right now. In summer this area is beautiful and covered with flowers but at this time of year it becomes very cold from the driving wind that blows up the valley."

Finna had no response as she watched her feet following along the path behind Catriona. The flat look of the valley was deceiving as there were crevasses and low rocky outcroppings--deep gouges hiding under the grass to the left and right of the trail. They walked for a long time, with just a slight cold breeze coming up from the valley on their left. It was an eerie place, with no birdsong and no sign of any life at all except for the grassy tufts and small wildflowers, now dry and withered. Finna kept scanning across the valley as they walked, but the distance did not seem to diminish; it seemed too far to calculate. She was in a daze, just putting one foot in front of the other when Catriona stopped abruptly.

"Listen, can ye hear that?"

"A high-pitched sound?"

"Aye, 'tis what I was afraid of."

"What is it?" Finna asked, peering at the trail ahead.

"'Tis a group of people."

"Can you see them?"

"Look...keep your eyes focused ahead and wait."

Finna did as she instructed and within a minute small figures came into view and then disappeared as the path dipped and rose. They seemed at least a mile away. "They're heading toward us."

"Aye, and they're running—'tis nae a good sign." Catriona squinted into the distance with a frown.

"What could it be?"

"Many things, but we need to be out of the way when they reach us."

"Should we just wait for them or what?"

As they drew closer, the keening cries became loud and discordant, an eerie dissonance that echoed. Catriona headed off the trail searching frantically among the rocks.

"What are you doing?"

"Finna, fit yourself into this crevasse--there is just enough room for one person."

"But what about you? I don't want to be separated." Fear rose into Finna's throat as she fought to stay calm.

"I'll find another hiding place close by. Do not leave this place until I come for ye!"

Finna ran across the tufts of grass and wedged herself into the narrow opening between two partially buried boulders. She watched Catriona hurrying away on the other side of the trail. The people were very close now; their screeching cries set her nerves on edge. Finna peeked out to see what it was they were running from but there was nothing visible behind them or anywhere around. They hurtled down the trail, two men, two women and a child around ten, their wide-open mouths in a perpetual scream.

As they came closer to Finna's hiding place she could clearly hear the whirring sound from the viciously whipping wind. A second later, icy fingers seemed to close around her throat. She choked and gagged, her hands going to her neck as she pressed herself against the rocks. The people were even with her now, their eyes wide and crazed. The wind whirled around them, tearing their clothes and pulling at the flesh of their bare arms and faces. Finna's mind emptied as she felt their terror and pain. She squeezed her eyes tight and put her hands over her ears to shut out the horror of the sounds. As the screams faded, she sucked in air, her throat raw. When she had the nerve to pull herself up, Catriona was heading toward her. Finna unwedged herself but her legs wouldn't hold her. She sat down heavily.

"What in the world was that?"

"The wind we encountered two days ago."

"It seemed so much worse, like it was pursuing them."

"It *was* pursuing them. This is why I told ye to be focused today. This valley has always been a place where the winds run rampant. By now those poor people's minds have been completely taken over. All they could do was run but there's no escape for them."

"What will happen?"

"Their energy will soon be depleted. They will not be able to think clearly for a very long time, maybe ever. Come now, we have wasted much valuable time, we must continue."

Finna thought she could still hear their terrible cries in the distance as she and Catriona began walking quickly in the opposite direction. The sky was a forebidding shade of gray, the clouds full of moisture—it was definitely cold enough for snow.

"Is this because of Vasilia?"

Catriona nodded. "Vasilia is the goddess of the wind, Finna."

"But why would she do this?"

"'Tis nae a matter of her 'doing this', 'tis more about minds that are nae prepared. Remember her warning."

Is my mind prepared? Finna wondered to herself. How could it be? Fear was always with her no matter how hard she tried to overcome it.

· · ·

THEY WALKED for a long time before the snow started. It was light at first, only a thin dusting, but soon it was coming down so thickly they could barely see. Wind blew hard up the valley sending stinging pellets against their faces and clothes. Finna's sweater became stiff with ice, her wool scarf barely managing to keep the cold off her face and neck. She was shivering despite the pace they were keeping. There was no way to tell how far they had come or how far they still had to go.

"Can't we find some rocky shelter along here to wait it out?" Finna yelled, trying to be heard over the wind.

"We canna tarry here. 'Tis a very dangerous place." Catriona stopped and opened her backpack giving Finna more herbs--high john for strength, mixed with hyssop for physical and spiritual protection.

When Catriona took some as well, Finna had a sinking sensation in her stomach. Until now her mother had never shown anything but confidence. Her hands shook as she put the herbs into her mouth.

"Ye have the strength for this, ye must let go of your fear!" Catriona called to her over the whistling wind.

They continued walking but now the snow was so thick that Finna could no longer see her mother ahead of her. Whispered voices were calling her name. She peered through the snow, imagining she saw strange human-like shapes forming and unforming in the swirl of white. As she came to a fork in the trail she didn't know which one to take. She yelled to Catriona but her voice disappeared--there was no answering call.

A moment later a screech pierced the silence. Finna looked up to see an enormous blue-faced figure flying over her. Her hand went to her mouth and then she was crouching, her head covered with her hands as the apparition flew in a small circle above her. Tangled gray hair whipped in every direction, dark ragged clothing billowing around her. She rode a gigantic black wolf, with eyes as yellow as the sun. Finna let out her breath when they disappeared, hoping fervently that they had moved on, but a second later two glowing red eyes, like burning coals, appeared out of the snow. Those eyes burned into Finna's, her breath an icy wind on the back of Finna's neck. Soaring close to the ground about five feet away from Finna, she touched the earth with an enormous stick, turning it all to ice. Finna opened her mouth, emitting an unearthly scream of terror that sounded alien to her ears. And then she was running through the pelting snow, her heart in her throat.

Shouting for Catriona, she veered off the trail, stumbling as her feet got caught in holes. She went down, landing hard on her right hip. When she stood again her hands were red with cold and bleeding. Above her the snow swirled in dizzying patterns. She gasped for breath. Her legs would not move anymore and a languor came over her. She couldn't find Catriona and the voices were telling her to rest; she must follow their advice.

She searched along the rocky area next to the trail. When her sore and shaking fingers found a slight opening, she followed it to where it widened. *Just enough room for my body,* her muzzy mind said. Inside the crevasse, the earth smelled musty with a kind of mushroom scent and something else that could have been animal dung. She knew the danger of hypothermia and struggled to stay awake for as long as she could, pinching herself and staring into the dark, but finally the cold and exhaustion took over. Finna closed her eyes.

She was falling down a long tunnel, down, down, the voices calling in dulcet tones; she could see their faces now. Long hair in wisps and ghost-like bodies, they pulled her by her hands into a small underground pool, a warm pool. It felt so good to be in the warmth after the freezing snow; she relaxed, sinking into the shallow water. She looked down to see an enormous serpent swimming toward her. Its green head was about five inches wide, the long scaled body glinting gold and green under the water. Terrified, she watched it approach, sure it would bite her and she would die. Yellow-green eyes locked on hers as the serpent's mouth opened. "Trust," it said. "The baby will protect you now." After the message it turned and swam away.

When Finna opened her eyes again she had no idea how much time had gone by. Her damp sweater offered little protection from the temperatures that were surely below freezing. As she raised herself up to look outside she noticed that the snow had stopped. An inky black sky lay above her, stars winking on and off. Crawling out of the opening she called out, her voice echoing in the pristine stillness. Waiting for a response but hearing nothing, she called out again. Her heart pounded loud in her ears as she surveyed the desolate landscape. What if something had happened to Catriona? Who knew what that terrifying hag in the sky could have done or what other horrible beasts roamed across this valley? Climbing out, she was immediately assaulted by the chill wind and gasped as its icy fingers went through her sweater. Hugging herself tightly she decided it would do no good to wander around looking for Catriona. The safest thing would be to remain here until morning. And she still felt weary to her core. Lowering herself back into the small space she pulled her sweater around her, bunching it up to get more warmth and soon fell into a deep and dreamless sleep.

CHAPTER 8

Finna stood up, blinking into blinding sun sparkling off the snow.

"Finna! I was so worried... I could nae find ye!" Catriona ran toward her and threw her arms around her, almost knocking her down. "I've been searching since daybreak."

"I got lost. I guess I took the wrong fork in the trail." Finna relaxed into her mother's arms feeling the welcome warmth from Catriona's body.

"I'm so glad ye found shelter. 'Twas a terrible storm." Catriona's translucent eyes looked seagreen today, the color of the ocean during a storm.

"Mother, I was afraid something had happened to you. I saw some kind of weird apparition in the snow..." Finna pulled her sodden sweater over her head, spreading it on a rock to dry.

"Can ye describe it?"

Finna sat down on a rock and hugged her knees. "A creepy hag riding a wolf. It made a horrible noise."

Catriona's eyes widened. "'Tis the Cailleach Bheur, the spirit of winter! She may nae be beautiful to gaze upon and can be very fierce, but she's also gentle; she guards the deer in the winter and brings the storms we need to fill our aquifers. This is the time of year when she arrives. Finna you're shivering." Catriona dug in her pack, pulling out a heavy gray sweater.

Finna took it from her, wondering how so much could fit in one small pack. Maybe it was magic, she thought, laughing to herself.

"Why didn't ye think to use the moonstone? It would have showed ye where to find me."

"I don't think I could have seen it, even if I remembered to look; where I hid was completely dark--I was so scared and cold..."

"At least we're together now and that's what counts." Catriona picked up her backpack and pulled out jerky and an apple. "Ye must eat, Finna. Ye look like ye may have lost some weight. You're in the second trimester now and the bairn needs food to grow."

Catriona handed her pieces of jerky, cheese and some bannock she had purchased in Tiadan. "Put some of the butter Duncan gave us on the bannock. Ye need the fat."

As Finna munched hungrily she noticed the worry lines creasing her mother's face. *Oh no*, she thought, *what now?* It had been so nice to relax for a moment feeling the warm sun on her skin--filling her empty belly—feeling safe. But as the moments went by and Catriona didn't say anything she put the food down. "What is it, Mahair?"

Catriona turned toward her, her expression somber. "Finna, my dearest nighean, I wouldn't be takin' ye on this journey if I didnae ken that 'tis absolutely necessary for ..." she trailed off.

"For what?" Finna asked. "Ye keep starting to tell me something..."

"It will become clear but I canna say more now. If something happens to me ye must use the moonstone to find your way to the Glass Mountain."

"Without you?" Panic shot through her mid-section.

"Finna, my daughter, I love ye so much. This is the first time I have truly recognized what I lost by leaving ye behind. I dinna want to lose ye again but this trip is more treacherous than I anticipated and anything could happen. I only want ye to be prepared if it does."

Catriona reached for her and Finna melted into her embrace. For the first time she experienced a deep unwavering sense of connection with her mother. It was as though something heavy had been lifted from her heart. She thought about the strength of this woman and vowed to become more like her.

"Mother, I had a dream about a snake. It told me that the baby would protect me now—what does that mean?"

Catriona's eyebrows shot up. "The serpent is a messenger, Finna. Did it say anything else?"

"Only that I should trust."

Catriona nodded. "And so ye should. Your baby is aware now and part of what we are doing."

"But how can that be true? I'm not even four months yet. And why do I need protection, anyway? I thought this trip was to have the moonstone and the baby blessed. What else is going on? It certainly seems a lot more dangerous than you led me to believe. Is this something about what I heard Mikdal and Herska talking about? They used a word--*fass-nik*, I think it was —is that the name of some horrible beast?"

"Ye heard them use that word?"

Finna nodded. "They said, *Remember the Fass-nik...*"

Catriona turned away and began searching around the rocks. "We need to make snowshoes for the rest of the journey across this valley. Help me search for twigs."

"You didn't answer my question."

Catriona straightened and turned her gaze on Finna. "All of this will be revealed soon enough. All I can tell ye is that faisnich is not the name of a beast. Ye must take the advice of the serpent, Finna, and trust." Catriona turned to dig in the snow behind Finna.

"But..."

"No more questions! Ye need to help me find sticks now. We have a long way to go."

Finna turned away, but her hands shook and her mind was racing. What could it all mean and why wouldn't Catriona tell her? In one breath Catriona told Finna not to behave like a child and then she kept things hidden from her as if she *was* a child. Anger gave her energy as she violently broke off twigs for the snowshoes. When she brought an armful to Catriona, her mother pulled out twine from her pack and began to weave them into large ovals, using the string to knot and tie them together.

"It looks as though you've done this before."

"Of course. I've needed snowshoes several times. These will nae last long but I'm hoping they will at least get us across the valley."

When she finished the knots, Catriona showed Finna how to tie them on to her shoes and then led the way back along the trail to the fork Finna had missed.

"WHAT HAPPENS NOW?" It had taken several hours to work their way across the valley in the cumbersome snowshoes. Finna's legs were wobbly and weak as she sat down to remove them. By now her irritation with her mother had been replaced with a weary resignation. Her emotions seemed to be on a roller coaster—one minute feeling safe and warm and the next, furious and angry.

"We're nae far from a settlement, just another short trek. We will surely get a warm meal and good shelter for the night. 'Tis time for ye to learn to focus your mind."

Didn't Mikdal mention something about the settlement? Finna felt a flutter within her belly. Was the baby trying to warn her or was that strange sensation just the normal movement of the fetus? "Can't this focusing be accomplished with the herbs?"

"Ye need more than herbs to control your thoughts. I can hear them in my mind as if they were my own."

Finna's face flushed as she remembered all the unkind thoughts she'd been having. Yes, more control was defininitely needed to deal with her mother's uncanny abilities.

"Ye must be able to clear your mind in an instant since your indecision and fear are what these forces prey upon. I will nae put ye in more danger without first knowin' ye can defend yourself."

"Defend myself against what?"

Catriona sighed. "I suppose 'tis time to tell ye about the child ye carry. I wanted to wait until ye were strong enough to understand but now that the serpent has come to ye...I've known about this baby since before it was conceived."

"What do ye mean? That's not possible." Finna thought about the large sweaters that Herska had made for her and the packets of herbs that Mikdal had prepared, the preparations for this trip that seemed to have been made months before she was even pregnant.

"I haven't told ye everything I know about this baby, Finna. 'Tis a magical child."

Finna stared at her. *A magical child? Would it be able to fly, or what?* Finna shook her head as her eyes filled and before she could stop herself, tears were running down her cheeks. Whatever Catriona told her now would put her completely over the edge. She put up her hand to silence her mother and then plugged her ears and let the tears fall. It was too late for anything but to keep going but if she had the will and the courage she would turn around right now and head home.

Nine

Finna followed her mother up a steep rocky path into a dense forest of hardwoods and evergreens. The understory of bright yellows, reds and orange were in sharp contrast against the deep green conifers. The only sound was the swishing of wind in the high branches, no birdsong, not even the scurrying of small rodents. Finna's mind was a riot of confusion. After her crying fit had passed, Finna had tried to question Catriona about the baby, *her* baby, but Catriona would not say another word no matter how much she pestered. She finally gave up in frustration and decided to wait until they reached the settlement.

"What made those?" Finna pointed to several huge prints in the snow.

"Wolves. There are many living here, in fact this forest is called *Faol Lann*, the area of the wolves."

"Have you seen them?" Finna asked, scanning into the trees nervously.

"Many times. Remember I told ye about them saving my life? They have been my guides and may be again on this trip."

Finna didn't reply to this, she was too busy visualizing the animals that had made the prints and wondering if there were any close by. When she peered into the trees she expected to see eyes, but instead, the forest grew thick and dark and stretched endlessly into the distance.

They walked on, heading deeper into the trees, following a path so narrow they had to go single file. Finna felt her baby moving about restlessly as if to communicate something, but she couldn't decipher what it was trying to say. The word *magical* kept appearing in her mind and making her feel light-headed.

THE WOLVES WATCHED *from the shelter of the trees, their golden amber eyes standing out in stark contrast to the dark gray fur in a thick ruff around their necks and covering their muscular bodies. The two older males acted like sentries protecting the females and the cubs, now almost full-grown, who had been born in the den before the snows had melted from winter last. They had caught the scent on the winds; humans, and they had come to investigate. Their territory had changed since the last time the forest woman was here--they had lost a large part of their hunting grounds to the fires.*

They had seen the woman who called herself Catriona many times. She spoke to them in their language. Now she walked with another who was not familiar. Was she the one who carried the future within her--the cub who would save this world? They had heard this whispered among the birds, through the bubbling of the water spirits and from the ancient trees themselves.

They knew what was at stake. They felt the change here in every one of their keen senses--the energy shift, the gathering of the dark. They had lived through the fires and the swarm of dark birds, heard the human and animal screams of terror. They had known to stay away, to stay far out of sight. And so they had traveled deep into the woods, farther than they had ever been before. Far away from the man who set the fires and burned so much of the sacred forest down, upsetting the natural balance. Now they had to be careful to not show themselves. This man and the others he called his pack hunted the wolves and their numbers had grown smaller.

The dark days of winter were coming and game was scarce. Soon they would feel their bellies growl with hunger and they would be forced to eat the nuts and dried berries they could find in the forests to the south. Lack of game caused by the man who wore black. He took everything for himself without sharing. He did not give back to the spirits and the spirits were becoming angry.

WHEN FINNA SAW a pair of amber eyes staring at her from between two small trees she froze in her tracks. It was all she could not to scream as she gestured wildly to her mother.

Catriona turned and began to speak in a soft murmuring tone. Finna couldn't understand what she was saying but she watched as the eyes blinked, softening in their intensity, and then they were gone. Finna's legs crumpled beneath her and she sat down, leaning back against a tree trunk.

"'Tis perfectly safe. They ken me."

"Did you just speak wolfish or something?"

"Something like that. 'Tis more of a tonal language and although they dinna speak and respond, they make themselves understood in other ways."

Finna sighed, her hands going to her temples where a headache pounded. "I'm glad they're friendly. What exactly did ye say?"

"I let them know we are passin' through and will be gone in a few days."

"What was their response? I didn't hear anything."

"'Twas in the eyes. They heard and recognized who I was and left."

"I only saw one pair of eyes, were there more?"

"Aye, maybe five or more. The others were hanging back, out of sight."

Catriona offered a hand to help her up. "We must continue

on if we want to get to the settlement by nightfall. Are ye feeling all right, Finna?"

"How can you even ask that? You haven't yet told me what's going on and then we encounter some huge and terrifying animals! I feel weak and sick and angry."

"Dinna be afraid of these creatures. They are the natural inhabitants of this forest along with bears, lynx and many other animals. They are only dangerous if ye are hunting them or doing something to hurt them or their offspring and then they are fiercely protective and rightly so."

Catriona let go of Finna's hand and headed up the trail. The heavy branches of the evergreens obscured the light; it was hard to tell where the sun was. Finna had lost all perspective in the gloom of the understory. As she glanced left and right, expecting to see eyes peering at her, her anger was replaced with an urge to get to the settlement as quickly as possible.

It was dusk before they reached the clearing and the river valley. A heavy fog hung over the mountains in the distance and it looked like snow was falling on the highest peaks. The sky was pale lavender, the air crisp and fresh. Finna's spirits rose as she gazed into the distance realizing how depressed she had become in the dark conifer forest. It was a good place to be a wolf, she supposed, running low to the ground with little chance of being spotted, but to her it was as though all the air had gone out of her world. She could never live in a place like this.

Up ahead, a few huts came into view, clustered together near the steep bank of a river. The grassy hills surrounding them were dotted with grazing sheep. It was warmer here with no snow remaining on the ground. Catriona told her there was an underground river that ran from an ancient volcano higher in the mountains that flowed into this valley, emptying into the wide waterway in the distance.

Finna followed her mother, aware of Catriona's cautiousness. She wondered why until several people came into view. Their expressions were somber as they hauled water and carried armloads of twigs to their dwellings. They seemed poor, their clothes stained and torn, and their hair unkempt and matted. There were no signs of children, nor any sounds of laughter. Smoke issued out of only one or two stone chimneys and the rest had a deserted feeling. Despite what Catriona had told her, Finna thought again about the *Fassnik*, imagining a fire-breathing dragon that terrorized human beings. It would explain the people's behavior better than anything else she could think of.

"Wait," Catriona said, putting out a restraining hand as Finna walked forward. "Let me announce our arrival, these people are nae used to visitors."

Finna stood where she was, watching Catriona approach the nearest hut. Her mother spoke with a man and woman who seemed around Catriona's age. As she spoke they held their arms stiffly by their sides and never once looked up. Finna could hear Catriona's lilting Gaelic but couldn't hear their responses; she was beginning to think they would be spending another night out in the cold when Catriona gestured for her to come down.

"Finna, this is Artur and his wife Thema, they have offered to share their house with us." There was a warning look in Catriona's eyes.

Finna smiled and said hello but they did not speak or smile in return. They turned abruptly, heading up a small path toward one of the huts. Catriona and Finna followed. On the way Catriona turned and put a finger to her lips signaling quiet. Finna sensed a tension here that she hadn't felt so far during the trip.

They followed Artur and Thema through a small doorway into a rudimentary dwelling. The inside smelled of goats and dirty clothes and was messy, with different cooking items and clothing strewn about on the floor. The couple turned to Catriona when they got inside, pointing to a room separated from the main room with hanging burlap. When Finna and Catriona pushed the flap aside, a putrid smell wafted out. It was filthy, filled with tools, rags and what looked like goat droppings. Finna held her nose as she followed Catriona inside and then took off her backpack and laid it on the floor. Once the burlap had fallen back in place Catriona put her finger to her lips and shook her head.

Catriona began moving rags and tools out of the way to make a small sleeping pallet for the two of them as Finna picked up a shovel and pushed goat droppings into a pile in the corner. The strong smell was nauseating and she breathed through her mouth hoping she wouldn't have to throw up. Once she heard Artur and Thema leave the other room she turned to Catriona. "What's going on?" she whispered.

"These people are very fearful. They expect bad things to happen at every turn. I'd forgotten about how superstitious they are."

"You don't know any of them?"

"I once had friends here but I just found out that they left a few years ago. And no wonder. Things have deteriorated drastically since my last visit."

"I can understand that. I feel so much tension here."

"We will only stay one night. I had planned to stay and teach ye some things but I canna do that here. We'll leave at dawn."

Despite the nausea, Finna's stomach felt hollow. "What

about food?" she asked, pressing her hands there to quiet the rumbling.

"I canna prevail upon them for a fire. They're very poor and wood is at a premium, even with the enormous forest standing behind us." Catriona looked down and shook her head. "They're afraid to cut the trees because they fear retribution from the tree spirits and so they gather what twigs and fallen branches they can find for cooking and heat."

"But why would the tree spirits harm them?" Finna asked, thinking about the 'Ghillie Dhu' and the innocent tinkling bell-like sounds they made.

"They would nae do so and especially with a small prayer of gratitude for what they take, but these people live with a negative view of the spirits around them. Instead of appreciating what the world has to offer, they fear it and live in a kind of self-fulfilling prophecy. This is a blessed place. Warm springs abound in this area, full of life-giving minerals, and yet these people dinna use them. They think because the water is warm it means it comes from a wicked place and so they avoid it, drinking instead from the river and the rainwater they collect. We will travel on tomorrow to the sacred spring and there I will teach ye what ye need to know."

Catriona began taking dried berries and apples out of her knapsack. There were still some tubers but no way to cook them.

"Where do these strange ideas come from?" Finna asked, helping her with the food and looking longingly at the tubers.

"Something has happened since I was last here. The people have always been a bit superstitious in these parts but this seems extreme." Her eyebrows drew together.

"Didn't Mikdal mention something about the settlement?"

Catriona stared into space for so long that Finna didn't think she had heard the question but finally she turned to

Finna. "I didnae heed his warning, Finna. I've come through here before and despite the superstitions the place was welcoming. If what he told me is true, 'tis not a place for us to remain for long."

"What did he tell you?"

She shook her head and sighed. "I will nae believe it till I see it," Catriona said, biting into an apple.

FINNA AWOKE to the sound of a loud gong. "What was that?"

"'Tis their call to prayer," Catriona mumbled, rolling over. A second later the older woman was up and stuffing things into her backpack. She pulled her hair back, braiding it quickly, binding the end with a piece of leather. "Finna, we must leave immediately."

Finna was surprised to hear the urgency in her tone and hurriedly pulled her things together. The night before, when Atur and his wife returned, Catriona eavesdropped, a warning finger to her lips. Finna watched her skin go from rosy to pale in reaction to whatever was being said in the other room. When she finally turned, Catriona had nothing to say, only whipering that the two of them neeed to sleep now since their departure would be early.

They opened the burlap curtain to find the small hut deserted and the fire cold. The desolate atmosphere was even stronger than the day before. Outside, a line of people, including Thema and Arttur, were headed toward a large building on top of the hill. A tall man dressed in black stood in the doorway ushering them in as they arrived. His pale face was without expression as he gazed in their direction. Next to him an older gray-haired woman pointed and gestured in their direction. "This is what I was afraid of," Catriona muttered. "My stubbornness has put us into danger."

129

Finna felt a sharp twinge of fear as she stared up the hill. The man seemed vaguely familiar but she was sure she had never seen him before. The woman smiled and beckoned for them to come with the others up the hill, but Catriona ignored her, pulling Finna down the hill toward the river.

"They want us to come up there, Mother. Who are they?" Finna craned her neck to get another look. The woman was slight, her hands pushing strands of gray into the bun at the back of her neck. She gestured again, smiling in Finna's direction and then turned to say something to the man. He bent his long frame to hear her and then looked again at Finna, his eyebrows raised in recognition. He nodded and smiled.

Finna felt Catriona's fingers dig into her arm. She pressed her toward a rickety bridge spanning the river. "Go quickly now."

"But who are they?" Finna whispered.

"'Tis my brother, Brandubh."

Catriona gave her a push toward the bridge. It looked flimsy, in disrepair and Finna stopped for a second to examine it. "Go!" Catriona urged from behind her. As soon as Finna stepped onto the footbridge there was a sharp crack and the board under her feet split and gave way. Finna reached frantically for something to grab onto but there was no railing. Catriona's hand missed Finna's by inches as Finna twisted and then fell, landing heavily in the river below. The water was ice cold, not fed from the warm spring, and the shock of it sucked her breath away. Her sweater quickly grew heavy as it absorbed water and began to drag her under.

On the hill she saw Brandubh with his mouth open, shouting and waving his arms. He started down toward her but the woman put a restraining hand on his shoulder. A second later Finna was pulled into the swift current. Over the din of rushing water she could hear Catriona calling her, her voice shrill and frantic. She struggled to keep her head above water but the heaviness of her clothes sucked her under and she was carried further and further away from her mother and the bridge. Viney waterweeds twined around her legs and arms, pulling her down as she fought for breath. She heard a shrieking voice, maybe her own, and then all was swirling greenish black.

CHAPTER 9

Finna opened bleary eyes to see Catriona's worried face looking down at her. Her mother's tears had mixed with the muddy river water leaving brown streaks trailing across her pale cheeks. Catriona helped Finna sit up and then pulled the heavy sodden sweater over her head while Finna struggled with her woolen pants and tights. Catriona helped her into dry clothes she had taken from her own pack and squeezed the water out of the others. She pulled Finna close, murmuring soothing words that Finna couldn't understand.

"Can ye feel the baby? Is she all right?"

Finna couldn't feel anything except pain in various parts of her body that had been cut and bruised on the rocks and sticks hiding beneath the water. She put her hands on her belly and felt an answering flutter as the baby swam in the sea of her womb.

"She's all right," she answered, and then she was sobbing, scalding tears streaming down her cheeks.

Catriona changed her own water-soaked pants for dry ones

and then put a hand on Finna's shoulder. "We must hurry away from here." She rolled the rest of the wet clothes into a ball and stuffed them in her pack.

Finna stood up shakily, picked up her water-laden pack and followed Catriona along the riverbank heading toward the bridge.

"Are we going back to the settlement?"

"Nae, Finna. Brandubh is there."

"But he seemed friendly—I thought he was going to help."

Catriona shook her head wrapping her arm around Finna's waist. Finna leaned into her, waiting for her teeth to stop chattering.

"He's really your brother?" It seemed weird that a close family member wouldn't help them. "I thought there were only women in this line."

"I did say that. And great spiritual power as well. He's the anomaly, my twin. All I know is that he's been corrupted. We are like two sides of the same coin. The Oillteil approached him when he was very young. They felt his vulnerability and wanted control over the spiritual power that runs through our line. At that time he would nae have anything to do with them. He told me all about it, how they approached him when he was out walking in the woods. He said they scared him with their misshapen bodies and corrupt ways of thinking."

Finna tried to make sense of everything her mother was saying but she didn't know what or who the Oillteil were. Her mind was still back in the water fighting with the weeds and trying to stay alive. She tried to pay attention because she knew what Catriona was saying was important, but she felt so drained and weak she could barely keep her eyes open.

"...and when Brandubh went into the priesthood," her mother continued, "I was worried and I told him so. He assured me that all he wanted was to do good outside this world where priests were given so much power. I saw a hungry look flash in his eyes when he said the word *power* and I knew he would succumb. I tried to dissuade him from his decision. But he treated it lightly and told me nae to worry. The connection between the two of us was strong, he said. *'Twill never be broken nae matter what I do*, he told me. But as the years went by he took any good he could have done as a priest and turned it to his own darker purposes."

"Like what?" Finna asked, coming out of her stupor.

Catriona stopped on the trail and shook her head. "He began taking advantage of people, most especially women. He's a good lookin' man and that combined with bein' a priest was just too much for him." She looked over at Finna, anger clouding her features. "I had hoped he would come to his senses. I thought maybe he had, since I hadn't heard anything about his behavior for some time. But this experience tells me that what Mikdal feared is true."

Finna mulled this over. Her experiences with priests and the church were limited. Alex's mother, Rose, was a staunch Catholic who tried at every turn to get her son involved. But Alex would not be swayed and Finna agreed with him. The church was too patriarchal. "Who are the Oillteil?"

"They're an extremely evil race of underworld dwellers who left the Otherworld centuries ago, were chased out and defeated by the Tuatha De Danaan. Their home is Torach, also known as the Dark Realm, in a dimension far beneath the Otherworld. If my brother has succumbed to their manipulations they are certainly making a comeback. They are able to manipulate the mystical and elemental powers and may be responsible for the ferocity of the winds we experienced. Vasilia rarely uses her power for destruction. Mikdal told me something about these changes but I dinna believe him."

Underworld dwellers? Finna's mind went to every frightening children's story she had read, imagining the Oillteil first as hideous dwarves and then as giants with misshapen heads and legs and arms too long for their bodies. She hoped she would not run into any of them on this trip. Was the faisnich in league with them? They had been walking steadily away from the bridge and the river and now Finna stopped and pulled away from her mother. "Are you serious? Why didn't you mention any of this earlier? Will we run into them?"

"Serious about what, Finna? I did tell ye about Brandubh after we left Clachencreid. I didnae tell ye the rest because I didnae wish to frighten ye needlessly. I had hoped my brother had come out of his dark place. When we were bairns he did something that left a mark on his soul. The violent act was done for me and so I feel responsible for what has happened to him."

"What did he do?"

Catriona's eyes darkened. A long moment went by before she answered. "He killed our father."

Finna gasped. "Why?"

"Because of what Fergus did to me." Catriona shook her head, her eyes wild. "I canna speak of this."

Finna was quiet for a moment watching Catriona's expression go from anger to despair. "And this Tuath de...? Who are they?"

"They're the first tribes who lived here. The original people."

"And they're good?"

"Aye. They were considered gods in the early days."

Finna tried to make sense of this new information. What had Catriona's father done to her that would cause her brother to kill him? And this new tribe she hadn't met who had lived here for centuries, what were they like? Images of enormous warriors, naked to the waist, carrying clubs and spears came to her mind.

A sickening feeling went through her mid-section. There was no way out of this—they were too far from anything familiar. She could have remained in Tiadan, she thought despairingly. If only she had known then what she knew now. So far she had accepted wolves that communicated with humans, a tribe of sentient ape-like creatures, a very frightening 'goddess' of winter, apparently *conscious* winds that wiped your brain, the fassnik that might or might not be a terrible killing beast, and the evil *twin* brother who Catriona had neglected to mention. And now the Oillteil and the Tuatha...de...whatever their name was. This place was more frightening and weirder than she could possibly have imagined when they started out. Her mother had lied, encouraging Finna to come on this trip with sweet words. And now the truth of what they were up against was becoming apparent. She had no sympathy for her mother's troubles or any of her latest rationalizations.

"So your brother is in league with these Oilteil and together they are what-- trying to take over?"

"Aye, that's exactly it. I did nae realize when we started this trip the extent of what my brother's been up to."

"Who was the woman with him?"

Catriona paled and shook her head, her fingers digging into Finna's waist convulsively.

Finna sighed at the gesture that was becoming all too familiar. Right now she didn't have the energy to push it. It took all her concentration just to climb the path. Her muscles ached and the scratches and bruises burned and throbbed. She tried not to panic. How would she get herself and her baby out of here alive?

"If ye can manage on your own we should hurry now. The spring is nae far."

Finna nodded as her mother released her. "I'll be fine." She wasn't fine at all but having her mother's arm around her waist had begun to grate on her nerves.

The trail entered another dark conifer forest where half buried roots and rocks were hidden under the fallen needles. They both stumbled several times. Catriona went ahead and was striding quickly away when Finna heard her sharp cry. By the time she reached her, her mother was on the ground with both hands around her ankle.

"What happened?" Finna crouched down beside her.

"I tripped over a root or something and twisted my ankle. 'Twill be fine if I rest for a moment." Catriona's face was ashen, contorted with pain. A fine sheen of sweat had appeared on the surface of her skin.

"What can I do?"

"We canna stay on this trail, 'tis dangerous." Catriona glanced back the way they had come, her eyes wide. "Help me up. We must get to the spring." As she tried to put weight on her foot she let out a cry of pain and crumpled to the ground.

Finna kneeled next to her, examining her ankle and feeling along the bones. "I think you may have sprained it. I don't think it's broken." Finna helped her mother up and looped an arm around the older woman's waist. "Lean on me."

"Take me over there, under the trees," Catriona said weakly, pointing.

Finna helped her hobble into the shelter of the trees and supported her as she lowered herself down, her back against a wide pine.

"Ye must get help. The herbs I have with me would heal this over time but we have little of that." Catrion gazed up at Finna, her eyes dark with pain. "We must call to the wolves."

"Wouldn't your brother help with this? Or maybe I should go back to get the older woman who was with him."

Catriona shook her head and grimaced. "Neither of them will help us, Finna, but there is a man I know who lives close. He has the power to heal with his touch but I canna find him with a hurt ankle."

Catriona gingerly pulled off her sock. Purple bruising had already appeared on the surface of her skin and the swelling was well under way.

"Finna, I know this scares ye, but we must quiet our minds and call to the wolves."

Catriona cupped her hands around her mouth and emitted an eerie high-pitched call. "Try to empty your mind. Picture the wolves coming here to us."

Finna couldn't imagine actually wanting the wolves to come. She was too frightened of them. She closed her eyes and tried to concentrate, but every time she saw a wolf in her mind she got shaky and couldn't breathe. Catriona leaned against the tree trunk with her eyes closed. She was shivering now and when Finna put a hand to her brow it felt clammy. Finna pulled the last dry sweater out of her pack and covered her mother's legs, tucking it in around them.

Out of the quiet she heard a rustling sound, like soft wind blowing through branches, and then stifled a cry as four enormous wolves padded silently out of the understory.

"Hello, my friends," Catriona intoned softly. They watched her, their perceptive eyes seeming to take in the severity of the situation and then listened intently, their ears pricked forward, as Catriona began to make the tonal sounds Finna had heard her use earlier. When she stopped, the wolves blinked their great gold-brown eyes and shifted their gaze toward Finna. She took a step backwards, her hand going reflexively to her belly. "Why are they staring at me?"

"I have asked them for help. They will lead ye to the caves, where Eron is."

Finna looked from Catriona to the wolves. "Ye mean I need to go with them?"

"'Tis the only way. I know you're still weak but 'tis nae far. 'Tis high time for ye to challenge your fears."

As much as she wanted to, Finna could not let go of the panic building inside her, but then one of the wolves wagged its tail and went to lie down beside Catriona. It looked like an enormous shaggy dog and Finna had to laugh. The fear was gone.

"This one will remain with me for protection, but the other three will lead ye."

Catriona gave a signal to the wolves and then Finna followed them into the forest. There was no trail and the underbrush was full of prickly bushes and vines that kept getting caught in her clothing. The wolves waited patiently as Finna disentangled herself and then they trotted off again, looking back to make sure she still followed. Her mind went to the Oillteil again and she hoped there weren't any of them lurking in the bushes. The wolves would probably know, she thought, hurrying after them.

When they reached the top of a ridge the wolves headed down the slope toward a streambed, but instead of continuing across the narrow waterway, they turned to the left, trotting down a well-used trail that paralleled the sandstone cliffs. Many small shelters had been dug into the soft ochre stone. Finna had a feeling they were getting close to their destination. As if reading her mind, the wolves looked back and then slowed to an ambling walk. Above them, dug into the sandstone cliff, was a large cave entrance.

After a minute or two, Finna made her way nervously around them and started toward the dwelling. Just as she reached the entrance, a man appeared from within. His gray-green eyes peered at her curiously from under thick dark brows. He looked strong, wide-shouldered and stocky, with long auburn hair lightly streaked with gray. His clothing was made from the hides of animals sewn together with careful stitches: pants and a long overshirt.

"Hello. I'm Finna, Catriona's daughter," Finna said in a small voice, hoping that the man would understand.

"Finna!" he cried, grinning widely as he came forward. His arms came around her, and she was pulled close to his chest in a strong embrace. From his shoulder where her face was pressed, she picked up the smoky scent of sage and the clean musky smell of damp earth. The slow and rhythmic beat of his heart calmed her almost immediately. When he finally released her, he held onto her forearms and looked searchingly into her eyes. "I am Eron."

It seemed as though he wanted some response from her, as though she would know him, but all she could think of was her mother lying helpless back in the woods. What if Brandubh came looking for them or even worse the Oillteil or the fass-nik? Quickly she blurted out why she had come. When she finished he held up his hand and went back inside the cave. He held a leather pouch in his hand when he returned a minute or so later.

"I will use yarrow leaves for Catriona's ankle if it is as you say." He gazed at her quizzically. "You are also injured." He put his hands gently on her bruised arm. "How did you get these scrapes and bruises?"

He spoke English as though it was not his native tongue, haltingly and with a heavy accent.

"I fell in the river and got washed downstream," she answered.

"Sit Finna, I will help you before we go." He took out a

small jar and some leaves from his pouch, moistening them with an aromatic salve before he placed them on her bruised hands and arms.

"Where else are you hurt?"

"I'm sore all over."

"Come with me." He reached for her, pulling her up.

When she grasped his fingers and felt the reassuring warmth of his calloused hands, she had a sensation of kinship. But this man was a stranger, just another old friend of her mothers.

Inside the cave two narrow wooden shelves held a line of small glass jars. Another wider shelf was laden with earthenware pots, bowls and cups. A woven rug in a geometric pattern of browns and grays lay on the dirt floor in front of a small firepit dug into the sandstone floor. Charcoal drawings of horses, wolves and something that resembled an emormous cow with horns adorned the walls. Had he done these? They were very different from the ones in the tunnels. An aroma of recently burned sweetgrass lingered in the air.

Eron instructed Finna to remove her sweater and lie down on the thick sheepskin on the floor. He then began to move his hands in the air above her body. She could feel energy, like waves, moving in little currents across her skin. When he placed his hands underneath her back she could feel the heat from his hands spreading out in all directions.

The pain coalesced around his hands and dissipated until it was completely gone. He told her to rest for a few minutes and then went outside where she heard him communing with the wolves, making little crooning and clucking sounds. A few minutes went by before she felt like sitting up. As she was pulling her sweater on over her undershirt, he re-appeared.

"Your baby is fine."

Finna looked into his eyes, noticing that they were the

same color as her own. "How did you know?" She looked down, placing her hands on her lower belly.

"I am a healer. As to the baby...I knew as soon as I laid eyes on you."

A fluttering sensation went through her. This man had just taken all her pain away with his hands and his dark eyes seemed to contain a deep wisdom that she could only guess at.

He helped her up and then packed a few things into the leather pouch around his waist. "Are you up to the trip back now?"

Finna nodded, following him out of the cave and down to where the wolves waited.

Eron made a signal to the wolves and they jumped up and were off. He told Finna to go ahead, he would be right behind her. She glanced back as they walked, noticing him scanning the underbrush. So there was danger around here. It felt good to have him there, his bow and quiver of arrows hanging across his broad chest. She could tell he was a hunter, a throwback to some earlier time when one's existence depended on keeping alert to dangers.

When they reached Catriona the wolves greeted the one left behind and then laid down a short distance away. As Eron bent over her, Catriona opened her eyes, crying out in delight before wrapping her arms around him. When they released each other minutes later, tears were streaming down Catriona's cheeks. Finna watched in surprise as they gazed into each other's eyes with their hands and fingers linked. Long moments went by before Eron opened his pouch, removing the leaves and the jar of salve. He took Catriona's ankle gently in his big hands. Finna watched Catriona's face for a sign of pain, but she looked serene, staring into his eyes. When he began to chant softly under his breath, Finna closed her eyes, feeling a shift in the atmosphere. When she looked again the swelling was nearly gone.

He put her foot gently down and began to speak quietly in Gaelic. Finna sensed that they loved each other deeply. With their heads together, they whispered, their eyes glistening with unshed tears. She thought about what she had witnessed with Catriona and Duncan and wondered about this new relationship; this intimacy seemed different somehow, with no room for her presence.

When Finna got up and walked back toward the path, the wolves followed and then went ahead, leading the way up a winding trail. The smell of sulphur filled her nostrils and a moment later the forest opened into a wide clearing. In the middle of the open space, a spring bubbled into a hollowed out pool of stone. With all the mud and detritus from the stream still coating her skin and hair, Finna didn't hesitate to strip off her clothes and climb into the warm water. But as she drifted with her eyes closed, an odd swooping sound, and then a low mellow warble came to her ears. Adrenaline raced through her. Was it the Fassnik? Her eyes flew open. A tall and stately crane was standing in the water just five feet from her. The bird shook out its feathers, fixing her with its orange eye. As she watched, the bird began to change, morphing into another shape, until she was facing a woman wearing a glossy dress of gray feathers. A small red crown lay elegantly atop thick silver hair flowing down her back. Finna scrambled backwards as the bird/woman began to speak in a singsong voice, holding her in its orange-eyed gaze.

Within you is the child of the prophecy; the one who will be known as Saille, the Willow. She will be called from a faraway land to her place of birth to fulfill her destiny. You must guard her carefully and keep her safe until that time.

• • •

BEFORE SHE COULD THINK of something to say, the woman's body began to change and shrink, her dress shortening and taking on the shape of a bird, long black legs appearing, the crown just a spot of red on her small head. She lifted gracefully into the air on wide wings and flew away.

Finna leapt from the pool. "Wait!" she cried, pulling on her clothes. As she ran toward the trees Eron and Catriona, their arms wrapped around each other, appeared in the clearing.

"What has happened, Finna?" Catriona grabbed her arm as she came to a stop in front of them.

"I...there was a bird..." She turned and pointed frantically at the spring. "It...she..."

"Slow down," Eron said. "Take a deep breath."

Finna drew in a couple of ragged breaths. Her heart pounded in her ears. "She...it...the bird...she said something about my baby...a prophecy... she said there was a prophecy...?" Finna heard the hysteria in her voice as though it was coming from someone else.

Catriona gazed at Eron before turning back to Finna. "'Twas Corra, the goddess of prophecy. This is her spring."

She took Finna firmly by the arm and steered her to a flat rock next to the pool that Finna was sure hadn't been there the moment before. "She said the baby was Sol-yay, the Willow."

"Part of the tree oracle. The willow is connected with water and the moon. 'Tis the tree that is most flexible, known for its healing properties. Your baby will be strong, intuitive."

Finna stared at her. "So you believe this...this..." she waved her hand in the direction of the spring.

"As I told ye I've known about the prophecy for a long time, Finna."

"No. You said ye knew of the baby but you didn't mention a prophecy or tell me any of this—why?"

Catriona hesitated, turning again to Eron. "I wasn't absolutely sure the prophecy referred to this baby, your baby, but now, 'tis been confirmed."

"She said I need to guard her—everyone keeps saying that, but how can I? Oh, I wish I had never come here." Finna felt the prick of tears and then they were sliding down her face.

Eron sat down next to her and put his arm around her shoulder. "It is fine to cry. You've had a shock." He held her as she leaned into him and sobbed into his shoulder. "I'm afraid I have some more shocking news, but this time I hope you will be happy to hear it."

Finna sat up and looked into his dark eyes. "What else?"

"Eron."

Catriona's tone of warning piqued Finna's curiosity. What more revelations could there be?

"Catriona, why have you not told her?" Eron sounded sad, his eyes, puzzled.

"Told me what?"

Catriona glanced at Eron and then at Finna. "I'm nae sure this is the right time."

Eron's eyes clouded. "When *would* be the right time? I want her to know the truth." He and Catriona's eyes locked together, neither one breaking contact as the seconds ticked by.

Finally Catriona looked down. "I suppose you're right, but do ye think it's

wise after what she's just been through?"

"Stop!" Finna shouted. "I'm right here, you can't talk about me like I'm deaf or something."

"Finna, your mother has told you that Angus is your father but this is not true." He paused, glancing over at Catriona for a moment who was shaking her head, in a resigned way. He faced Finna again, his hand going to her shoulder. "I am your real father."

"What?"

Catriona sat down on the other side of Finna, picking up her hand. "'Tis true, Eron is your father. I didnae tell ye because I hadnae expected to see him again, at least not on this trip, but now that we've re-connected, well..." She gazed at Eron, her eyes alight with love.

Finna pulled away and stood up. "This is just too much. How could you?" Her shriek seemed to bounce across the glade, echoing into the trees. "We've been traveling together weeks and weeks and you've never mentioned the prophecy, hardly spoken about Brandubh, my uncle, or the most important thing of all, my real father." Tears welled up but she willed them away, brushing a hand angrily across her eyes. Rage sent adrenaline coursing through her body as she continued to shout. "What else have you kept from me, Mother? And how, exactly, did all of this happen, anyway?"

"'Twas unplanned, Finna. Eron was married at the time." Catriona wiped tears from her cheeks with the back of her hand.

"I am not ashamed of what we did, Catriona--'twas never wrong. We loved each other and we still do. Just because I was married did not mean we shouldn't have shared our love. You of all people should know that." Eron turned toward Finna. "Finna, your mother did what she thought was best for you at the time. She married Angus."

Finna felt dizzy from all the lies stacked up against each other. How could marrying Angus be a good idea? And then to go off, leaving Finna with a man who wasn't even her real ffather. "Does he know about this?"

"I told him," Catriona said. "But he thought there was a possibility that ye were his, even though I assured him this could nae be true. He was always in denial about it. And he adored ye and that was that."

"Is that why you left me? Because he thought I was his?"

"Finna, dearest. Angus loved ye to distraction and could nae bear the idea of me takin' ye away. I left ye because it would have killed him if I had brought ye here with me."

"But how do you know for sure? I mean that Eron--that I'm--"

"Finna...I knew the moment ye were conceived and of course I was sure when my menses ceased. Ye must at least understand something this simple. When did ye ken about your own bairn? Ye were meant to be--to come from our love." Catriona gazed up at Eron standing next to her. As her fingers reached for his, he bent to kiss the top of her head.

"So, what you're saying is that you were sleeping with both Eron and Angus?"

"I'm sorry if this shocks ye."

"Your mother has always been a free spirit. I shared her with others, knowing that I could not possess her. I just appreciated her when she was with me."

"What about your wife, Eron? Does she know?"

"I never told her. That's one of the reasons your mother decided to marry Angus, she did not wish to disrupt my family."

Finna was reeling with this new bit of information. First Duncan and now this? She couldn't understand her mother sleeping with a married man much less two men during the same time period. "What about Duncan?" she cried out.

"What is your question? Ye mean why did we make love if I love Eron?"

"That and...I don't know...it's just wrong! I can't listen to any more of this," Finna cried. "I'm leaving tomorrow, going home. I cannot stand to be around either one of you or any more of this crazy immoral mysticism!" She ran into the woods, collapsed under a tree, and burst into tears. Nothing made any sense. If her mother was such a free spirit, why did she think it was necessary to marry at all? *And why did she abandon me if I was the child who came from their love?* Finna grabbed her head to stop the whirling emotions—anger, followed by confusion, followed by an acute longing for the calm solitude of her little cottage. But it was very far away now, too far to travel by herself.

Finna must have fallen asleep, she realized, because it was dark when she opened her eyes again. The smell of wood smoke and roasting meat wafted her way, making her stomach growl. She heard voices and laughter. She didn't want to be anywhere around the two of them but her stomach told another story; it had been a long time since she had eaten any real meat.

WHEN SHE REACHED THE SPRING, she found Catriona and Eron sitting on the ground in front of a small fire pit. Catriona had changed into a long blue shift that clung to her curves, the thin fabric revealing her nakedness beneath. She leaned forward, placing tubers into the fire where the meat had already browned. Her loose hair swung across her cheek and she pushed it back behind her ears. Eron whispered something into her ear, his hand on the small of her back, his fingers tracing the curve of her spine. Catriona giggled and then turned, spying Finna.

"Come eat. Eron has brought us a rabbit."

Finna didn't say anything as she imagined the two of them wriggling around on the ground, lost in the throes of passion. Her mother was what was known as a harlot. And having a mother who slept around did not appeal. Catriona and Eron continued their conversation in Gaelic as though she wasn't there. They were laughing about something now and Finna's face grew hot. Anger was still right on the surface and she knew if she opened her mouth, all of it would come spilling out.

Once they finished eating, Eron brought out a small bottle of mead, pouring a little into three earthenware cups. He brought one over to where Finna sat alone, and handed it to her.

"To toast this unexpected night with Catriona and my daughter Finna and the special new life that Finna carries, our grandchild." He lifted his cup as Catriona picked hers up and then he and Catriona linked arms and drank together. Finna took a tentative sip. It tasted of wildflowers, honey and herbs. She drank deeply, feeling soothed for a moment by the delicious nectar.

That night Finna dreamed again about the dark and shadowy figure. Fires raged, blocking her escape as she ran down one trail and up the next. Just as the flames were about to engulf her, she woke up. Her heart pounded, leaving her limp with terror and helplessness. She raised herself on one elbow noticing Catriona and Eron sleeping beside her. Covered with a blanket of felted wool, Eron's arm lay protectively around Catriona--her head on his shoulder, her body curved into his. Finna rose quietly and went to the spring.

Re-uniting with her mother had allowed something wonderful to be born and now it was all gone, all her feelings of love and connection, lost in an instant. Catriona wasn't the person Finna thought she was. If Finna couldn't trust her, who could she turn to? How had her father coped with the knowledge that Finna wasn't his child? And yet he still had raised her and let Catriona go off to have her affairs. He must be a saint.

The moon had set and stars glittered bright cold blue in the wide sky. The air was completely still; all she could hear was the bubbling of the water as it poured over the rocks into the pool. She lay down next to the spring and drifted into a twilight sleep. *Starlight reflected off each green-gold scale as the snake glided toward her. When it was very close it looked at her with its intelligent serpent eyes and began to speak in a garbled, under-water voice. "You must let go of the past and forgive what you do not understand. Trust yourself and look to the moonstone for your answers." The snake turned and disappeared into the mist on the other side of the pool.*

CHAPTER 10

W hen she woke again the sun was up and Catriona was close by her building up the fire.

"Guid mornin', Finna," Catriona said, her voice calm. "When did ye come out here?"

"I don't know. It was still dark. Where's Eron?"

"He's gone to check his snares. He asked me to let ye know how sorry he is that you're upset. He didn't mean for this to happen."

"He should have thought about that a long time ago."

"Finna!" Catriona said sharply. "There isnae time for this emotional nonsense."

"That's fine for you to say. I'm the one ..." and then she remembered what the snake had said, *let go...forgive...* "Oh never mind. I'm just...I don't know...shocked, I guess."

"With your sheltered upbringing, it's understandable, but 'tis done. Eron is your Da and I might never have told ye. Would that have been better?"

"Probably not. I don't know. I've spent my whole life thinking about things in a certain way and then I met you and I had to adjust and now it's all changed again. And I thought you were different."

"Different than what? Maybe ye had me on some sort of pedestal." Catriona sighed, pulling her hair back and weaving it into a loose braid.

"Where's Eron's wife, anyway? She probably wouldn't be too thrilled that the two of you...that..."

Catriona held up her hand. "I must tell ye the rest of this story."

"There's more?"

"Aye--concerning what happened to Eron's family. He told me about it all last night. Brandubh burned down the settlement while they were living there. Both Eron's wife and nine-year-old boy were killed."

"Oh my God! When was this?"

"Just three years ago. Eron was living in the cave at the time so he wasn't there to protect them. He blames himself."

"What could he have done? It's not his fault." When Finna pictured Eron's kind and open face tears filled her eyes.

"I tried to tell him that, but he carries a lot of guilt and shame. This spring is powerful and I'm glad that Eron has been able to spend time here. It has the capacity to heal what still lingers."

"What do you mean, 'what still lingers'?"

"I mean the negative energy from that time is still present. It needs to be healed and yet the settlement canna be healed while Brandubh is there. But Eron can heal."

"I still don't get how a priest could behave this way."

"Finna, ye are very naive. Brandubh has been taken over by something dark and malevolent. His thirst for power has eroded his conscience. He had this side to him when he was a young boy but it's grown stronger over the years and becoming a priest fed some part of it. He wields more power through the kirk."

"What did your parents do? Didn't they discipline him?"

"Brandubh and I were very close when we were young. We are psychically linked, at least we used to be. My father abused me from the time I turned thirteen." Catriona paused and looked at the ground. When she gazed at Finna once more, her eyes glistened. "Brandubh fought and killed Fergus when he discovered what he was doing.

'Twas an accident, really. He left after Fergus's death and then Adair, our mother, told me to leave. She blamed me for all of it. Adair always doted on Brandubh--he could do nae wrong. Apparently, from what Eron tells me, she's reunited and aligned herself with my brother."

"You told me your mother was dead."

"To me she is. My mother is a powerful and evil woman who helps her son in what ever way she can."

"Even though he killed your father? I would think she'd be completely distraught and beyond furious with him. What about the authorites? Wouldn't your brother get arrested for this?"

Catriona shook her head. "'Tis nae how this place works, Finna. I thought ye would understand that by now. We have never needed anything resembling authority of that nature. To Adair 'twas an accident and Brandubh is nae to blame--and in a way it was. Brandubh pushed Fergus away from me and he fell and hit his head."

Finna didn't know what to say. Somehow this terrible childhood of Catriona's seemed to make up for all the secrecy and lies. No wonder Catriona was into free love. She hadn't experienced any nurturing at all as a child. A new and more sympathetic view of her mother emerged into her consciousness.

"Can you tell me the rest? I'm just beginning to understand."

"I havenae told anyone about my childhood except Eron. I think this should wait for another day."

"Were others hurt in the fire in the settlement?"

"The fire killed more than a third of the villagers. After that, the others were so afraid they did whatever my brother told them. Brandubh made them believe that the village burned because of their wickedness. After the fire Eron never went back." She wiped at her eyes with the back of her sleeve. "The last time I was there it was more like Mikdal and Herska's village, a good sized bustling town. As I mentioned earlier, the people were a bit superstitious, that's all. Eron told me that when Brandubh arrived he forbade them to celebrate the festivals that mark our year and had all the shops closed down."

Catriona put a pot of water on the fire and then added some tealeaves. She sat down next to Finna, her green eyes clouded. "He refused to allow the people to practice their trades and set them to work in the fields instead, raising vegetables for food. This alone was nae such a problem but the loss of their creative work was. They were used to getting together with other villages for festivals and trading goods but now were utterly isolated. It explains why there was so much tension when we came through there. People need a creative life, without it they wither. My brother likes it that way," she added, frowning. "It keeps the people weak and easily controlled."

Finna thought about her threat from the night before. There was no way she could find her way home from here, not without Catriona. And besides that there were too many dangerous animals and people roaming around. She wished she didn't know about the settlement, the prophecy, Brandubh or any of the other horrible things that now filled her mind. "When are we leaving the spring?"

"As quickly as we can. Even though this sacred spring has magical protections, I still worry about being so close to Brandubh. With our psychic connection, well...who knows what might happen? And, according to Eron, the Morrighan was involved in the burning of the settlement three years ago."

"The Morrighan? Who's that?"

"She's the goddess of war." Catriona turned away, tears falling unchecked down her cheeks.

Finna wanted to console her but something kept her away. Her mother's grief was solitary, not something that Finna could do anything about. Brandubh was her mother's brother, her uncle. How much of this evil nature might be inherent in her own psyche? And what about her grandmother, Adair? The entire scenario made her feel slightly sick.

Finna went to the fire and poured tea into two cups. As she handed one to her mother she saw the immense sadness on Catriona's face. Guilt washed over her for all her unkind thoughts. Finna wanted to wrap her arms around this woman who had endured things Finna couldn't even imagine. But the shell around Catriona held her back. They sipped together without speaking, listening to the soothing murmur of the spring.

A MELANCHOLY ATMOSPHERE hung over them as they ate a breakfast of oatmeal. As Catriona disappeared into the woods to meditate, Eron arrived, bringing supplies for their trip: deerskin jackets, blankets and food. He joined her by the fire.

"Can you come with us, Eron?"

"I cannot."

"But why not?"

"I belong here. This is a trip for you and your mother."

"Why did you let my mother go? Did you know about me?"

Eron looked away away for a moment and Finna could see the effort it took to keep his emotions under control. "'Twas a hard decision, my daughter," he finally said. "One that your mother and I talked long and hard about. We decided that our love and the birth of a baby between us would be too painful for Grita, my wife, to deal with. She was a fragile soul and it would have hurt her deeply."

"But I don't understand why my mother left me with Angus. She could have brought me back here with her. Then I could have had a relationship with you. And why didn't she just raise me on her own instead of marrying?"

Eron eyes were dark with pain. "Catriona married Angus for Grita as well as for you. I was surprised when Catriona left you, though. She's never been afraid of anything in her life but somehow raising a child seemed to overwhelm her. She told me she would not be a good mother."

As Eron finished his sentence Catriona emerged from the woods. "What are ye two talking about?"

"I was trying to get Eron to come with us, but he won't."

Catriona went to Eron and linked her arm through his. "Eron has his own life here. He's a healer and he's needed, especially now with what's going on in the settlement; those people need him more than they know. I have many friends. They'll look out for us."

Eron nodded. "As your mother said, there are many to help you. And if you're in need I'm sure I'll hear Catriona's call. Rest assured I will see you at the blessing ceremony."

If we make it that far, Finna thought. Her brain felt overtaxed as though too many conflicting thoughts and emotions were jostling for recognition. As she left the clearing to go pack

her things, she heard Eron say, "I'm not fit company anymore."
She stopped to listen.

"What are ye talkin' about?" she heard Catriona say softly.
"You're just as good company as you've always been."

"Nay, Catriona, I feel old. Every time I think about..."

"Eron, shh." Catriona placed her hand on his mouth and
then kissed him. "It takes time to get over these things. Ye need
to stop blamin' yourself, 'twas nae your fault."

"Then whose was it? I should have been with them."

"She chose to live there. Ye tried to get her to come to the
cave."

Finna saw the haunted look in his eyes as he turned his
head toward her mother. "I didn't try hard enough. All I really
wanted was you."

"Dear Eron," her mother said tenderly, putting her head on
his shoulder.

CHAPTER II

"Where will we shelter tonight?"

"There is a city nae far. We should be there by nightfall. The people who live there are called the Crion. They are like us, but smaller, since they have adapted to living in tunnels."

"Dwarves?"

"Nae, not dwarves."

"Do they speak English?"

"Some do but they have their own language."

More strange beings to meet, Finna thought tiredly. She felt depleted both physically and emotionally.

They had left Eron at the spring at midday, heading down the hill toward a valley filled with heather and broom. Different shades of faded purple and mauve interspersed with yellow made a pleasing carpet in front of them. Tiny creeks flowed under the low growing bushes and the murmur followed them as they stepped carefully around hidden rocks and holes. Part of this valley was a peat bog so Catriona had gone ahead, searching for the narrow paths made by animals. Peat could be like quicksand.

Finna had placed the moonstone in her pocket for quick reference and took it out now to look into it. "The stone is pointing in that direction," she said, gesturing toward the north where snow-covered mountains sent their peaks toward the sky. She didn't look at her mother as she spoke, still aware of a strain between them from the revelations at the spring--a troubling estrangement that she couldn't completely shake despite the sympathy she now felt. Ominous dark clouds hung above the mountains in the distance, giving a sense of foreboding despite the warm sun and the bucolic scene that stretched before them. It seemed a good place to encounter the *Fassnik*— Finna looked into the sky, expecting to see it flying out of the gray clouds, flames roaring out of its open mouth. She missed the safety of the spring and the comforting presence of Eron.

"It's even warmer here than back by the spring." Finna reached down, picking a tiny flower from the coarse heather at her feet.

"This entire area is influenced by the sulpher springs and because of this the heather and broom grow year round. The Crion use if for their dyes. They're weavers," she added.

They walked until close to sunset with Finna constantly checking their progress in the stone. The heather and broom had given way to low scrub grass and the streams had long since disapppeared. She was tired and hungry and had twisted her ankle several times on hidden rocks but she refused to complain, summoning a new determination.

When a chime rang out, a bright clear tone like a bell, Finna looked west toward the sound. Two figures stood in silouette about a quarter of a mile away. Catriona hurried toward them with Finna trailing reluctantly behind.

The figures waited beside a round opening in the ground, the entrance to their tunnels. Drawing closer, Finna was struck by their unusual amber-colored eyes. There was something fox-like about them with their triangular shaped faces and eyes that slanted up slightly at the corners. They stood around four feet tall, dressed in woven wool tunics in muted tweeds, their feet and legs encased in high sheepskin boots.

Catriona chattered away, ignoring Finna as she followed them down steep dirt stairs. When they reached the bottom she turned to make sure Finna was following and then relayed the information that the city was dug out of compressed volcanic ash. Torches made of the long stalks of mullein lit the way as they followed the Crion into a narrow tunnel on the right.

This new passageway took them by several rooms filled with bright woven tapestries and rugs. The smell of the blazing torches was strong in the damp air. In one of the rooms, Crion sat at miniature looms, their nimble fingers moving the shuttle back and forth as they worked the pedals with their bare feet. In a corner of another room a pile of unspun wool sat on the floor next to a vacant spinning wheel.

The Crion took them to the entrance into a large open room and then vanished down a side tunnel. Finna ran into Catriona who had stopped abruptly in the doorway.

"What's the matter?" Finna whispered.

"Look."

"Well, well, look who's here, my long lost sister," Brandubh drawled. He was sprawled in a chair, his long legs stretched in front of him.

Finna backed away. Now she was able to see his uncanny resemblance to Catriona. His lips were shaped like hers but slightly thinner, and had formed into a sneer that Finna had never seen on Catriona's face. It was like looking into a funhouse mirror--everything beautiful in Catriona's features, twisted into its polar opposite.

Three brightly dressed Crion women hovered nervously around him. There was a mug next to his chair and a plate covered with cheese and bannock. Finna looked over at Catriona, waiting for her to say something, but she just stared at him with an unreadable expression on her ashen face.

"No greeting for your twin, sister dear?"

"What exactly are ye doing here?" Catriona finally asked, her voice shaking.

"Probably the same thing ye are, sheltering for the night," he replied languidly, a cat-like smile on his lips. "And who pray is this delightful creature with ye? Is she perhaps my niece? Why haven't ye introduced us, sister?" Brandubh stared at Catriona, his eyes going dark with barely contained fury.

Finna flushed. His oddly seductive tone terrified her. When his eyes met hers she felt unable to move. She struggled to get control of herself.

"My dear, ye had a slight mishap at the river. Sorry I couldn't be more help."

Finna searched his face to see whether he was being sarcastic. She had seen the look of concern on his features that day, his urge to come to her rescue. He couldn't be all bad. "I..."

"Come, Finna." Catriona grabbed her hand and tugged her toward the tunnel.

"Do ye have to go so soon?" came Brandubh's voice. "I havnae had a moment with my niece."

"Mother, why can't I talk to him? He..."

Catriona shook her head violently. "Ye dinna understand," she whispered, pushing Finna ahead of her down the tunnel. "He wishes ye harm."

"I didn't get that feeling from him."

"Ye dinna ken him," she said in a hoarse whisper. "How did he do this?"

"Do what?"

"Gain access to these people."

Finna didn't know what to say. Brandubh didn't seem to be doing anyone any harm at the moment. The Crion seemed to accept him in their midst. It wasn't a question she could answer.

Catriona put her head into a doorway and began speaking in the lilting language that was the Crion's native tongue. And then she turned to Finna. "We have to leave immediately."

OUTSIDE, Finna tried to keep up with her mother's fast pace. "What's going on? Is Brandubh coming after us?"

Catriona stopped and pulled out the moonstone. "See for yourself." Finna looked over her shoulder, noticing two figures and a silver thread zigzaging across the surface. Finna sighed in relief. "But I don't understand how to follow the route it shows. Where are we going?"

"Notice where the mountains are? They're our touchstone. Always keep the mountains to the right of the line in the stone. There's another Crion village around here somewhere. I'm trusting the stone to lead us there."

As she struggled to keep up with Catriona, Finna kept seeing things out of the corner of her eye--shapes and shadows, small movements--but when she turned to look, there was nothing there. Maybe the *Fassnik* was like the creatures she and Catriona had encountered early on--the shadow creature that preyed on fear. This new image didn't have wings, it was amorphous like smoke, moving and enveloping everything in its path like whatever pursued those poor people in the valley. A chill went down her spine. She ran on, trying to keep her mother in sight.

"Listen," Catriona ordered, stopping abruptly in front of her.

A faint tinny sound could be heard coming from beneath the ground, sort of like the distant clanking of cowbells. "We are very close now."

Close to what? When Finna caught up with her, Catriona was pulling on a chain attached to a round piece of wood set flush with the ground. As she lifted it out of the way, a steep stairway came into view, leading down. Finna followed her into the darkness, a hand grasping Catriona's sleeve. They worked their way along, feeling the sides of the tunnel in the pitch black, but it was barely a minute or two before the heavy rock in the tunnel ahead of them slid aside and bright light spilled in, along with the chatter of excited voices. Catriona said something in their language and then they were surrounded with small people and escorted into the warm and well-lit tunnel.

"What are they saying?" Finna whispered.

"They know about the prophecy."

"How do they know?"

"The prophecy is well known by most of the inhabitants of the Otherworld and especially the Crion. These people are the keepers of the wisdom, along with the Amuigh."

"Keepers of the wisdom?"

"With their purity of heart, gratitude and appreciation they keep the atmosphere and energy of the Otherworld in balance. This village contains thousands of Crion. They have been telling me about Brandubh. He's been making the rounds and trying to convert them. 'Tis one reason we ran into him at the first village."

"Is he succeeding?"

"Nae, they have held on to their belief system, as I was sure they would."

"What system is that?"

"They believe in the ritual celebration of the changing seasons and offerings to the spirits that dwell within everything. They are an intrinsically happy people and shy away from conflict. Let me recite a poem from the 1300's by St. Catherine of Siena that explains what I'm tryin' to say."

All has been consecrated.
The creatures in the forest know this.
The earth does, the seas do, the clouds know
As does the heart full of love.
Strange a priest would rob us of this knowledge
And then empower himself
With the ability
To make holy what
Already was.

FINNA GAZED into the Crion's shining faces, noticing the light in their eyes as they listened to Catriona. Tears blurred her vision. It seemed that crying had become a daily event. When the small ones noticed her tears they came close, patting her and making crooning sounds. As Finna wiped the last of her tears away, the Crion rose from where they had crouched next to her, heading off in different directions. The few remaining ones chattered in high, agitated voices gesturing with their delicate hands.

"Catriona, is something bothering them?"

"They're asking me many questions, but then Aila here,"

Catriona gestured to the woman standing next to her, "warned that the next person to ask a question would be made king or queen."

"King or queen? That sounds like a good thing."

"Nae, Finna. These beings have no hierarchy. They live together in harmony. That would be the worst thing they could imagine."

"What are they asking?"

"About Brandubh—they worry that he's so close."

A disturbing image of Brandubh's shadowy hunched over figure making its way down the low tunnel went through Finna's mind.

Catriona put a hand on her shoulder, gazing into her eyes. "But he canna enter here. The stone is in place, it can only be opened from the inside."

Even with Catriona's comforting assurances, Finna was frightened. It seemed like her visions were arriving from some future time—maybe when her baby was a grown woman? Was she becoming clairvoyent after all? Whatever it was, she didn't like it.

COREY AND HIS MATE, Aila, led the women down the tunnel to a room with two where they could sleep. Along the way they passed by a large space enclosed by a low gate, housing a dozen small sheep with bells around their necks. Catriona and Finna paused to watch them munching contentedly on their sweet smelling hay mixture—the movement of their heads had the bells chiming, a pleasant music. Catriona answered her question before she could ask it.

"They keep their sheep in here for the coldest winter months so they can give birth to their lambs inside, away from the hungry wolves. Their manure heats up the room where they are housed and then is piped into other areas of the village. See the holes in the walls? 'Tis a good way to keep them warm since peat gathering around here is very difficult and virtually non-existent during winter."

"What about feed?"

"They have another room where they store the sweet grass, heather and wild oats that grow out here in the summer."

"Why doesn't it smell bad?" Finna asked, sniffing the lavender scented air.

"They clean up the urine quickly, covering it with a type of soda that absorbs the odor." Catriona pointed to the ceiling where herbs had been hung to dry. "They collect lavender during the growing season, lavender and heather. This is the scent ye are picking up."

"Where do they get the dyes for their wool?" Finna asked, looking into the weaving room they were passing. Brightly colored skeins lay scattered across the floor. A weaving had been started on one of the looms in a complicated design of orange and blue.

"They collect many plants to use for their colors: goldenrod, madder root, heather, broom and the heartwood of the Yew."

At the end of the hall Cory and Aila led them into a room and gestured toward the table where a food tray had already been left. Before the couple turned to go, Catriona thanked them in their language, making a small bow with her hands together. The two Crion bowed back and then turned to Finna. They said something unintelligible and then Aila used gestures to indicate Finna's baby, crooning and rocking her arms as though they held the invisible child.

"What are they saying?"

"They hope to meet this bairn when she's wee so they can enjoy a baby again. Aila is barren. It seems that many of the

Crion women are becoming barren and I dinna understand why. I have treated them with the herbs for this condition but they dinna seem to help. I canna say whether it is a low sperm count or something with the women, but 'tis disturbing."

After Aila and Corey left, the two women turned toward the table where two bowls of soup, fresh bannock and apple slices had been carefully arranged on the tray. A sprig of heather lay next to each bowl. "Vegetable soup!" Catriona exclaimed.

Finna, ravenous, sat down and began to pull off pieces of the crusty bannock, dipping it into the soup of carrots, potatoes and beets.

While eating, Catriona explained to Finna that they would need to make an early start in the morning. She hoped to make it to the Rowan village by nightfall and that meant leaving before dawn.

SOMEONE PULLED ANNOYINGLY at her shoulder. Finna tried to roll over but then she heard Catriona's urgent voice calling her name.

"What's the matter?" Her body felt like it had been in a war and her head was splitting.

"We need to keep ahead of Brandubh."

Her eyelids burned as she opened them to look blearily up at her mother.

"Finna! Now!"

Finna reached for her sweater on the floor, pulling it over her head. "What time is it?"

"Sometime just before dawn. Please hurry."

Yawning widely Finna rose and finished dressing, wondering what all the fuss was about. It was pitch black in the little room and she could hardly see her hand in front of her face.

"I have your pack," she heard Catriona say from the direction of the doorway.

They emerged out of the tunnel to a rumble of thunder rolling across the sky-- heavy storm clouds covered the peaks of the mountains in the distance. The air was decidedly colder than the day before and Finna pulled on an extra sweater. At the eastern horizon a thin line of orange signaled the dawn-- above them a violet sky with a few stars still visible.

Finna woke up quickly in the cold air. She was hungry and tired and did not want to think about the possiblility of Brandubh coming after them. He seemed more than powerful; there was something almost supernatural about him. *As though he could sprout wings and fly to where she and Catriona were*, she thought, making her heart speed up. And then she remembered the *Fassnik*. There would be no defense against a smoke-like being who preyed on fear.

Her hands went to her belly where the baby's kicks were becoming more obvious by the day. Due to the circumstances, she wasn't taking proper care of herself and was surprised she hadn't come down with a cold. As this thought went through her mind she sneezed. Catriona looked back.

"Are ye all right?"

"I need to eat something."

"I was in such a hurry I nearly forgot about breakfast." Catriona stopped and dug into her pack, handing Finna a small piece of cheese and some of the bannock they had gotten from the Crion. "I'm sorry to hurry ye but this day is most critical."

"What is worrying you? I know Brandubh is a bit creepy, but why would he follow us?"

Catriona's eyes darkened. "I'll tell ye the reason when we're safe again. Right now we need to focus on getting to

Rowan." Catriona put on her pack and turned toward the trail. "Are ye up to this?"

Finna nodded, slipping her arms through her pack. She chewed on the bannock as she followed her mother up the trail. Her headache had not gone away and all of her joints ached. Her eyes burned as though she hadn't slept at all.

THE SUN APPEARED above the low hills to their right, streaming across the valley and illuminating the low growing bushes and plants. Finna stopped for a moment to absorb the pastoral scene, thinking about what paints she would use to depict the different shades of muted greens and grays and the brighter outlines where the sun touched them. Payne's gray and maybe Thalo green—burnt sienna for some of the bushes--some purple for the shadows...it was hard to feel any kind of urgency in the warmth of the beautiful morning air.

"Finna! What are ye doin'?" Catriona stood in the middle of the trail with her hands on her hips.

"Just taking in the sunrise."

Catriona hurried toward her, a frown marring her usually smooth brow. "Finna, please listen to me. We *have nae* time to spare."

Finna's stomach contracted when she saw the worry on her mother's face. "I'm sorry," she mumbled. "I didn't realize..."

Catriona shook her head and turned back to the trail. "Please try to keep up."

Now Finna was worried again, her calm feelings replaced with a pounding heart and clammy hands. She looked behind them, expecting a smoke being to be hard on their trail. There was no sign of the fassnik or of Brandubh and she returned her attention forward, trying to keep up with Catriona.

The terrain gradually rose, scrubgrass replaced by larger bushes and spindly trees. Boulders dotted the landscape. Finna paused at the crest of a small hill, scanning into the distance. A wave of dizziness made her sway and right after that she broke out in a sweat. She peeled off her sweater, tying it around her waist. "How much farther is the Glass Mountain?"

"It will still take us a number of days from here, but Rowan is nae far. We should be there by dusk if we keep this pace."

"Rowan—isn't that some kind of tree?"

"Aye. The people there revere the magical rowan trees growing in that area. They have welcomed me in the past and I am hoping they will do so again. They live simply, raising sheep, hunting and working with their hands--many are expert woodcarvers."

A tree-covered hill in the distance took Finna's attention, giving rise to an image of people with tree limbs for arms and legs and leaves all over their bodies. She laughed, pointing. "Is that it?"

"Aye, just beyond the beginning of the treeline." Catriona peered at her, a look of concern on her features. "Finna, your face is bright red."

"I feel like I might be catching something." A second later Finna sneezed was overcome by a violent sneezing fit.

Catriona placed a hand on her forehead. "You're burning up!"

The sneezing had made her dizzy again. Finna grabbed Catriona's arm to keep herself upright.

"Put your sweater back on and lie down for a wee minute. I have some willow that I collected at the beginning of the trip. 'Twill help with the fever." She pulled off her pack, frantically rummaging through it. "Chew on this," she said, handing Finna a woody stem.

Finna sat on the ground and did as she was told, despite

the bitter taste. When Catriona took out the moonstone and stared into it with a frown, a tremor went through her body. What now?

Catriona laid her hand on Finna's forehead and then helped her stand. "We have to go on. I'll support ye as much as I can but if we stay here any longer we will nae make it to the village before dark."

"What did you see in the stone?"

Catriona didn't answer, only putting her arm around Finna's waist and tugging her foreward.

Finna's condition got progressively worse. Catriona stopped often and made her drink little sips of water but the fever and dizziness increased. Finna felt as though she was in a dream as she put one foot in front of the other, struggling up the uneven terrain.

"'Tis nae far now," she heard Catriona say. By this point she could barely focus on their surroundings and spasms racked her body every few minutes. Catriona pulled another sweater over her head and pressed her foreward. Every step was agony and Finna couldn't imagine how she would take another. They struggled on.

Had it turned dark or had her vision dimmed? "Are we there?" she asked, her voice raspy and weak.

"Aye, child, very close now."

Finna fell, going down hard and landing on her back. She did not want to get up but Catriona was shouting in her ear making her head hurt even more. She protested when Catriona's fingers pressed into her upper arm, pulling her to her feet. "Ye must try, Finna. I canna carry ye."

Rowan sat on the top of a hill with an unobstructed view on all sides. It was originally built with protections in mind but also for the many rowan trees, which were considered auspicious. Catriona pulled Finna by the hand, heading toward the closed gate. Sheep and goats grazed on the hillside and they lifted their wooly heads to stare as the women passed by.

An enormous rowan tree grew next to the wide ornamental gate, its graceful branches reaching out in all directions as though to embrace the world. The fence of intricate entwined branches that enclosed the settlement was also made of rowan and had been worn to a fine-grained silvery-gray by the elements.

Finna, almost delirious, could barely keep her eyes focused--she saw the gate and her mother as though they were made up of wavy lines.

A man approached from the other side carrying a lantern. "Hello! What have we here?" he asked, swinging the gate open.

"My daughter has been taken ill--I hope ye can help us."

"Of course," he answered. Finna felt a cool hand on her forehead and then his distressed voice. "We must take her to the healer immediately." Strong arms came around her and then she was lifted. From a distance she heard shouting, but could do nothing but focus on the pain shooting down her spine as he ran. It wasn't long before he stopped and she heard his knuckles rapping on wood.

"Aye, Janus? What is it?" Finna heard a woman say.

"A visitor who is very ill," he said in a tone of urgency and then she was lowered onto something soft. She tried to open her eyes but they refused to focus. Warmth was behind her, a fire perhaps. Urgent hands removed her sweater. Her teeth began to chatter as her undershirt was also pulled over her head. She tried to sit up. "What are you doing?" she asked, feeling embarrassed to be undressed in front of these strangers.

"Ye are in competent hands," she heard the man say.

"Fetch my herbs, Janus," came the woman's peremptory command. "What has happened to this woman?"

Finna opened her mouth to tell her but all that came out was a mumbled croak.

"Mostly nae enough food or rest," Catriona answered.

"And who are ye?"

"I am Catriona, and this is my daughter, Finna. We are on a journey to the Glass Mountain...we..."

Finna heard the conversation but could not contribute. A dark fog had entered her brain and she struggled to maintain consciousness.

"Aye, I have heard all about ye and your daughter."

Something about the woman's voice scared Finna. But as she opened her mouth to say so, a wave of dizziness almost made her black out. Their voices went in and out of her consciousness. She heard her mother ask, "Have we met before?"

"Nae, Catriona, but many who come through here speak highly o' ye."

"Aye. I have also heard tell of your skill, Brianag. I am glad my daughter is in your hands."

"Before we talk more I must tend to your daughter, she is very ill. She could lose this baby." Finna felt something come into contact with her skin, something cool and soothing. "Please wait outside, Catriona, I must concentrate."

"I would rather stay and help."

"Please. Brianag needs to be alone when she is working her healing," the man added. There was the scrape of a chair and the sound of a door closing. *Don't leave me.*

Finna felt hands on her body, rough hands that pressed

and hurt. Mumbled incantations were being said but she couldn't make them out. Sometime later arms came under her body and she was lifted and carried, the sound of the door creaking open. "What's happening?" she heard her mother ask frantically and then there was a chill wind on her bare skin. Her teeth chattered so hard it made her head hurt. *Mother*, she tried to say, but she was too weak to get the words out.

"We're taking her to the spirit cabin where we can build up the fire and try to purge the illness from her body," came the hurried reply from the man.

"I want to go with ye..."

Finna couldn't hear anything anymore...*she floated above her body watching the two people carrying her. Her skin looked so pale. She wasn't afraid, just kind of interested in the proceedings. The little house where they took her had rowan trees twined together over the entrance. She saw the woman stop just before the threshold and hand Finna's body to the man, who carried her inside.*

The room was very warm and smelled like herbs: sweet grass and sage. The man built up the fire and sat next to her, replacing the herbs on her chest and bowing his head as though in prayer. She wondered if she was already dead. Pungent smoke lifted from the fire as the man placed leaves into the flames. Her mother was not here, not with her, and she wondered why.

She went into a strange white fog-filled place for a while and when she became aware of things again she had been moved back into the first house. She was on a bed in a small room and a stout gray-haired woman was sitting next to her, knitting. The rhythmic clickity clack of the needles made her feel slightly sick. Where was her mother? Murmuring voices came from the other room and she tried to focus on them but she kept drifting in and out. But then Catriona shouted, "I want to see my daughter!"

"Oh heavenly days," the woman said, as the clickety clack, clickity clack continued rythmically. A little while later she distinctly

heard her mother say the name 'Brandubh' and then the murmur of the man's reply. When she moaned the woman came over next to the bed, lifted her head and gave her a sip of some terrible tasting tea and after that she felt very sick and was gone for a long while into the white place.

Much later she was in the air close to the ceiling and could look down on herself again. Her face was deathly pale and bluish shadows lay under her closed eyes. A small smile curved at the corners of the gray-haired woman's lips as she regarded the limp body. She watched the woman pry open her lips and force some liquid down her throat. "This will fix ye right up," the woman whispered and then she chuckled.

Finna was suddenly in her body again, feeling the liquid burn the membranes of her throat. She choked and coughed as she recognized the acrid taste of hemlock. She knew this plant—knew it could be used to help her but if misused it would kill her. Bile rose up and somehow she managed to turn her head and vomit, but enough had already begun to seep into her bloodsteam and she felt the narcotic effects begin to descend over her consciousness.

"Ye little bitch," she heard the woman say as she came over to the bed and pried open her lips. It was no good, more of the noxious herb was going down her throat and this time she couldn't fight it. She fell into a drugged sleep.

Finna struggled to open her eyes. She heard her mother talking with the woman but her eyes seemed stuck shut and her throat was so dry and sore she couldn't speak.

"Janus just told me that Finna was better," her mother's worried sounding voice said.

"She was a little while ago but this last few minutes she seems to have relapsed," she heard the woman answer.

Finna thought, no, this isn't true, and struggled to become more conscious so she could tell her mother what was happening. She was finally able to croak out her mother's name.

"I'm here," she heard Catriona say. Catriona's hand took hold of one of her, pressing it reassuringly.

"MOTHER...I....OH...." Finna moaned, a wave of nausea going through her.

"She's still feverish," Catriona said sharply. "And it smells as though she's been sick. What have ye been giving her? Ye ken she's pregnant."

Finna did feel extroadinarily sick with a languor that she couldn't seem to come out of. She wished she could throw up again but she could not move. Her arms and legs felt rubbery and almost paralyzed.

"I know this. I'm only giving her herbs to help with the fever and dizziness," the woman replied, her voice calm. "There's nothing to be done, Catriona. She needs to sweat out the illness now."

Finna felt her mother's gentle hands on her, moving the quilt back.

"Leave the quilt where it was." Finna felt the quilt pulled back up and tucked tightly around her body. She felt like she was going to suffocate and tried to make a sound but all she could manage was a croak.

"Get away from my daughter!" Catriona shouted. "She's getting worse, not better. If ye harm her or the baby she's carryin', ye will be very sorry."

With a vast effort, Finna opened her eyes. "I...you must..." Finna tried to sit up but the effort cost her and she fell back, dropping into a dark place and then she was falling...falling... soft hands shook her but she could not rouse herself from the torpor and lay very still, unable to move or speak.

"Not to worry, Catriona. She'll be all right, she just needs to sleep..." was the last thing Finna heard.

. . .

FINNA WAS on the ceiling again but this time she was deeply afraid. The woman was giving her another dose of the poison and she didn't have the strength to fight her off. Why didn't Catriona see that this woman was poisoning her? She was hot, so hot and she wanted to throw the covers off but now she couldn't even move her fingers. Terror shot through her as she realized she was totally paralyzed.

"I want to take her to the spirit house!" Finna heard her mother's shout from a distance. "I think she's having an allergic reaction to what you've given her." Finna felt the covers come off--her mother's hands trying to lift her inert body. Please help me, I don't want to die.

"Wait!" The woman's shrill voice hurt her ears. "Leave her for now. If she's not better in an hour we can take her."

"Aye, let's wait a short while," the man's voice agreed. "Sometimes after a healing the body has to come back into balance. If we interfere it could be harmful."

Finna tried to move her hand but it would do nothing but lie there. She was terrified. And then she thought about her baby. She had not felt her kick for a very long time. Was she going to die without Catriona realizing what was going on? She called silently to her mother, 'please, please help me'.

"Did Finna say something?"

Finna felt her mother's presence close by her and reached out with her mind. "She's poisoning me...please help me!"

"Why don't we have some tea, Catriona," the man said. "Ye need to calm your nerves or ye could be our next patient." There was the sound of a chair scraping across the floor. "Have faith in Brianag—she's very skilled. The worst is over, I'm sure of it.

"The tea will revive ye," Finna heard the woman say. *Oh my god they were going to poison Catriona too. She tried as hard as she could to move, using every bit of her will but she was unable to even lift her hand. She called out in her mind again—'don't trust them, please don't trust them'-- The sound of a jar being opened and then the clunk of the pot being placed over the fire. 'Don't drink it, mother'.*

"Catriona, put some honey in your tea, 'tis good for the nerves."

"I know all about what's good for the nerves, Brianag. I should never have let ye tend my daughter."

Finna was going to die if her mother didn't do something. Her body was numb now and no feeling came from her belly. She was sure the baby was dead and she was soon to follow. Something warm and thick was being poured down her throat and it soothed the burning thirst

A few seconds later she was awake and retching into the bucket that her mother held next to the bed. "That's right. Get it all out, Finna." Another wave of nausea hit her and she threw up violently and then coughed and choked as the acrid bile clogged her throat. Catriona held her securely, keeping her hair out of the way as wave after wave hit her. Finally, exhausted, she fell back and closed her eyes.

A LONG TIME went by before Finna woke again. This time she was able to pull herself up to a sitting position. Her mother watched worriedly from a chair next to the bed.

"How are ye feeling now, my daughter?" she asked, taking Finna's hand in hers. Her eyes were red-rimmed, her face pinched with worry.

"Awake at least. And I can move."

"'Tis so good to see ye awake. You've been in and out of consciousness for nearly three days. Are ye hungry? Can I get ye something to eat?"

" I...still feel sick...as though...I hope the baby's all right."
She placed her hands on her belly, waiting for the familiar kick
but there was nothing. She started to cry.

"Finna, my dear one." Her mother reached down and
pulled her close. "I've been so worried."

"Well, Finna, you're lookin' better!" Brianag said brightly,
entering the room.

"Mathair!" Finna grabbed Catriona's hand, holding on
tightly.

"Get out of here, Brianag," Catriona ordered. But the
woman ignored her.

"Don't leave me." Finna clung to Catriona's hand, trying to
lift herself out of the bed.

"Finna, ye must stay in bed, you're too weak to be walking
around. Ye don't want to lose that special bairn of yours, do
ye?" Brianag said, her voice sweet as honey. "And Catriona, this
is my house and I am the healer here. Ye have nae right to order
me about."

"It may be your house but this is my only daughter."
Catriona helped Finna up, looping an arm around her waist to
support her. They walked together into the kitchen. Catriona
lowered Finna down onto the bench by the table. She took off
her own sweater and pulled it over Finna's head to keep her
warm in the chilly room.

"Any change in your appetite? How about some soup?"

"Maybe a little soup if you make it, but no tea, please."

Brianag made a small disapproving sound as she walked to
the door. "I'll be back later," she said, slamming the door
behind her.

Finna turned toward Catriona. "She's trying to kill me."

"I know," Catriona said quietly as she brought over a small
bowl of soup. "I just wish I had realized it sooner. I knew of
Brianag from others who had high praise for her skills, so I

trusted her without question. The effects of hemlock in small doses can be medicinal but what she was giving ye was way over that. I'm just glad your body managed to expel most of it."

"I don't know if my baby is still alive." Finna started crying again her hands on her stomach.

Catriona came to her and placed a hand over hers. She was quiet for a moment, listening. "She's fine, Finna. I can feel her heartbeat as strong as ever."

"Are you sure?"

"Feel for yourself." Catriona placed Finna's hand on a spot on her belly. "See?" she said, as the fluttering heartbeat became obvious. "This baby is strong."

Finna put her head down on the table, sobbing with relief.

Catriona kneeled in front of the fireplace building up the fire with kindling and and adding two larger logs on top. The kindling caught fire easily from the remaining coals and soon there was a crackling blaze as the larger logs began to burn. The chilly room warmed.

"Don't leave me with her no matter what."

"I will nae leave your side."

CHAPTER 12

Finna woke as a nasty smelling cloth came over her mouth and nose. She struggled, but the strong noxious odor had already done its job and she fell into a twilight sleep. Fingers dug into her flesh as her body was lifted. In her semi-conscious state she heard shouting and growling dogs. It was dark and the wind was cold, blowing through the light shift she was wearing. A vaguely familiar voice shouted, "Bring her here, bring her to me! Hurry!" Through a haze of drugged dizziness Finna saw Brandubh standing on the other side of the rowan wood fence. He held his arms outstretched as Finna was carried quickly toward him. This must be a dream, she thought to herself, but the cold air on her was sharp and she felt goosebumps rising on her arms and legs.

"Goddamnit!" Brandubh yelled as he tried vainly to get through the fence.

"I'll take part of the fence down," Brianag offered. She shifted Finna to the person behind her but Finna couldn't see who it was.

"Just hand her to me. Where's my sister?"

"We took care of her meddlin' ways," Brianag answered. "Nae need to worry about her."

A sharp pain shot through Finna's back as Brianag and her helper twisted Finna's body and ran down the fenceline. Her tears were hot on her cold cheeks. They had killed her mother and now they were going to kill her.

Their gripping hands were on her belly, pressing painfully. She cried out but they ignored her. The beasts came into her line of vision on the far side of the fence. They could rip her thoat out in an instant. In a panic, her hand went to her throast and she screamed as loud as she could.

"Shut your mouth, girl!" Brianag pressed a hand across Finna's mouth and nose. "I look forward to seeing ye on the ground with those snarlin' animals rippin' ye to pieces. Can ye see their teeth, Finna? They'll make short work o' ye."

Finna tried to breathe--the lack of air was making her dizzy. She still felt the effects of the drugs and her mind seemed unable to conprehend what was happening. Across the fence the beasts waited with their mouths open, showing bloodied yellow teeth. Two villagers lay on the ground next to them, their eyes wide and staring. Bile rose into Finna's throat as she took in the masses of blood and gore. She twisted her neck, managing to dislodge Brianag's hand and drew in a ragged breath. It was then she noticed the men with filthy dreadlocks who circled around the beasts. They grunted, their pale eyes on her as they moved closer to the fence.

A burst of adrenaline shot through her as she watched one of them climb through a hole in the fence and head her way. She twisted and kicked as hard as she could. How could this woman in her fifties have this much strength? Finally managing to get one hand free, she punched the older woman in the chest as she tried to get her head and neck out from under her arm. But it was too late, her adrenaline was spent, leaving her weak and limp.

"Ye are nae getting' away from me, girlie," Brianag said, smacking Finna's face with the back of her hand while she shifted her body into another uncomfortable position. "Can ye help me?" Brianag called, her voice frustrated as she struggled with Finna's body.

Finna heard a grunt from a person she couldn't see. A hand went under her ribs making her shriek in pain. A gray-haired man was running toward her and she braced herself for the impact but instead he struck Brianag on the back of the head with a club. Finna twisted her head enough to see Brianag's features go slack and then she was falling and Finna was going down with her. As they landed, her other captor let go and ran before she had a chance to see his face.

Finna rose to her knees and retched until there was nothing left in her stomach and then wiped her face with the hem of her thin shift. She kneeled on the ground, her entire body trembling uncontrollably. Her savior was gone, disappearing into the mahem around her. Villagers ran in all directions and as the dawn light began to shine across the hill, their terrified faces became clear. Many had been injured, bitten by the beasts, and blood ran down their faces and arms in rivulets of red. Bodies lay crumpled and bleeding and she could see that many of them were dead.

She felt too weak to get up, too weak to do anything but watch helplessly as the fight continued. Above the din, she heard Brandubh scream and looked up to see him climbing through a hole in the fence. His eyes were intent on her and there was nothing she could do.

He was almost upon her when she heard a battle cry and looked up to see her mother running toward him. Catriona hurled herself at her brother but Brandubh had already grabbed Finna's arm, dragging her toward the fence. She shrieked as his other hand took hold of her braid, pulling her behind him despite her screaming. When he reached the fence his enormous hands came round her waist, squeezing until she gasped for air. He pulled her with him through the broken branches of rowan and deposited her on the ground, weezing from the effort.

Amid the snarling beasts, Finna rolled into a ball, covering her face with her hands. A high-pitched cry rent the air and then her mother was upon them, attacking Brandubh, her fists pummelling his chest.

"What the hell, woman!" he cried out as she kicked and bit and pounded him with all her strength.

But Finna had to turn away as the beasts closed in for the kill. Paralyzed with fear she watched their pack behavior, their snarls and the way they moved as one, drawing closer and closer. Just before they lunged, a form jumped the fence and came barreling toward her. Janus. He had a club in his hand that he used to beat off the animals. When he reached her, he dropped the club and picked her up, despite her feeble attempts to get away from him. Her sounds coming out of her mouth sounded wild, animal-like to her ears, but she couldn't stop as he hoisted her into his arms and began to run.

They were through the fence and heading up the other side when Finna twisted to look back. Catriona and Brandubh were on the ground struggling in what looked like a life and death fight. Her mother resembled a war goddess, her white face filled with hate, her wild hair a nimbus of red. Finna heard her high-pitched yell as Brandubh's hands came around her neck. The man outweighed her by several stone—there was no way she could win.

Tears ran down Finna's face as she lost sight of them. And then Finna howled, the sound high and keening, as she realized her mother's imminent death. Janus clamped his large hand across her mouth and slung her over his shoulder. Her body went limp.

Janus had reached the top of the hill--where he was taking her was a mystery. Maybe he would throw her off the cliff. Finna no longer cared what happened. Her mother was dead. A pain like a knife went through her upper chest and tears flowed down her face and into Janus's shirt. Blood rushed into her head. In the distance she heard her mother's death cry and then all went black.

FOURTEEN

"'TIS ALL RIGHT, FINNA," Catriona's voice said, "ye are safe now."

Finna pushed herself up and focused on her mother. Janus stood behind Catriona next to an older man who looked vaguely familiar. "I was sure you were dead!" Finna reached toward Catriona, tears welling in her eyes. Catriona pulled Finna into her arms.

"Brandubh is nae as strong as he thinks he is, especially against the magic of rowan wood," Janus remarked.

What was Janus doing here?

Finna stared at her mother. "But the last thing I saw was you struggling with Brandubh. How did you get away?"

"'Twas Roc and a few of his friends--they helped repair the hole while I somehow kept my brother from getting through again." Catriona laughed shakily. "I was filled with supernatural strength for a few moments. Unfortunately the struggle still continues which means we need to get away from here as fast as possible."

Finna turned to view the two men and then looked back

toward her mother. "But Janus—he was taking me—I thought he…"

Janus smiled. "I am sorry Finna. I had to get ye out of there. There was no time for explanations. My roughness didn't do any permanent damage but ye may be a bit sore. I checked ye when we got here, managed to get some warmer clothes on ye. Ye were unconscious for quite a while but I think it was more due to fear and the aftereffects of the chloroform. Although I'm only an apprentice I'm learning to be a healer. I can tell these things."

Finna's attention went again to Catriona, who had scratches on her face and a purple bruise next to her temple. "I heard Brianag say that she had taken care of you or something, but then you were there…"

"Brianag used the chloroform on me as well and I didn't come to until she had taken ye." Catriona's hand went to her temple. "I guess I bruised my head when I fell. And thank ye, my dear friend," she added, looking at Janus. "Without ye I dinna know what I would have done."

"Nae need to thank me. I just wish I had known sooner about Brianag, or should I call her Adair?"

"Adair?" Finna looked from one to the other.

"My mother is a sorceress, Finna," Catriona answered. "She took the shape of the healer and fooled all of us."

"Are you saying that Brianag was actually Adair? The entire time?"

Catriona glanced at Janus. "'Tis hard to ken. At the beginning she seemed…"

"I think she was Brianag until we took Finna to the spirit house. I should have noticed her reluctance to enter. The rowan will nae allow evil to cross the threshold."

"But why do they both want to kill me?"

"Because the child ye carry is the one prophesied to save this world," Janus

answered. "I'm afraid things here will get worse before they get better. But maybe with our combined effort we can protect some areas. I've already begun a plan to reinforce the fence. With the help of Airmid we might be able to cast a spell to add even more protection."

Airmid—had she heard that name?

"Airmid is the goddess of healing, Finna. She presides over a spring that brings the dead back to life."

Finna let out a gasp as the baby kicked. "She seems to be all right

despite everything that's happened."

"She's a strong one." Janus smiled, his gaze warm.

Catriona came over and wrapped her arms around her daughter, her head against Finna's cheek.

"Everyone keeps saying that," Finna muttered. "I hope they're right."

"Thank the spirits," Catriona whispered into Finna's ear. "That hemlock could have caused ye to miscarry."

Finna glanced toward the other man standing behind Janus. When their eyes met, his weathered face broke into a wide smile.

"I am Roc," he said, coming next to her and holding out his hand. "An old friend of your mathair. I have something for ye," he added, digging into the pocket of his trousers. "'Tis a talisman of rowan wood to keep ye and your baby safe until ye reach the moon goddess." He handed her a small carving of a coiled snake. A black velvet ribbon had been threaded through a tiny loop at the top next to the carefully rendered head of the serpent. Chips of a greenish gold stone made up the serpent's eyes and each scale had been delicately carved. "I've been

waitin' a long time to give ye this. 'Twas meant for your thirteenth birthday."

"Is this the necklace my mother brought me...?"

"Aye, 'tis the very same one. Catriona brought it back to me
for safe-keeping."

"But what about the snake?" Finna asked no one in particular, as she recalled the message at the spring. "If I had gotten
this when I was thirteen it wouldn't have meant what it does
now."

"The serpent represents our instinctual self, our true self.
The snake holds wisdom and magic. It sounds as though whatever you've experienced lately gives an added dimension to the
talisman. Strange how things happen." Roc looked over at
Catriona and winked.

Finna pulled the ribbon over her head. The carving hung
neatly in the hollow below her breastbone. "Thank you for
this," she said, feeling the inadequacy of the words as she ran
her fingers over the scales.

"We need to get you two on your way," Janus said urgently,
as the sound of shouting came from across the hill. "I know
you're still very weak, Finna, so I've made something for you as
well." From beneath a small bush he pulled out a small
wooden wagon. Their packs were already in it. "I made this out
of rowan wood to help speed you on your way. There's an old
tunnel along the side of this hill that leads to the river. I used to
play in it when I was a boy. It was built long ago to provide an
escape route during sieges."

He pulled the wagon behind him, heading quickly down
the hill. Catriona helped Finna up and supported her,
following Janus toward the thick bushes growing in front of a
rocky overhang.

· · ·

"Here it is." Janus pulled aside the bushes, pointing the wagon toward the opening.

Catriona peered into the darkness. "I dinna have a torch."

"Ye'll be all right without one. The tunnel is small and there's really only one way to go. 'Twill take an hour to get from here to the river. After that ye'll need to find the bridge that lies downstream. On the other side, head up the hill to the copse of trees directly in front of ye. There ye can pick up the trail north. We'll hold off Brandubh as long as we can."

Catriona embraced him, her eyes misty. "Thank ye, Janus, we will nae forget your kindness, nor yours, Roc."

"I'm glad things turned out the way they did," Janus replied. "The situation could have gone very awry. This will nae happen again, I promise ye. I'm nae sure how things will be when Brianag comes out of this. 'Twill be difficult to trust her, even though she had no control over what happened. Now hurry," he urged, looking over his shoulder in the direction of the shouting and eerie whining of the beasts. "There is nae time to spare. Why don't ye get onto the wagon, Finna?" Janus helped her get settled, resting on the backpacks with her knees up.

She smiled at him, embarrassed by her earlier lack of trust. He pushed his long hair back away from his face, his espression kindly. "All will be well."

Many of the people she had met so far spoke English easily, with the heavy brogue Finna was becoming used to, but Eron and Janus both spoke hesitantly, as though English was their second language. And then there were others who didn't speak English at all, like the Crion and the Amuigh. Her mother seemed to have an affinity for language, conversing with everyone, even the wolves.

Catriona crawled into the narrow opening and pulled on the rope attached to the little wagon. It moved lightly as though on a cushion of air. "Thank ye, again," she called as they left the opening behind.

The tunnel darkened as they worked their way deeper inside and soon it was black as pitch. Terror gripped Finna. She wanted to go back--anything to get out of this dark and tiny space. As they came to a fork, Catriona chose the one on the right.

"I thought he said there was only one way," Catriona grumbled to herself. The space narrowed down until Catriona had to crawl to get through. "Can this be right?"

Finna's throat closed down. She could barely breathe as they inched their way along. "Shouldn't we be there by now?"

"Maybe we should have gone the other way."

Sparks danced in front of Finna's eyes. Was she hallucinating? "Did you see that?"

"See what?"

"The light, the little sparks of light. They keep coming by me and then they disappear."

"Finna, we need to get out of this tunnel. Try to focus on that."

"Wait! I have something in my hand!" When Finna opened her fingers, lights, like tiny fireflies, sprang from her grasp to dance around them, providing enough illumination for them to see each other clearly. The sparks then joined others, heading in a line of brightness, like the beam of a flashlight, back the way they had come. "Follow the lights," Finna yelled excitedly. "They're helping us!"

Catriona reversed direction, struggling to turn the wagon and then followed the line of light as quickly as she could. Once they reached the fork, the lights headed down the other tunnel.

"At least this one's higher," Catriona said. "'Tis nice to be able to stand up."

"I feel a lot better!" Finna's voice reverberated off the tunnel walls. "I think the little light beings gave me some energy."

AROUND A HALF AN HOUR later they came out of the tunnel into an area of dwarfed oaks, maples and birch. Trees dotted the surrounding hills, interspersed with large gray boulders and dry weeds. Winter sunshine dappled the ground, casting odd shadows from the twisted and stunted trunks. The only sound was the murmur of the river as it wound along the bottom of the shallow ravine in front of them. Finna got out of the wagon and raised her arms above her head, stretching into a small backbend.

"Finna, ye do look better." Catriona smiled, her eyebrows raised in surprise.

"I don't know what happened in there but--something. Do you think those lights could be the Ghillie Dhu?"

"I suppose they could have been. I've heard them variously described as elf-like, fireflies and such. I'm just glad you're doing so well. It seems that every being here knows about the magical child ye carry."

There was that word again, *magical.* "Why do you call her magical? What will she be able to do?"

"We will find that out after she's born, Finna. There's no tellin' the extent of her powers. I just know they will be formidable."

Formidable and magical. Finna imagined the discussion she would have with Alex when she got back. In her mind's eye she could see the astonished look on his face as she used the words, 'prophecy', 'magical', 'formidable'. He would never believe her.

• • •

191

THE TWO WOMEN walked downstream until they found the bridge. It was just wide enough for the wagon and Finna went ahead, pulling the wagon behind her. On the other side, a path wound up the hill.

"Do ye want me to pull the wagon for a while, Finna?"

Finna shook her head. "It seems so light and it feels good to walk."

At the top of the hill they found the copse of trees Janus had mentioned, easily locating the wider trail heading north. The terrain had leveled out and the two women were able to walk side by side.

It was close to an hour later when they heard a dull rhythmic thumping in the distance. At the crest of a hill in the distance, the outline of a rider came into view, heading toward them at a gallop. A herd of horses followed. Catriona and Finna glanced at each other nervously, both hoping it had nothing to do with Brandubh; there was no way to outrun them and no place to hide.

The rider fast approached the closest hill and they could now make out the bright golden dress and black hair of the woman who rode the magnificent gray mare. Her waist length hair shone like dark silk against her milk white skin. A dark purple cloak covered her shoulders, fastened at the neck with an intricate silver clasp. She rode bareback, both legs draped to the left, her fingers twined through the horse's thick mane. Boots of the softest doeskin encased her feet, with wide leather straps that wrapped around her calves and disappeared beneath her long skirt. The horse's coat gleamed in the sunlight, its color the deep purple-gray of a storm cloud, its eyes dark and ringed with black. Birds of every hue circled above the woman, singing in melodious voices that rang out in the still air.

As the horse galloped toward them, Finna went to hide.

Catriona stood her ground as the woman came to a stop in front of her. "I am Rhiannon, " she said, her voice booming into the quiet. "I have come to give you a message."

Finna peeked out, struck by the unusual violet eyes staring at her mother.

"This is for the one who calls herself Catriona."

Finna glanced at her mother who had turned very pale. "I am Catriona," she said.

Rhiannon nodded, shifting her weight on the horse. She pointed toward Catriona with fingers covered in rings, the light glinting off the facets of the precious stones."Your anger is blinding you and cutting you off from your special gifts. You very nearly allowed your daughter into the clutches of the sorceress and her son because of this. You cannot fight this man on his terms. Your power can only come through a clear heart. You will prevail over the dark only if you give up the dark place inside you. You will need all your power for what is to come. This new life," she said, gesturing toward the tree Finna hid behind, "is all that is important now, not your own petty grievances and guilt, even though they be true." Rhiannon paused and her stern expression softened. "You have lost faith in yourself, Catriona. And because of this, your light has dimmed. It is obvious to all who can see your true essence. I hope my words will reach into your heart."

Her eyes focused piercingly on Catriona's face before she smoothed her full skirt and shook out her hair with an elegant movement of her head. As she turned the mare with a subtle command, she looked over her shoulder. "Take good care." Her dark eyes regarded them calmly. And with that she galloped off without a backward glance. Her long hair lifted behind her like a flag as the birds wheeled and followed her. The rest of the herd galloped after her.

Catriona walked unsteadily over to an oak and sat down,

her head in her hands. Tears coursed down her cheeks. Finna didn't know what to do. She hadn't seen this side of her mother and she was still reeling from the larger than life woman who had just spoken to them. What Rhiannon had said was shocking considering what Brandubh was up to. Why wouldn't Catriona be angry with him? She should be, he was a horrible person.

It was many minutes before Catriona stood up and turned to Finna. Tears still glittered in her eyes. "Are ye ready to go on?"

"Have you met Rhiannon before?" Finna asked as they prepared to leave.

"Aye." Catriona wiped her eyes and then straightened her shoulders. "Rhiannon is the horse goddess but she also represents fertility and inspiration. This child ye carry is under her domain. Remember I told ye she would release the horses from the spell? The gray mare must have consented to be her mount."

Catriona shook her head and then gazed into the distance. "She is appealing to me because of my fears and confusion about my brother. Now is nae the time for me to be thinking of myself. I must protect ye at all costs." Catriona paused for a moment, her expression resigned. "I'm thankful for her message."

"But how can ye be so sure? I mean that this baby is the one?"

"Do ye still doubt it, Finna? After what Rhiannon just told me? After everything that's happened?"

The look on Catriona's face was bleak and full of pain. Finna breathed in, trying to slow the wild hammering of her heart. It was time to stop questioning and accept the truth.

．　．　．

THE WAGON FLEW UP and down the hills. Finna rode while Catriona pulled it, but from what Finna could see, Catriona's effort was minimal. Going up it seemed to float, and coming down it seemed to have some internal resistance that kept it from going too fast. *Rowan wood*, Finna thought, *the magic of rowan wood*. Catriona had been silent after the encounter with Rhiannon and Finna decided not to press her. It was obvious from the set of her jaw that she was still very upset.

They had been steadily gaining elevation for the past couple of hours and the hardwoods of the lowlands had been left behind, replaced with tall pines, larch and firs. It was rocky, the area littered with boulders--coarse shale mixed with dirt and pine needles on the narrowing trail. Ahead stood enormous mountains, their steep sides in shadow as the sun dipped below the horizon. Beyond this range was the tallest peak of all. It stood alone, its jagged tip obscured by clouds-- the Glass Mountain.

At dusk they began searching for a place to spend the night, finding a shallow cave beneath a large group of boulders. They pulled out the blankets Eron had given them and made their beds away from the direction of the wind. Catriona dug a firepit and they spent some time gathering wood to make a fire. That night they feasted on pemmican, dried berries and the oatcakes Janus had given them and warmed themselves by the comforting flames.

Finna felt closer to her mother now that she had witnessed her vulnerability. And even though she was sure Brandubh was probably hot on their trail, there was a tranquility here that had seeped into her psyche. When she mentioned this to Catriona, her mother told her that there were beings living in this area who kept the forest safe. Catriona had felt their presence in the past as well as on this trip.

. . .

LATER THAT NIGHT, just before they went to sleep, Finna finally summoned the nerve to bring up what Rhiannon had said. "I don't understand her words. How could ye not be angry with him? He's evil and wants to do harm to the baby. We barely escaped."

"Aye, 'tis true, but if I succumb to anger, I will nae see him. It clouds my perceptions. I've always been psychically linked with my brother," she said with a sad smile. "When we were little, we could read each other's minds. Now I need that skill more than ever in order to keep ye safe."

CHAPTER 13

Catriona and Finna woke early the next morning and traveled east, leaving the shelter of the conifers behind. A small rise marked the beginning of a different region, one with undulating low rocky hills and sparse, scraggly trees. A wide river lay at the bottom of the valley and on the far side, a deep green carpet of forest stretched east and north.

Catriona grabbed the wagon's rope and made her way carefully down the hill. Finna followed, feeling more vulnerable now that they were leaving the protection of the tree spirits.

"This is the great middle valley. The forest there in the distance is called the Frith, the deer forest—'tis home to the red deer and reindeer and also the oxen known as aurochs. This forest and these creatures are protected by Cernunnos, the horned god. We are two days from the border of the Caer Sidi, if everything goes according to plan."

A light mist fell around them as they reached the valley, the air sweet with the scent of damp earth and the last of the wild-

197

flowers that still bloomed among the dried grasses. A few grasshoppers and insects buzzed about, landing on the flowers and drinking the droplets of dew.

"It's lovely here," Finna said, as a faint rainbow appeared within the mist.

"This area is under the protection of the Horned One. The animals drink from this river and it flows deep and wide from here to the sea. We will make camp on the other side of the river tonight, where the forest begins." Catriona pointed toward the east.

"But don't we need to go north toward the Glass Mountain?"

"We shall, but we will be safer if we stay close to the Frith. Tomorrow we will head to the Caer Sidi."

As they started across the meadow a child came into view sitting amongst the wildflowers. Finna tugged her mother's sweater pointing.

"Madainn mhath!" Catriona called.

The boy looked their way and then stood up. He looked to be around eight or nine, with fair skin, an angelic face and shiny blonde curls hanging to his shoulders. He waved and came toward them. As he drew closer he broke into a smile. "Catriona! I know you," he said in English.

"Pryderi!" Catriona exclaimed, bending down to hug him. "What are ye doin' out here by yourself?"

"I am perfectly capable of being alone now that I am nine," he said with a scowl.

"Finna, this is Pryderi, Rhiannon's son."

Finna smiled at the boy, struck by how handsome he was. Of course he would be, being the son of a goddess. "I have just recently seen your mother," she said.

Pryderi looked away. "I am mad at her. She always has things she wants from me and Pwyll is even more annoying."

"Who's Pwyll?" Finna asked, looking toward her mother.

"He's my father."

"Pwyll is a human who came to marry a goddess, Finna. This child is half human and half god."

"I am not a child." Pryderi smiled and then did a little dance. As he twirled he held out his fingers and caught some of the grass on fire. "I am a god, I am a god!" he chortled.

"Pryderi this is nae a good idea. Ye have destroyed some of the wildflowers and with it the bees that drink the nectar."

"What do I care about that? I can do anything I want." He pursed his lips and put his hands on his hips, glaring at Catriona.

"What if I tell Rhiannon what you've been up to?" she said, glaring back.

"Go ahead. I am tired of being bossed around. I have powers and she will never let me use them." He looked like he was about to cry.

"With powers comes responsibility, Pryderi. Rhiannon wants ye to be respectful of everything around ye."

"My father lets me. He likes what I can do. Sometimes we go hunting and he asks me to kill the animals. I do not even need a weapon, I can do it with my mind."

Finna sucked in her breath. This was a very dangerous child and she didn't like him. "Can we go now?" she asked.

"Just a minute, Finna," Catriona said putting up her hand. "Pryderi ye need to mend your ways. I will certainly let your mother know what ye have done today and I dinna like how you're behaving. This area is part of the Frith. Has Cernunnos witnessed your insolence? Because I would imagine he would nae put up with it."

Pryderi looked around furtively. "He is not here, is he? I like this place. There are a lot of insects to practice on. I have learned to zap them with my fingers."

"Mother, please." Finna walked away, pulling the wagon with their belongings behind her.

"We're leaving now but if I find out you've been cruel, I will certainly tell your parents." Catriona turned and joined Finna who had walked ahead. Finna heard the boy's contemptuous laughter as she and her mother headed down the path.

"That child needs to be reined in," Finna said vehemently. "He's going to be dangerous later on if his mother doesn't discipline him now."

"Finna, I've never heard ye sound so certain! Ye are correct but I do nae think 'tis as bad as all that. He is, after all, very young, and boys do these things. Rhiannon will take care of him, I'm quite sure."

Finna shook her head. She had a very strange feeling in her belly like the baby was trying to tell her something. All she wanted was to get to the Caer Sidi as quickly as possible.

ONCE THEY REACHED the river they walked in silence along the edge. "I was sure there was a bridge along here," Catriona finally said with a puzzled look.

"How long since you've been this way?"

"A very long time. I suppose something could have happened to it. Maybe it was taken down for defensive purposes."

Finna stopped and pointed. "There's a little boat heading our way."

Catriona's face lit up. "'Tis the boatman come to take us across."

"Who is the boatman?" Finna whispered, but Catriona didn't answer.

"Do you wish to go to the other side?" The man standing in

the coracle looked ancient, with long white hair and beard and deeply etched and weathered skin.

Finna looked into his milky unseeing eyes but when he turned toward her she had the oddest feeling that he could see her thoughts.

"Aye, we need to get to the forest," Catriona answered.

"And what is your purpose here?" the boatman asked.

Catriona took Finna's hand and pulled her closer to the edge of the water where the little boat bobbed back and forth. "We are heading to the Caer Sidi to have my daughter's baby blessed."

"You may get in," he said at once. "I feel the pureness of your heart and that of your daughter. Arianrhod is expecting you."

"What about the wagon, Mother? Should we leave it here?"

"It will nae fit in the boat, so I suppose we must." She picked up the packs and put one on, giving the other to Finna.

As Finna stepped into the boat the boatman asked, "And what will you give me for my services?"

Finna glanced toward her mother in bewilderment.

Catriona stepped into the little boat. "Do ye have any use for the wagon?"

"Is this something you value?" he asked.

"It was made especially for us out of rowan wood."

"Then I will come back for this," he said.

The ride did not take long and the boatman steered the little coracle easily, despite the fast current of the river. When they reached the other side, he brought the boat into an area of weeds next to the bank.

"Thank ye," Catriona said, helping Finna out of the boat.

He nodded and then turned the boat skillfully around, heading into the current. One second he was there and in the next he had disappeared. "Where did he go?" Finna asked, staring up and down the waterway.

"He goes where he's needed. He could be a hundred miles from here by now." "But...how?"

"'Tis one of the mysteries of this place, I canna explain it more than that."

CHAPTER 14

I
t was dark by the time they reached the edge of the great
forest. They made camp under the trees, using the soft
pine boughs that Catriona gathered for their beds.

In the morning they awoke to a heavy charcoal sky. Tracks
of animals were visible in the soft ground around where they
slept. "I didn't hear any animals, did you?" Finna asked, gazing
wonderingly at Catriona.

"They were careful not to wake us."

"What did they want?"

"Just to see ye, I expect, the mother of the child destined to
bring the balance back."

"They know of the prophecy?"

"The animals know, as well as the trees, the spirits, and all
the beings who live here."

Finna examined the many prints. Some were cloven-
hoofed, some the soft pads of wolves, others were smaller like
foxes and badgers. They knew about the child before she did.
How strange all of this was. Lightning lit up the dark clouds for
a moment, taking her attention to the north.

"Is that the Caer Sidi?" From where they stood the land slanted down and then leveled off. Beyond that, rolling hills undulated across the valley ending at the ocean.

Catriona nodded. "The area known as the Caer Sidi begins where the forest ends. See the natural curve of the land beyond the forest? 'Tis the boundary."

Finna gazed west where sage grasses faded into low purple hills in the far distance. To the east the conifer forest stretched into mountains covered in heather. A flat open valley lay to the north; the silver ribbon of the river flowed down the center, narrowing as it headed toward the sea. Closer to where they stood, cattails and bright yellow flag hugged the river's edge, moving gracefully as the light breeze touched them. The distant landscape curved like a shell, shimmering in the misty sunlight and echoing the soft curve of the shoreline beyond. Further still was the deep blue stone of the sea and a small island, its sheer snow-covered peaks reaching into the sky. Against the backdrop of mountains stood the shining castle made of ice.

"Finna, I need a bit of time alone. You'll be safe here. I'll be back very soon." Catriona smiled before she walked toward the forest.

Finna watched her mother disappear under the trees and then returned her gaze to the magical scene that lay before her. The breeze felt like thistledown where it touched her cheek. Her nostrils flared as she picked up the scent of pinesap and the deep primordial aroma of rotting vegetation from the river. Her body felt heavy, rooted and relaxed, and she could feel the tingling hum of energy inside her fingers and all around her.

As she rested her hands on her belly, she could almost see the child. Tiny movements under her fingers made her aware of the living person inside her. At this moment the baby rested quietly, asleep in the water of her womb. Her belly had grown bigger in the past week or so and Finna felt it like a tether to the earth. Something had changed. She was changed. She felt close to the earth in a way that seemed sensual, instinctual and almost primitive. A distinctly sexual feeling went through her and there was no guilt, no shame. Instead, it felt like a cause for celebration, an awakening.

Alex's face passed in front of her mind's eye and she wished she could share this moment. The past seemed to disappear as she imagined his arms around her, his lips on hers. Now it seemed like a failing on her part that had prevented them from coming together as a man and woman should. It was wrong of her to place all the blame on Alex.

Without thinking, she walked into the forest. Through the trees she spied her mother dancing under the protective boughs. Catriona's arms were flung out like branches, moving sinuously, slowly. Her upturned face held a rapt expression. Finna wished she could dance with her, that her own movements would have that liquid grace. She moved her body, trying to get the rhythm as she watched her mother. And then she closed her eyes and got in touch with the emerging part of herself. Her body flowed like water as she allowed herself to be taken by the primal impulse.

By NIGHTFALL they had not reached the end of the forest. Without the wagon, Finna became exhausted; she had not yet recovered her strength. The stars had come out in the wide dome of the sky but no moon was visible.

"Are ye all right, my daughter?"

"I'm very tired."

"We'll camp here. Tomorrow we will reach the protection of the Caer Sidi."

"What about Brandubh? Do ye think he's following?"

"Ye can be sure he's following, Adair as well. He may not know our route though, and the boatman would surely not bring him across." Catriona stopped and took off her pack. "I know of a spring deep in this forest. I wonder if I can still find it."

"A warm spring? I would certainly love a bath," Finna gazed at her mother hopefully. Her hair felt thick and dirty from the sweat of her illness.

"'Tis a warm spring that flows from the mountains to the west. Airmid has been known to frequent it."

"The healing goddess--is this her spring?""

Catriona shook her head. "Hers is far from here in the west."

"I hope we won't need to find it." Finna glanced at Catriona, the ordeal at the Rowan village racing through her mind.

"Dinna worry now, child. As I said, we will be in the Caer Sidi tomorrow and Brandubh and my mother can nae work their evil there. Are ye up to a little more walking? We can camp at the spring."

"I suppose so, but I hope it isn't far."

They followed a narrow animal path that wound its way through the forest, going deeper and deeper into the trees. The trail was barely visible in the gloom.

"Mother, if we don't get there soon, I won't make it."

It was only a moment before the light gray of the limestone formation came into view. The musical sound of water reached them as it poured over the rocks and emptied into the deep pool hollowed out of the stone. They took off their clothes and climbed in, listening to the hoot of owls, the scurrying night sounds of small animals, the occasional deep mooing call of an auroch. Finna's muscles relaxed in the warmth of the water. She put her head back letting her mother shampoo her hair with amole, reveling in the deep pleasurable sensation of

Catriona's fingers scrubbing her scalp. Afterwards she squeezed out the excess water and rebraided it.

After bathing, the two women made a fire and brewed tea, talking late into the night. Finna felt completely at ease, her mind calm, as she sat cross-legged in front of the fire. The baby was very active, kicking and moving, making her laugh for the first time in weeks. "I think she likes it here," she told Catriona.

"The firth is a special place. Cernunnos takes good care of his forest."

"Have ye ever seen him?"

"I have not, but I have heard that he is fearsome to look at, enormous, with horns growing out of his head."

"If we had stayed with Duncan, we could have met Cernunnos and Habondia." Finna thought back to the earlier time. It seemed as though a year had gone by since then.

"Aye. A lot has happened since we were with Duncan." Catriona gazed at Finna, her eyes soft. "Many changes for both of us, both emotional and physical," Catriona added. "It won't be long now before this little one will be with us. Just two months after the solstice. You will be a mother, Finna."

Finna laughed and then picked up her tea and took a sip. It was good to look back and see things in prospective now the trip was nearly complete. Despite her own weakness and whining, she had made it this far—and she'd seen her mother's vulnerability as well. Despite the encounter with Rhiannon, she knew Catriona's strength and she'd learned a lot from her, especially in the last few weeks. She sighed, realizing that the trip would soon be over, her child protected. Would Catriona stay with her in Bailemuir and help with the birth? She now recognized her need for this wise woman.

"Thank you, Mathair, for getting us this far," she said, reaching to squeeze her mother's arm.

Catriona looked surprised. "I'm glad ye still have faith in

me, in spite of the last few days. 'Tis nae been the trip I expected, but we are very close and now under the protection of some very powerful beings."

"Ye mean the moon goddess."

"Aye. The moon goddess, Cernunnos, and the many druids who watch over the Caer Sidi."

When they finally bedded down, Finna fell asleep quickly to the murmuring sounds of the spring.

DEEP in the night the horned god came to Finna in her dreams. He was just as Catriona had described him but his large hands were gentle as he caressed her body. His naked torso glistened like amber in the soft light of the moon as he looked down on her with his strange feral eyes. When his lips touched hers, she was suddenly on fire, her mouth opening eagerly under his. She felt no fear when their bodies became one, sending wave after wave of sensation through her. When morning came, Finna woke feeling completely rested, as though some magical healing had come to her during the night.

"This is very auspicious," Catriona remarked after Finna told her about the dream. "The horned god has infused your child with his essence. Your baby is now part of this place and connected with his forest."

"Are you saying this was more than a dream?"

Catriona nodded, her expression serious. "Everything that happens here is real."

Finna's cheeks burned. She turned away, her thoughts going again to the dream. It did feel as though something had changed. She felt like a woman for the first time, no longer the naive girl she had been when she left the safety of Bailemuir so many months ago. The image of Cernunnos bending over her awakened a hunger, sending shivers up and down her spine.

Had she truly made love with a god? Catriona hadn't said it but Finna had also been inbued with something new and wonderful. She smiled, hugging her arms around her body.

THE SUN WAS high by the time they left the spring. Neither one of them had wanted to hurry. It was the first time they had truly been able to relax. Catriona gathered some special herbs that she told Finna only grew close to the spring while Finna washed out some underwear and repacked her backpack.

They had been walking along the edge of the forest for an hour or so when Finna noticed the worried look on her mother's face. "Do you think Brandubh is following us?" Finna finally asked, scanning nervously back the way they had come.

"I have felt his presence." Catriona shook her head. "But I canna let go of my anger. Making contact with his mind is impossible."

"But ye said he wouldn't be able to get across the river."

"There are other ways besides the boatman, Finna. Brandubh is a clever man--he will find a way. And Adair has powers far greater than his. The sooner we get to the Caer Sidi the better."

Catriona changed coarse, following a new path leading toward the valley. The ground was muddy, and Finna slid, going down on one knee, soaking her pants with the brown-red mud.

"Hurry, Finna!" Catriona called over her shoulder, making her way nimbly down the slick trail.

Finna's hair was plastered to her head and rain trickled down her face and into the collar of her sweater. Her anxiety had come back with the mention of Brandubh, and the rain and darkening sky were only making matters worse.

Directly ahead lay an area of softly rolling hills criss-crossed with low stone fences. Within the enclosure sheep grazed, and further on a small house came into view, smoke curling out of the stone chimney. From what Catriona had told her ealier this looked like the boundary of the Caer Sidi. "Who lives down there?"

"I once knew an old druid who lived around here but that was at least twenty years ago."

"I don't know much about druids."

Catriona turned. "They've lived here for centuries, serving as protectors of the land and acting as "priests", officiating at the ceremonies. Their spiritual beliefs are linked with trees. The word 'druid' means 'knowing the oak tree' in Gaelic. They hold many of their rituals in the sacred groves as well as the stone circles that were built thousands of years ago. Remember the ogham writing ye saw at the circle where we had lunch? 'Tis their ancient language. They are psychically connected with the spirit world and many are able to manipulate the elements such as wind, fire and water. They move from place to place through the ether and can travel between the spirit world and this one. Just as ye were allowed into the Other-world, the Druids are able to enter places that we as regular human beings only dream of."

"What are you saying? That I might not have been allowed in here?"

"Aye, my daughter. But because your heart is pure 'twas easy to bring ye here."

"But what about Brandubh? He doesn't have a pure heart."

"Brandubh was born here and so he can come and go as he pleases."

Finna thought about her reverie of the white-robed people at the standing stones. If it was a real vision, they were the Druids of old. There was a grandeur about them that made

Finna wish she had been part of the ancient culture that lived here in the distant past. What did Brandubh want here? It made no sense to her that he was trying to take over. Take over what? The place was backward, filled with empty spaces and people who basically had no material goods. The land was beautiful, though.

Maybe Catriona was mistaken. Maybe Brandubh was pretending to go along with Adair but in reality he was working against her. Brandubh was Finna's uncle, her mother's twin. From what Finna had read about twins they were so much alike that their lives would follow similar paths, even if they never knew one another. Despite all the stuff that had happened at Rowan, she wondered, mainly because of the look she had seen on Brandubh's face when she fell into the river. That had not been the expression of an evil person. But then again, at Rowan Finna had been under the influence of several potent drugs and a lot of her perceptions could have been skewed.

And Brandubh had been schooled outside this world. In Edinburgh, Catriona said. If his nature was basically evil then why wasn't he out *there* trying to take over? Many priests had gotten away with all sorts of despicable things. You heard about them every day on the news. What Catriona had mentioned about her brother didn't seem that bad in comparison.

Drawing closer to the cottage revealed a warm glow coming from the small windows. Someone was definitely living there. As they climbed over a low stone wall and walked across the pasture, a man with long white hair and beard emerged onto the front stoop.

He looked their way and then called out something unintelligible, motioning for them to come inside. A minute later his face lit up and he yelled, "Catriona!" hurrying forward to embrace her. "Kim-mer-uh Hah shiv?" he exclaimed, holding her by her forearms. Catriona answered him in the same language and then turned to Finna.

"This is Finna, my daughter," she said carefully. "Finna, this is the druid I told ye about, MacCuill."

MacCuill turned to Finna, his deep blue eyes crinkling with pleasure as he smiled. "Aye. She is as I expected. Beautiful like her mother." Finna struggled to understand the heavy brogue.

'Tis is a special joy to meet you." He surveyed her like a kindly grandfather and turned again to Catriona. "You both appear to be well—you have taken good care of her."

At these words Catriona colored slightly, a guilty expression coming across her features.

MacCuill led them into the house, inviting them to sit in the small chairs facing the warm fire. The pungent scent of mint and sage permeated the one room cottage, coming from the many herbs hanging from the ceiling beams. Woven rugs covered the earthen floor, and against the wall, shelves held jars and strange objects made of wood, bone and glass. A long wooden flute rested on two hooks protruding from the wall.

"Vervain--good for the both of you," MacCuill said, placing leaves into two wooden cups. He added hot water from the kettle hanging over the fire.

"Why vervain?" Finna asked.

"Good for the nerves, Finna, 'tis a woman's herb," Catriona answered, taking a sip from her cup.

""De tha thu a deanamh?" MacCuill asked Catriona.

To Finna it sounded like *Jeh hah oo uh Jee-ah-nur.* She looked questioningly at her mother.

Catriona caught her glance and then addressed MacCuill in English. "We are on our way to the Glass Mountain, but we are being pursued."

MacCuill nodded, pulling his hand over his long white

beard. "I thought as much. The goddess has come to me in her owl form to enlist my help. Caer Sidi is not as safe as it once was."

Finna looked from her mother to MacCuill, aware of an unspoken undercurrent between them. Even when they spoke English she felt as though things were being communicated that she couldn't understand. Apparently the goddess Arianrhod was a shape-shifter, another fact that seemed impossible to swallow. *Maybe I misheard*, she thought to herself. It would be easy to do with the strange speech patterns of this man.

MacCuill paused and glanced at Finna as though he was trying to decide whether to go on. Finally he said in English, "Adair is grown stronger still and helps Brandubh in his dealings with the Oillteil."

MacCuill began speaking in the other language and Finna distinctly hear the word *fassnik*. Finna ran to the window. "Is it here?" she cried, frantically scanning the area.

MacCuill and Catriona turned to her. "Is what here?" Catriona asked.

"The fassnik! I heard MacCuill say..."

Catriona laughed. "I told ye the faisnich was nae a beast, Finna. Have ye been worrying about it all this time?"

"Well then, what is it?"

"Faisnich is the Gaelic word for prophecy. The first time ye heard it I was nae sure ye were ready for the truth."

Finna frowned in embrrassment. They were both looking at her with kindly smiles making her feel like a complete idiot. "Ye should have told me. It could have saved me from a lot of sleepless nights."

"Ye should have asked if ye were unsure, Finna. Keeping these fears to yourself does nae good."

Finna stared at her, thinking about all the times she had asked questions only to be rebuffed.

"What we need to focus on now is Adair and Brandubh. MacCuill has told me more details about their dealings with the Oillteil. I had nae idea they had breached the securities in the Caer Sidi."

Finna gazed into the distance, visualizing Adair and Brandubh arriving on black wings, grabbing her and taking her away to some horrible prison. This image was much more frightening than any vision of the fassnik. "How did that happen?"

Catriona looked down at her hands curved around her cup. "Adair taps into a source of power that has lain dormant for millenia. The Oillteil were defeated by the Tuatha De Danann but now she summons them back. 'Tis what I felt when we came through the tunnels. Remember I mentioned something had gotten through? Adair is pulling in malevolent energy that has never been in this place before and 'tis disturbing the balance. The prophecy speaks of a time in the future when the child ye carry will come here and battle these forces."

"But she hasn't even been born yet! If things are already deteriorating now, how can she be of help?"

"All I know is what the prophecy says. Maybe the forces for good can hold the darkness at bay until she comes. 'Tis been said that our consciousness can work miracles. What do ye say to this, MacCuill?"

"Druantia, queen of the druids, is holding a great gathering to speak to this very issue. The druids have always been the gatekeepers here in the Caer Sidi but due to Brandubh and Adair the protections are weakened. Many more will need training if we are to keep the Caer Sidi safe."

"But what of the rest of the Otherworld?" Finna asked, her mind going to the Amuigh, the Crion, and all the beauty she had witnessed on the way here.

"My job resides here. Others are keeping the vibrations pure. I'm sure you met many of the inhabitants on your way."

Finna nodded even though she couldn't imagine those innocents dealing with anything as bad as this. "Will ye come with us to the castle?"

"Aye, I will accompany you as far as the shore. From there the boatman will carry you safely to the island."

Finna thought about the ancient blind man. She would feel a lot safer it it was MacCuill taking them to the island. Something about those milky eyes gave her the creeps. And what weren't MacCuill and her mother telling her? She could hardly wait for the blessing ceremony. She made a promise to herself to stay strong despite a creeping sense of doom.

FINNA WOKE to Catriona and MacCuill talking together in whispers. "Please stop trying to shield me."

Catriona and MacCuill turned in surprise. "We were only whispering so as not to wake ye," Catriona answered.

"MacCuill has just told me that the beasts were here in the night."

Finna jumped out of bed. "They're here?"

"Not now. They were only scouts, but now they know where we are and will report back to Brandubh."

Finna felt weak. "What are we going to do?" All her earlier resolve faded as fear blanketed her mind. She paced from one side of the cottage to the other, her hands on her belly. She jumped when MacCuill's hand came down on her shoulder. Her restless energy was gone in an instant. Her feet felt rooted to the earth as energy coursed through her from his fingers. His eyes met hers. She breathed deeply in and out.

"That's the way, Finna. You've learned your lessons well."

He took his hand away and turned to the fire. "Come have some tea."

"There's fresh goat cheese and milk to go with the delicious bannock that MacCuill has made."

Finna turned to see her mother smiling, her face aglow. She didn't look at all afraid. The spring and being with MacCuill seemed to have revived her. The druid did have a special way about him.

Shortly after the meal they prepared for departure. Picking up his walking stick by the door MacCuill said, "This stick is fashioned out of hazel wood, the tree of wisdom and sacred to druids." As he slung his flute bag over his back he added, "And this flute of alder contains many magical properties." He winked at Finna, leading the way outside. Once Finna and Catriona were out, he closed the door and then touched it lightly with his walking stick. Before Finna could think to ask a question he was walking away, heading north.

Because of the cold overcast day Catriona and Finna had donned their warm deerskin coats. MacCuill was dressed as always in a pale hooded robe of wool, his feet encased in leather sandals. The trail was narrow and they went single file. Between her mother and MacCuill, Finna had the impression she was being protected. She scanned behind them, her nerves on edge. There were many hills in the distance that could hide Brandubh and the beasts.

"Mother, do ye think Adair is traveling with Brandubh?"

Catriona shrugged. "The encounter at Rowan is the first time I've come into direct contact with her since the day she told me to leave my childhood home. I was barely fifteen."

MacCuill turned. "Adair will not waste her time tracking you, Finna. Her talents lie in other directions."

"Like what?"

MacCuill hesitated, looking at Catriona for a moment

before he continued. "Adair is a sorceress whose only wish is to rid the Otherworld of the leanabh...the child of the faisnich."

"Child of the prophecy," Catriona translated.

"But you just said she wouldn't..."

"Her methods will be more subtle than that. Adair is not one to show her hand. I will keep you safe. I have a number of tricks up my sleeve as well." He winked and smiled, pulling a long dagger out of his wide sleeve and holding it up. It shone dull silver and looked very sharp. Finna had an image of the dagger flying though the air and shook her head. Better to concentrate on each step she was taking toward the blessing ceremony. It was several minutes later that she thought to take the moonstone out of her pocket.

"Mother!" she yelled. "Look!" A tiny line led across the surface. At one end were three figures, at the other end it looked like a number of people as well as something smaller gathered together. "Is that what I think it is?"

Catriona and MacCuill examined the stone and then exchanged a look. "How far away do ye think they are?" Catriona whispered.

MacCuill's eyebrows drew together and he scratched his head. He drew in a deep breath and let it out. "Hard to tell, but I think we should go as quickly as we can."

They increased their tempo, hurrying up one hill and down another. At the top of the next hill MacCuill stopped and took a spyglass out of his sleeve. "They are about a half mile away," he said quietly, slipping the glass back into his sleeve.

Finna's heart pounded in her ears. The beasts could travel very fast. She looked ahead where more hills obscured any view of the water. "How far is the shore?"

MacCuill didn't answer as he pulled his flute out of the bag and began to play. The notes were haunting and mysterious, lifting and falling in the still air. The wind moved around them, pulling at her hair and lifting the hem of her coat and she had the distinct impression it was being summoned by the music. The tune changed, the notes coming faster with more force, and the now visible wind leapt down the path behind them in a long pale gray mist. There were angry shouts and yelling and when she squinted, Finna could see the beasts and people running in all directions. "Who's with Brandubh?" she asked, watching the chaos.

"'Tis the wildmen who control the beasts. Apparently they have been recruited."

Oh, yes, Finna had seen those men at Rowan. Finna looked toward MacCuill who had put his flute away.

"Alderwood has the ability to control the winds. It will delay them for a short time. Follow me." MacCuill hurried away, his robe billowing around him like a pale cloud.

Finna trotted after him, her hand on her necklace. Hadn't Roc said it was to keep her safe until the blessing? She hoped it would do its job.

CHAPTER 15

They followed the trail down a steep hill, arriving at a strange boggy area very different from the dry grassland behind them. MacCuill gave the opaque greenish-brown water a wide berth, holding his hazel stick in front of him like a dousing rod. As they passed by, yellow eyes just above the surface peered out at them.

"What's in there?" Finna asked MacCuill, making a detour to avoid getting too close.

"Sea serpents. Did you see something? They do not show themselves. They may be aware of who you are."

"Are they dangerous?"

MacCuill smiled and nodded. "If they take you down to the underworld you will not return."

Finna moved behind her mother and watched where she put her feet, stepping neatly into her tracks.

"These sinkholes connect with the seas that lie around Caer Sidi. They are not just the mud puddles they appear to be," MacCuill told her. "These creatures are ancient and provide a link with what lies beneath."

"Do you mean we could have fallen into one of these holes?" Finna looked at her mother who seemed unconcerned. "Did ye know about this?" she demanded.

"Finna, calm down. The Caer Sidi is looking out for ye. Ye need to believe in the magic that exists here."

"Sea-serpents? I can't see how the place is looking out for me. And what about Brandubh? The beasts?"

MacCuill took hold of Finna's arm, staring into her eyes. "Your mother is right. You must trust. There are dangerous forces at work but the forces for light are also strong. The serpents exist to keep the inattentive out, those corrupt people or beings who do not belong here. Believe me, the serpents are well aware of who you are. They would not choose to harm you but if you stepped into one those holes...well...but you would not do so, that is the point. Didn't I see a necklace of a serpent around your neck? You have a connection with them, Finna. Even if you were alone you would watch out if you saw them. And your mother has made this trip before and has managed to get you this far. She's capable of conveying you to the Glass Mountain."

Finna turned back as they left the boggy area, thinking about MacCuill's words. If she were running from something like Brandubh and his men and beasts, she could easily see herself falling into this bog. She shuddered, her fingers going up again to trace the serpent hanging around her neck.

At the top of the next rise, the island came into view--a crystalline jewel in the deep blue of the sea. An enormous castle glittered against dark mountains stretching into the sky, their tops obscured by gray storm clouds. Massive arches that looked like glass decorated the walls, circling windows and doorways.

Almost there, Finna thought with a shot of adrenaline. "Is the castle made of glass or ice?" Finna asked, shielding her eyes to get a better look.

"'Tis called the Glass Mountain because the mountains are so sheer and covered year-round in ice. Inside, the castle is crystal but the outside is ice."

"How far back do you think Brandubh and the beasts are?" she asked MacCuill, struggling to catch her breath.

"I hope far enough to give us time to get to the boat. Once you're on your way to the Glass Mountain he has less of a chance of using his power against you."

Less *of a chance?* Finna thought she would be safe here. It's what her mother had told her constantly during the course of the trip. As they reached the top of the last hill they looked down on the green water lapping against the rocky edge of the shore. Tucked into the cliff was a tiny harbor, just big enough for one or two boats. They peered into the darkening gloom, trying to see the boat. It wasn't there. The sky darkened and turned black as an enormous raven glided soundlessly over them.

Finna cringed and screamed. "What is that?"

"'Tis the Morrighan, the goddess of war. If she's helping Brandubh we have even more to contend with."

The raven dropped toward the hill behind them and Finna watched the huge bird begin to shapeshift just before its graceful landing in front of Brandubh. Even from here Finna could see the glossy feathers turn into filmy layers of an uneven dress of black. A woman with a long mane of glossy black hair stood in the bird's place. Light glinted off a wide circlet of gold around her neck. Finna couldn't see her features but she could hear the booming voice.

"*What do you want mortal? Haven't I done enough to help you?*

Finna shot a glance at Catriona and MacCuill to guage their

reaction but they were both fixated on the frightening apparition.

"*Well, what is it? Speak up.*" There was a pause while Brandubh mumbled something and then Morrighan said:

"*I know all about the prophecy, mortal, now what do you want?*"

A few minutes went by while Brandubh talked and gestured with his hands. "*And what will you give me in return?*"

Another pause, this one longer. Brandubh's head bobbedas he told her what he

intended but his words were not audible.

"*What* you *are doing? What is it that you think you are doing?*" Morrighan sounded scornful. Brandubh said something else and then Morrighan replied, this time even louder:

"*And what about the help I gave you at the settlement? The thousand crows sent to help you with the killing? How have you repaid me for that?*"

Brandubh's head was bowed as though in supplication as he replied. Finna heard an intake of breath and glanced at her mother. Catriona's face was blanched of color and her eyes had filled with tears. The realization suddenly dawned on Finna that this man had received help from Morrighan to kill Eron's wife and child and all the others at the settlement. Her insides churned and she thought she might be sick.

Do you think you will stop the prophecy?"

Finna wrapped her arms protectively around her belly as Morrighan's words rent the air.

"*You cannot stop what is foretold.*"

"*But...*" Finna heard Brandubh say, and then the word, "*dead*". Finna turned toward MacCuill and Catriona. "Mother..."

"Wait." Catriona held up her hand.

"*I am not interested in arguing with you. You do not know how this world works. I will help you this time. But I warn you, do not expect this to change the prophecy, it will not. For payment I will expect three things from you. I will let you know when I need them."*

There was a pause while Brandubh replied, but none of his words could be heard.

"When the time is right I will let you know.

Morrighan's body began to transform, growing feathers and becoming larger and larger. *"Where do you wish to go?* she rasped from her thick black beak.

Finna watched Brandubh climb onto her back. A deep chill went through her body as she watched MacCuill scan for the boat, concern puckering his forehead.

"We better get out of here because Brandubh will arrive any minute." Catriona grabbed Finna by the hand and dragged her toward the shore.

"But what's he going to do? What did Morrighan mean?" she asked, trying to keep up with her mother.

Catriona did not answer. They reached the miniscule harbor but there was still no sign of the boat. MacCuill stared out to sea looking through his spyglass. "I see it."

Finna looked in the direction he was pointing where a small dot headed their way.

Darkness enveloped them like the blackest night as the raven flew over them. The bird made a most terrible screeching cry as it banked not far from where Finna and the others stood and then the small figure of Brandubh came into view. Finna screamed as the bird landed on the hill behind them. Her horrible vision of Brandubh with wings had come true.

Brandubh slid off awkwardly and then the bird lifted and flew toward the east. He dusted off his clothes and headed quickly toward them, his dark eyes fixed on Catriona.

Catriona grabbed her head with both hands. "He's trying to get into my mind!"

"Be strong, Catriona," MacCuill said quietly.

Finna couldn't move.

Brandubh cupped his hands around his mouth and let out an eerie howl, calling to the beasts. Finna remembered the sight of their sharp teeth and strong jaws. They could rip her to shreds in an instant. She looked at Brandubh where he waited. It was disturbing to see those familiar features and know the depravity that lay behind them. She cowered behind MacCuill, pulling her sweater around her, hoping for a miracle. MacCuill stood as still as a tree waiting to see what Brandubh's next move would be. He whispered to Catriona and Finna to stay behind him. They obeyed, knowing that there would soon be a confrontation. They were all hoping the boat would get there before it happened.

A few moments later the beasts arrived on the hilltop in a group. Their matted fur looked dirty yellow in the fading light, their eyes glowing red. Their high shoulders were hunched in anticipation as they swarmed around Brandubh, waiting for his command. A second later he raised his hand and they tore toward the beach with their mouths snarling, showing long yellow fangs. MacCuill didn't move. He held his stick pointed at them and when they got close enough, flames came roaring out of the tip, catching the lead beast's fur on fire. He yelped and ran back, rolling on the ground. The acrid odor of singed hair filled the air. The others stood at a distance, watching MacCuill warily.

A sudden flick of Brandubh's hand brought a knife flying through the air toward MacCuill, who yelled, "Watch out!" as he sidestepped nimbly out of the way. The knife flew past and sunk deep into Finna's shoulder. She shrieked and crumpled over. A second later Catriona was on the ground beside her, pulling the knife out. With a roar of rage, MacCuill ran toward

Brandubh, his hazel stick emitting fire. Brandubh backed up the hill looking around for the beasts.

Catriona removed Finna's sweater and undershirt to examine the wound. The knife had gone into the soft part of flesh between the shoulder and the clavicle. It was deep but hadn't penetrated to the bone. She pulled a piece of clean muslin from her pack and bound it. By the time her mother had helped pull the sweater carefully over Finna's injury, the boat was slipping into the harbor. The boatman put up the oars, grabbed the rope and pulled up on the other side of the beach. This man was young, dark haired and bearded with a heavy gold cross around his neck. Catriona grabbed Finna by her good arm and dragged her toward the boat.

"We must get to the Glass Mountain!" she ordered, helping Finna over the side.

The boatman looked bewildered as Finna fell into the boat.

"Can ye please help us?" Catriona's voice was high and hysterical as she climbed in behind Finna.

On the hill Brandubh and MacCuill faced each other, the beasts circling around them.

The boatman turned toward the men on the hill. "What's goin' on here?" he asked suspiciously, in a heavy brogue.

"That man, the one in black, is trying to harm my daughter. We need to get to the Glass Mountain as fast as possible."

The man turned to stare at Catriona. "Aye, we've been expectin' ye." He pushed the boat off the shore with one of the oars and they glided backward. He was putting the oars back into the oarlocks when MacCuill turned toward them and began to shout.

Catriona stood up. "What is it?" she cried. But all they could hear was the sound of the waves slapping against the side of the boat. MacCuill was shaking his head and gesturing but his voice was lost to them. Catriona gave up and sat down next to Finna. "What is your name?" she asked the boatman.

"I am Dallas."

"Well, Dallas, can ye row any faster? My daughter is injured as ye can plainly see."

When Finna glanced back, blue fire was erupting from MacCuill's stick. Terrible howling and furious unintelligible shouts and screams from Brandubh rent the air. Night fell and the sounds faded as the boat headed away from the protected waters and out to sea. All that was visible now was the white foam of waves as they coursed gently against the shore.

Dallas bent over the oars and rowed with all his might. When they got a distance away from the shore Catriona suddenly stood up. "Where are ye takin' us?"

"To the castle, of course."

"The castle is in that direction," she said, pointing east.

"I try to avoid the tides, they can force us onto the rocks."

"Who are ye?" Catriona asked shrilly, grabbing one of the oars out of his hand.

He looked at her silently.

"Get out of this boat!"

"I'll freeze in this water." His eyes were wide.

"Ye either get out right now or I will..."

"I'll take ye to the Castle...just please...don't..."

"Mother, don't hurt him," Finna pleaded from where she huddled on the floor.

"He works for Brandubh."

"I...he gave me money...he said...he would give me more if..." Dallas maneuvered the boat toward the island using the remaining oar. "I'll take ye, just please dinna hurt me."

"If ye so much as veer off I will throw ye out of this boat." Catriona handed him the other oar and watched him carefully.

• • •

IT WASN'T long before the castle loomed up in front of them. The moon had risen, providing enough light to see the intricate sculpted designs on the high walls of ice. Carvings of different animals surrounded each window and the enormous double doors were covered in designs of vines interwoven with serpents. Each door corner contained a circle enclosing triplicate spirals within spirals. The outside layer of ice glistened pale blue in the light cast by the waxing gibbous moon.

The boat pulled up alongside a wooden walkway and Catriona helped Finna out of the boat. "You're a fool to work for Brandubh," Catriona said. "He will never give ye what he's promised."

Dallas didn't answer, just held his head down and pushed the boat away, disappearing into the night.

Catriona supported Finna up the path to the entry. A design in the shape of an owl had been carved into the wide doors so that each outstretched wing became a handle when the doors were opened. Before they had a chance to knock, footsteps could be heard and the doors swung in to reveal a small woman with long hair the color of spun gold. Her vivid green eyes were filled with kindness as she held out her hands to draw them both inside. Once she had closed the doors, the thick ice that encased the front of the palace shone pale green through the walls of crystal. Small iron sconces set into the walls held lit candles, and many more candles stood on tall wooden tables. The flames flickered, casting shadows that undulated in strange patterns.

"I am Arianrhod, the ruler of the Caer Sidi. I have been expecting you. Welcome to my castle." She looked at Finna's white face, the expression of pain etched into her features. "What has happened?"

"My daughter has a knife wound in her shoulder."

"Accompany me to my healing trees." Arianrhod led the

way toward a dark room on the right. As soon as she stepped over the threshold the cold fireplace began to burn brightly and flames appeared in the many candles that lined the walls. Catriona and Finna followed Arianrhod across the room. When she touched the wall on the other side, a small door appeared, opening at her command. The sweet smell of flowers to wafted out on warm, humid air. On the other side an arboretum stretched upward, the vast domed space filled with trees and plants of every kind. The moon shone pale blue through the clear crystal ceiling, illuminating glossy leaves and vines that climbed and twisted through the branches of the trees.

"Come Finna, sit here." Arianrhod pointed to a carved wooden bench. "Please remove your sweater," she asked, kneeling in front of her.

Arianrhod picked a few leaves from a nearby tree and placed them directly on the wound, covering them with her hands. When Arianrhod lifted the leaves from Finna's skin a few moments later, the wound had closed, with only a thin line of red to show where it had been. Finna took her first deep breath, savoring the lack of pain. "Thank you," she said, gazing into Arianrhod's luminous eyes.

When Arianrhod smiled and then grabbed her hands to help her stand, Finna was surprised to see that the goddess was no taller than she was. Golden combs held her shining hair back. She wore a velvet emerald dress nipped in at her tiny waist, and flowing in soft folds to the ground. Upon her head lay a crown of crystal, etched with a crescent moon and stars. Despite her small size, she held herself regally with an aura of power and strength.

"Finna, the fair, the child you carry is a very wise being. Here in this world she will be known as Saille, the Willow. I cannot stress enough the importance of her coming into the world at this crucial time. She will have the power within her to bring peace and balance. By the time she has reached maturity, this world will be in dire peril. You must guard and protect her carefully. Come. My cook has prepared a feast for your arrival."

They followed the moon goddess back to the main hall and into another room where a wide oak table stretched almost its entire length. Green and white candles adorned the surface set with crystal goblets and pewter plates. Wall sconces held more candles and silk tapestries hung on the walls. A fire blazed in the wide fireplace at the far end of the room. Finna's mouth watered as the smell of roasting meat came to her nostrils.

Arianrhod led the way toward the fireplace and sat down at the head of the table, motioning Catriona and Finna to the chairs on either side of her. Almost immediately another door opened and a gray haired woman entered, carrying a large pewter tray. On it was roast boar surrounded with potatoes, carrots and parsnips. The empty crystal goblets were instantly filled with sweet tasting nectar.

Arainrhod indicated the food with an expansive gesture. "Please help yourself." She picked up her goblet and took a small sip. "The full moon arrives in two days. Until then you are free to go about the castle and into the garden, which contains a maze as well as many fruit trees that do not grow anywhere else. All the fruit is edible; the drink we are having tonight is from them. I must attend to my duties so I shall often be away from the castle, but Arabelle will bring you anything you wish from the kitchen. All you need do is think about what it is you want."

CHAPTER 16

Finna woke in the night after a dream in which her baby was a grown woman and fighting terrible monsters. She shivered, looking over at the fireplace where the fire had long since burned out. Wrapping a shawl around her shoulders, she went to the window. The moon was up and as she gazed into the distance, a gigantic owl flew by. She turned to see Catriona watching her.

"I hope I didn't wake you."

"You're cold, Finna, come back to bed."

"I think I just saw Arainrhod fly by."

Catriona nodded, patting the bed next to her. "She often patrols at night in this form. It does seem incongruous—she's such a wee thing."

Finna walked to the bed and climbed in. "Are we safe now?" Finna asked, her hands going unconsciously to her belly.

Catriona nodded. "Adair and Brandubh canna enter this sacred space."

• • •

THE NEXT DAY the two women picked fruit, savoring all the unusual flavors. They napped in the garden with the sweet perfume of flowers in their nostrils. The moment they thought of different foods they might like to have, sliced meats and cheeses and fresh bannock, Arabelle appeared carrying a tray. After eating, they wandered through the vast garden until they found the Yew maze and walked its pebbled paths in meditative silence, letting the magic of the place seep into them. It was a day of recuperation that they both sorely needed.

In the late afternoon Finna opened the door to go back into the castle, but instead of the room she was expecting, she was greeted with a dark tunnel. Dim light came from some indeterminate location ahead of her.

"What's this?"

"I have nae idea," Catriona answered from behind her. "Maybe 'tis the wrong door."

"Let's go back." But when Finna turned she was greeted with a solid wall of rock. "What should we do?" she cried in panic.

Catriona pounded on the stone and shouted but there was no response.

"You told me we were safe here."

"I dinna know where 'here' is, Finna. Maybe 'tis where Arianrhod has her prisons."

"Prisons?"

"In the olden days the goddesses punished those who went against them. I doubt this happens these days but the prisons might still be here, somewhere beneath the castle."

Finna thought Catriona sounded uncertain and it worried her. What if this was some kind of trap set by Adair or Brandubh? She tried to breathe through her fear as she followed her mother ever downward into the tunnel. When a loud click shattered the silence she turned. "We're trapped," she said in a small voice stopping to stare at the wall of rock closing in behind them.

"We were trapped before, Finna. We must keep going." Catriona did not even turn.

Finna ran to catch up hearing the clicks and shifts in the rock as she moved forward. "Maybe if we stop here Arianrhod will find us. I don't want to go on." A sharp painful kick had Finna doubled over, clutching her belly. "The baby doesn't like it either." Shadows flickered eerily on the walls from torches somewhere ahead of them.

"Ye heard what Arianrhod said, this castle is protected."

"But what if we aren't in the castle anymore?" Finna shivered as the truth of these words settled into her.

"How could we be out of the castle?"

"We've been heading down for quite a while, maybe we're in some underneath labyrinth or something that isn't part of the castle and the protections." As though in answer to Finna's worst fears the air turned suddenly thick and foul. Finna coughed and held her nose."What is that horrible stench?"

When a dark figure appeared in the tunnel ahead Catriona shrieked. She put herself protectively in front of Finna.

"How nice to see ye fell for my little trap," Brandubh remarked, approaching them. He grabbed Finna's arm. "Come with me, my dear, I'll show ye the way out...no no, don't worry about your mother, she'll be along in a minute." He dragged her into a small room off the main tunnel. "Give me one reason not to kill ye right now." His dark eyes bored into hers as he fished a knife out from under his robe. His other hand went round her neck.

Catriona appeared in the entrance to the room, her face a mask of white. "How did ye find your way in here? The castle is protected."

Brandubh's lips curled in a sneer. "With the help of some

friends of mine I was able to cast an enchantment that connected to the door. I must say that Dallas has come to be quite useful and of course, our dear mother. Ye should know she's always one step ahead of ye, Catriona. Her abilities are quite beyond mine and certainly way beyond yours. We are far below the castle in a place that Arianrhod has forgotten. I needed to draw my niece to me."

"Ye canna prevent what is already in place, no matter what ye do. If it isn't this baby it will be another."

"No, dear sister, I'm fairly certain that this will make a big difference." When he brought the sharp blade up to touch Finna's neck she let out a terrified sob. Tears welled and then slid silently down her face.

"What has happened to ye, Brandubh? Remember how close we were? Why would ye wish to harm your niece?"

Finna looked at her mother's distraught face, the emotions that struggled beneath the surface as she gazed at her twin.

"Ye don't know anything about me, sister dear. Ye don't know what I've become, how much I've grown. Killing Fergus was what led me to this life. So in some ways ye can blame yourself. Did ye know that Adair never blamed me for it? She told me 'twas ye that seduced him, 'twas ye who drove your own father to what he did by being a filthy whore."

"Why would ye believe her? Ye were witness to what he did to me. Ye saved me from him, Brandubh. What about our connection? All our years of readin' each other's minds? The games we played..."

Finna watched as her mother moved closer, her eyes locked on Brandubh's face. The knife withdrew from her skin making her hopeful that Catriona was having an effect.

"Why do ye let our mahair have power over ye, Brandubh? Ye joined the kirk to do good and even though I dinna believe in the hierarchy, I knew ye would be an asset because you're a good man underneath all of this."

"I am nae the same..." Brandubh's voice sounded unsure for the first time.

"Ye *are* the same person! Growing up we were united against our mahair—she hurt ye just as she hurt me. Adair is cruel, Brandubh. I know ye can see it."

There was a pause as Brandubh shifted his stance. He let out a long sigh and Catriona moved even closer. "Dinna do this terrible thing. This child, my daughter, is your niece. Ye haven't even had the chance to know her. And the bairn..."

Brandubh stiffened. "Ye are tryin' to get into my mind. I can feel ye pokin' about in there. It will nae work. Adair showed me how to close my thoughts from ye. She told me ye would try to sway me to your way of thinkin'." The knife came close to Finna's throat again. "With Adair's help I have the power now to do what I want and what I want is for ye and Finna to die. Right here and right now. Without the two of ye in the picture I can get on with our plans."

Finna squirmed trying to get away but as she moved, the knife penetrated the skin of her neck. She moaned as blood trickled down her neck and into her sweater.

"Dinna try to get away from him, Finna. 'Twill only make it worse. He'll come to his senses."

"This room is too cramped. Let's continue down the tunnel, shall we?"

Brandubh moved toward the door, his forearm wrapped around Finna's neck. She arched backward, trying to keep her balance on the slippery rock. Her heel caught between two rocks, wrenching her foot and making her cry out in pain.

"My dear girl, how weak ye are. My sister has nae taught ye anything. I must say as a girl, Catriona would nae bow down to anyone or anything. Too bad she did nae join me in my

venture. With the three of us, we would be unstoppable—
three is a magical number, did ye know this, Finna? Most likely
not. Ye were brought up by an old man who didn't see fit to
teach ye any of your heritage."

"How do you know anything about Angus?"

Brandubh laughed, a chalky scraping sound. "We all knew
who the mahair of the Willow would be. I wanted to kill ye
years ago but Adair said to wait, that it would be better if the
child had been conceived. Otherwise, another person would
give birth to this child of the *faisnich*. And that would mean an
entirely new witchhunt."

It took only a few minutes before they came to a wide stone
ramp at the end of the tunnel. Waves washed in and out, slapping darkly against the stone. Brandubh dragged Finna to the
edge and looked into the murky depths. "I will slit Finna's
throat first. That way ye can watch your daughter die--a fitting
end for ye, my sweet, sweet sister. What kind of mother have
ye been, anyway? Leaving her so that ye could whore around
with any man ye met along the road. Ye are a disgusting slut,
Catriona, and ye dinna deserve to have a daughter!"

He reached out and grabbed Catriona with his free arm.
"Stand here by the water next to my niece and the baby who
will never see the light o' day." He released both women and
stepped back from the edge. "Ye are both lovely to look at—
seems a shame to do away with such beauty. And ye, Finna, are
the spitting image of your grandmother--did my sister tell ye
how much ye resemble Adair?" He pointed the sharp knife
toward Finna and smiled. "I do wish our mahair were here to
share this moment, but unfortunatley she is working on some
other important matters for the future."

"Brandubh, remember the treehouse we shared? Ye canna
have forgotten our time...please stop this. Think about the
past, our past together!"

"Stop talking. I am nae the same person as that mealy-mouthed frightened mouse I was then. I wear the robes of a priest--I wield power in the kirk and out of it. What have ye done with your life, Catriona? Do ye think a bit of herb gathering is enough?"

"Ye were nae afraid to stand up for me, Brandubh. 'Twas ye who saved me."

Brandubh shook his head. "I should have let him have his way with ye. Maybe then he could have been part of the cause instead of lyin' cold and dead in a grave in the middle of those dark woods. Give up, Catriona. I will nae come back to ye as your loving brother or anything else except one who despises ye. I want to see ye die."

"I dinna understand what has become of ye. Has Adair shifted ye so much that ye canna remember who ye are? Ye have nae children, we are the only family ye have." Catriona was crying now, tears flowing down her cheeks and into her shirt.

Brandubh threw his head back and roared with laughter. "Ye dinna know what I have, sister. I could have heirs scattered across the land and outside of this world as well."

"What about your vows?" Finna asked in a small voice.

"Do ye think I would let that stop me?"

"And yet ye talk of me bein' a whore," Catriona mumbled through her tears.

"I am the man I was always meant to be," Brandubh went on. "Any bairns that come from me will be strong, not like this daughter of yours, Catriona. Look at her—she's weak and terrified as she faces her death. What happened to your influence, the fearsome girl I grew up with?" He laughed again, the ugly sound resounding through the stone. "Ye are the one who does nae see the truth, Catriona. Now stay your jibber-jabber, 'tis time for your daughter's death. And make no mistake, yours will follow soon after."

Finna cried silently, knowing she would die in the next few minutes. If Brandubh didn't slit her throat he would surely throw her into the water that swirled in dark eddies below where they stood. Her hands went to her belly where the baby moved restlessly. Glancing toward her mother she saw that Catriona's eyes were bright with tears. She reached for her mother's hand, holding on tightly.

As the man came toward them again, Finna gave a strangled cry and began to scream in earnest when she saw the voracious look on his face. Her hands went to her neck to fend him off, but he pulled them aside and pressed the blade against her, this time making a deep cut that began to bleed heavily. At the same moment Catriona lunged at him but he was too quick for her, hitting her full in the face with a closed fist. Catriona crumpled to the floor.

Finna edged away, but Brandubh grabbed her, turning her to face away from him and pulling her head back against his chest exposing her neck. He let out a long sigh of pleasure as he slid the knifeblade along her neck, his other hand pushing painfully against her middle as he held her secure. She writhed and twisted, trying to escape as the baby kicked and turned inside her.

"Don't fuss so, Finna. Ye canna get away, I'm too strong. I can feel the bairn inside ye—she knows what's to come." He laughed, the sound ugly and distorted as it bounced off the walls of rock. "This is like food to me--ambrosia. I can feel the heartbeats of you and the child through my fingers. Your fear feeds me and gives me strength." He sucked in air, his fingers moving along her neck and throat. "I should do this now but the longer I draw it out the more pleasure it brings me." He pulled her close, his fingers digging into the flesh of her belly as his other hand explored the skin of her upper chest. "Ye are so fragile. I can feel the bones beneath your skin. How could the child of a whore be carryin' a bairn of such importance?" The knife tip dug into her throat and Finna screamed as the pain ripped through her. Blood poured down her chest but she could do nothing to stop it. Why didn't he just get it over with? Her mother lay still now—she must be dead. "Do it!" she screamed, her voice wild and terrified.

"Well, well. Ye have some gumption after all. I'll do it when I've my fill, not a moment sooner." Finna stopped struggling as the realization hit her—there was no escape. Her mother lay unmoving on the floor and the man had a grip of iron.

"What, no more fear? Come on, Finna, I haven't fed from you enough yet. To bring your anxiety to the surface, let me describe exactly what I have in mind. The knife will slide along your neck, digging deep and severing your jugular. I will then let you drop to the floor and watch as your eyes glaze over. Your bairn will die with ye. Your grave is there," he motioned with the hand around her middle toward the dark water.

When his hand loosened, Finna wriggled, trying to extricate herself. Just at that moment the baby gave a heavy kick and Finna flung her body against him. In the second that he hesitated, she slid down and away from him. There was a terrible sound as the stone began to rumble, moving and sliding under their feet. Brandubh lost his balance and lurched off to the left as Catriona rose to her knees. She reached for Finna's hand, pulling her safely away from the water's edge.

When Brandubh regained his balance he headed toward them again. He reached out for Finna, but just as his fingers grazed her arm, a deafening roar resounded through the stone. The floor shifted and cracked, throwing him backward. Catriona and Finna watched as he was pitched into the water and sucked down into a whirlpool. His mouth opened in a scream that was never heard as he disappeared beneath the dark surface.

The tunnel had opened and Catriona didn't waste a moment, pulling Finna behind her as she hurtled up the dark shaft. They didn't stop until they reached the door into the castle. As soon as they emerged, the tunnel sealed itself behind them. Arianrhod stood there with a fiery look in her eye. Her arms opened to embrace them both.

"How did Brandubh manage this? What about the protections?" Catriona blurted, as Arianrhod examined her bruised face.

"The tunnels have been here for millennia. It was a weak spot, but now I have sealed them off for good."

"Is Brandubh dead?" Finna looked at her mother, seeing the pain etched on her face, the emotional toll the confrontation with her brother had taken.

Arianrhod shook her head. "He has forces helping him and they will have rescued him by now."

Finna felt her hope drop like a stone down a well. There seemed to be nothing that could get rid of this man. Not even that dark freezing water could do him in. Was he supernatural, a demon? With Morrighan helping him who knew what other horrors he could accomplish. And what about Adair, her role in it all? She shuddered, wondering if what Brandubh told her was true—that she was the spitting image of her grandmother. How could her newly found family, her own flesh and blood, be so horrible? The narrow escape, the realization of how cruel and heartless her uncle was made her cold inside.

"What has he done to you?" Arianrhod cried. She reached up and picked a leaf from the arching tree above her, placing it gently over the wounds. A piece of muslin materialized in her fingers and she wound it around Finna's neck. "I'm so sorry this happened. I had hoped for a restful time for you both."

Finna reached up, tracing the covering around her neck. Her serpent necklace had disappeared. Her eyes welled as she thought of Roc's kind face. He had kept the necklace safe for her for seven years and now it was gone. And she and Catriona had barely made it out of the tunnels alive.

CHAPTER 17

It was late morning by the time Finna woke. The winter sun had reached its zenith. Tonight was the blessing ceremony, but it was difficult to focus on it in light of everything that had happened the day before. The conversation between Brandubh and her mother made her wonder about the past and what her mother's childhood had really been like. From her mother's accounts, Brandubh had been defending her when the accident happened. But how Brandubh described the scenario was very different. Finna wondered about Adair and her role—what if she appeared at the blessing ceremony?

As Finna began to dress, she noticed the blue velvet gown trimmed in gold lying across the chest at the bottom of the bed. Its simple design would work perfectly for her current body shape. When she slipped it on, the soft material settled comfortably over her hips and belly. Catching her reflection in the mirror, she twirled, her mood lifting. While she was putting on her sheepskin boots, the door opened.

"Finna, ye look lovely!"

Finna smiled in pleasure. "I love the dress."

"Can I fix your hair?"

Finna nodded, turning so her back was to her mother. Catriona undid her braid and combed out her hair before adding a gold head piece.

"Now ye look perfect!" Catriona said, stepping back.

Finna looked into the mirror, surprised at her reflection. She had never worn her hair like this, never dressed it with any ornament. But the blood-tinted muslin ruined the picture. "Can I take this off now?"

"Let me," Catriona said. In the mirror, Finna watched her unwrap the bandage, going slowly so as not to cause pain, but as the last of it was removed there was no sign of the knife wounds.

Finna felt along her neck. "I can't believe it's all healed!" she caught her mother's eye in the mirror.

Catriona was smiling, her eyes bright. "Arianrhod is a miracle worker, for sure. We wouldn't want ye to be marred for the ceremony."

Finna laughed and shook out her long hair. "I feel beautiful."

When she turned from the mirror, Finna noticed that her mother was wearing a velvet dress similar to her own, but Catriona's was deep red, tight past the waist, ending in a V in front—a very medieval design.

"Gifts from Arianrhod," Catriona said, spinning. The wide skirt whirled around her slim legs.

"How did she know our sizes?"

Catriona chuckled and then grabbed Finna's hands. They twirled in a circle, both giddy with the release of tension, until Finna became dizzy.

She fell on the bed, her arms and legs splayed. "I feel so happy!"

When they entered the dining room, Arianrhod was seated at the head of the table. Her crown of crystal had been replaced with a wreath of leaves, her hair braided to form a Celtic knot at the nape of her long neck. She gestured to the platters filled to overflowing on the table. "Come enjoy this food. We will not eat again for many hours."

As they sampled the array of delicacies, Arianrhod described the trip they would be taking later in the day. The dresses they wore were made of a special material and would keep them quite warm for the hours it would take to reach the *nemeton*, the sacred grove. Arianrhod told Finna not to be alarmed no matter what she saw on the way to the spring, that magical beings would certainly come to witness the ceremony for this special baby.

Arianrhod led the way out the wide front door. As they approached the water's edge she stopped and turned back. "Finna, this trip will take several hours. Do you feel strong enough for this?" Arianrhod's eyes strayed to the significant bulge now protruding from under Finna's velvet gown.

Finna gazed into Arianrhod's green eyes. "I feel rested and quite wonderful today, considering everything." Finna pressed her hands into the fabric as the baby gave a happy kick.

"If you wish to ride, I'm sure one of Rhiannon's horses would be honored to carry you. Let me know if you become tired." Arianrhod smiled and pressed her fingers lightly against Finna's cheek before she turned once again toward the shoreline. At the sea's edge, she turned right, following a narrow path of rock that led along the steep cliff. They went single file for a hundred yards or so before the cliff curved inward, opening into a narrow valley between two ice-covered mountains. Here a wide stream rushed down and tumbled into the ocean. They crossed at the narrowest point where an arching ice bridge lay across the water, following a path up the hill.

The valley narrowed as they climbed, the walls of stone rising high on either side until they were completely in shadow. Catriona came to walk beside Finna, taking her hand to keep her from slipping. They passed by several entrances to snow caves deep inside the mountain. The silence was immense, broken only by the hollow echo of their footfalls on the thick ice of the trail.

When an unexpected noise behind them caused Finna to turn, she drew in her breath sharply--a long line of animals headed up the trail behind them. First in line were the wolves, their pelts like burnished pewter, their amber eyes gleaming. Behind the wolves came the ermine, white fur shining brighter than the ice, eyes like small black beads. Red deer came next, and behind them, badgers, slung low, their distinctive black and white heads standing out against the ice around them. More animals loomed in the distance, including the enormous aurochs from the eastern forests, and a herd of horses. The line stretched down the mountain as far as they could see. When a black horse with soft eyes appeared by them and nuzzled Finna's shoulder, she took the opportunity, allowing her mother to boost her onto the wide back. She sat sidesaddle, her long skirt spread around her, her fingers threaded through the thick mane for balance. Finna had never been on a horse in her life but she didn't feel any fear, in fact the rhythmic movement soothed her nerves.

As they moved on, Finna became aware of semi-invisible beings floating in the air around her. They moved like smoke, evaporating and re-forming, their round faces and dark eyes appearing and disappearing in the blue air. The little light beings that had helped them in the tunnels circled around her as well, moving in groups like fireflies.

After several hours the trail began to level out and they entered an area filled with many trees. The trail widened and turned muddy and the temperature warmed. The stream next to them had narrowed, and steam now rose from the water.

"This is the sacred cedar grove," Arianrhod announced. "These wise and ancient trees have witnessed all the ceremonies." The enormous trees reached high into the space between the mountains, their upper branches disappearing into the clouds of vapor rising from the spring. Finna felt their energy flowing around and through her and was awed by their magnificence.

A wide natural arch between the trees led into the grove. Once inside, an invisible and benevolent presence seemed to hold them close in the warm and resinous air. Finna slid off her mount and she and Catriona followed Arianrhod to the sacred spring. The crystal water bubbled into a shallow rock basin about three feet wide, spilling over to flow underground before it met the stream on the outside of the grove. On the far side of the spring, branches of three ancient rowan trees intertwined to form a Celtic knot. Within their branches rested an owl, the symbol of wisdom and change, a raven for healing and protection, and a crane, representing secret knowledge.

The sun had set but the moon was not yet visible; no light made its way into the deep shade of the trees. As Arianrhod walked in a circle around the spring moving her hands, green and white candles appeared above her, glowing softly in the dusky air.

"Come Finna, to the place of honor." Arianrhod took her hand and led her to a raised stone in front of the three rowan trees.

Finna sat down and arranged her velvet skirts carefully around her. She felt light-headed and closed her eyes for a moment, trying to concentrate on the moonstone. She reached into her pocket and pulled out the small velvet bag and held it in her hand. When she opened her eyes, she gasped in surprise. In a semi-circle around the spring stood many magnificent larger than life gods and goddesses, too many to count. They disappeared into the shadows outside the circle of candlelight.

Rhiannon was there, her glossy black hair held in place with a circlet of thin gold, and Corra, goddess of prophecy, her gray feather dress glowing in the soft light, a red crown standing out brightly against her shimmering silver hair. And there was Vasilia, goddess of the wind, in her gossamer dress, her gold eyes bright in her pale face. She didn't recognize Aife, the Queen and Goddess of the Isle of Shadow, who was there for protection, or Nimue, the pale-eyed water goddess dressed in a rose colored gown, or Airmid, the willowy goddess of healing, whose light dress floated around her like flower petals. Nor had she seen Modrun, the Welsh mother goddess, dressed in a simple white gown, her thick white hair piled on top of her head and twisted into ropes interwoven with green vines. Nantosuelta sat next to her, the goddess of nature, valleys and streams. She was dressed in pale green, and her fresh face shone under a mass of cornsilk hair. Her eyes were clear like the water she protected, and on her shoulder rode a glossy black raven.

And there were gods too: Cernunnos, the horned god of nature, whom Finna recognized, and close by him, his consort, the beautiful harvest goddess, Habondia. Her wheat-colored silky hair flowed like water down her back. And there was Lugh, the sun god or shining one, Grannos the god of mineral springs. And MacCuill, looking like a god himself with his long white hair and beard, stood in the first row, and next to him stood a tall and elegant older woman dressed in similar robes, Queen Druantia. On his other side stood Catriona, radiant, her arm linked with Eron's.

Finna looked around at the many faces with their strong and elegant features, dressed in richly colored robes of reds, purple and gold and made of magical materials she could only guess at and felt overcome with inadequacy and shyness. She hoped she wouldn't have to do anything but sit here because she knew if she opened her mouth to speak nothing would come out except possibly a squeak. How could she live up to this display of grandeur and all of these special beings? She caught movement on the outskirts of the grove and noticed the animals slipping in to take their places behind the gods and goddesses.

Arianrhod came to sit next to her and took her hand in hers. She began to speak to the gathered crowd in a carrying voice.

"You all know why we are gathered together here at the sacred spring on this auspicious night with the full moon above us. This is the beginning of something very powerful and good and even though we are bound by our natural laws to not interfere with humans, this child will be the exception to those rules. She will come among us as an equal and we will work with her to bring the light back to our world. The period of darkness has only just begun. We have had many other times of war and terrible upheaval here in the past. We have all seen through our gifts of prophecy what may come to pass in this future time. In this child to be born, the soul of Brigid resides, not only the human being she is related to, but our own Brigid, the goddess of fire, healing and unity. She returns to us in this soon to be born girl-child who will come to be known as Saille, the Willow. Now we will chant the words and do what we know to do to bless this child and also bless the moonstone, which has protected this unique line of women through these many years."

Arianrhod reached over and took the small velvet bag from

Finna's hand and removed the moonstone. She took it with her thumb and first finger and placed it in the air above the basin of water where it remained, shining like a bright star. The group around the spring began to chant and as the sound grew, the earth beneath them began to rumble. Finna felt the resonating vibrations go up her spine and into her head and she felt dizzy with a buzzing in her ears. She closed her eyes, imagining the moonstone in her mind's eye, and tried not to feel the fear surging through her. The chanting went on, sometimes low murmuring and then building in volume as the voices rose and fell. As the volume rose she could feel the music of it filling her every pore. When she laid her hand on her stomach an answering hum came from deep inside her.

She opened her eyes as Arianrhod brought over a large silver cauldron and filled it with water from the spring. As she began to sprinkle this water on Finna's head, Finna saw and felt each droplet like a tiny exquisite kaleidoscope of light, as though in slow motion. Arianrhod offered her the cauldron and she drank deeply of the water, tasting its sweetness on her tongue. Finna gazed into the ceremonial vessel, seeing many faces looking back at her; kindness and love shone from their dark eyes that reflected the light from the moon above her. The chanting began to build to a final crescendo that boomed around her, carrying her with it into a vast space where there was nothing, but at the same time everything. Tears flowed down her cheeks.

As the sound gradually died away, the light from the moonstone grew stronger until it became a dazzling brilliance that encompassed the entire glade. A sound came from the light, a high-pitched drone that coursed through her in waves. She closed her eyes for a moment and when she opened them the moonstone was gone, leaving only a soft glow in the air where it had been. When she looked around, all the gods and goddesses had disappeared, as well as the animals, Eron and MacCuill. Her mother and Arianrhod stood by her, next to the spring. Had minutes or hours gone by? She didn't know.

"Is it over?" she asked, feeling a sudden unexpected sadness.

"Yes, my child, the blessing is complete. The child is protected," Arianrhod answered with a smile.

"I felt the light come into my body...and more than that... much more...all sorts of strange sensations... but where is the moonstone?"

"The stone's power has been absorbed into the baby."

"But what does this mean? I don't understand."

"It is not necessary for you to understand, Finna. Come now," Arainrhod said softly, holding her hand out. "It is time to head down the mountain to our beds. Tomorrow after the banquet you will begin the long journey home to await the birth."

As they left the sacred grove behind, Finna's thoughts returned to earth. Her mind scattered back over the past months and everything she had seen, the strange beings and people she had met. "Mahair, you never told me who that woman was--the one at the settlement with Brandubh?"

Catriona turned toward Finna, her eyes dark. "I thought ye knew. That was your grandmother, Adair."

"Your mother?"

Catriona looked away before her darkened gaze met Finna's. "Yes."

www.ingramcontent.com/pod-product-compliance
Lightning Source LLC
Chambersburg PA
CBHW022036240626
47154CB00007B/2425